VAMPIRE RUNNER

Nightshade Vampires

ROWAN HART

D1737714

ALSO BY ROWAN HART

Nightshade Vampires

Vampire King

Vampire Enforcer

Vampire Savage

Vampire Runner

Vampire Solider

———

Knights of Hades MC Security

BLAZE

BONES

CONTENT WARNING

Vampire Runner is the fourth book in the Nightshade Vampire series, a gritty semi-dark vampire mafia series. This alone implies that there may be scenes that can make a reader uncomfortable.

Such scenes may include:

- Near death of a loved one
- Violence
- Religious tyranny and witch hunts
- Murder of a mother and infant, off page (*by antagonists and briefly mentioned*)
- Self-sacrifice for a loved one, multiple times.
- Angry sex (*100% consensual*)
- Light torture scene on page, implied moderate torture off page

- Implied intended infidelity (*while undercover*)

This list is not all-encompassing and readers should understand that this book features vampires who rule a seedy underbelly of a city with their considerable power. I trust each reader to make their own decisions when it comes to what they read.

Chapter One

ASHE

Bullets slam into the side of my Jaguar. I don't flinch but I do curse mentally at the damage. I glance out the driver side window, noting the approaching SUV in a perpendicular alley. A man dressed in white leans out of the window, an automatic rifle tucked against his shoulder. Pressing the gas pedal harder, I swerve around the sedan stopped at the red light and into the intersection.

"Holy fucking shit, Ashe!"

Eris slams her hand against the roof, gritting her teeth as I weave us between traffic and through to the other side. Looking in the rearview mirror, I'm satisfied that there's enough chaos now to slow our pursuers down. There are collisions, and likely mortals have been hurt, but they're collateral damage I have to accept.

1

I've accepted a lot worse while protecting my mate and wife these last hundred and fifty years.

"I would think you'd have more faith in me after all this time," I tell the demoness possessing my wife.

She grits her teeth and shoots me a glare. It's so reminiscent of the looks Cassandra would give me after I deliberately pissed her off that my heart stutters, aching like it's been sprained after tripping. I shake the pain off, too familiar with it to let it hold me down.

Especially not now. Not when we finally have a chance at fulfilling the bargain Cassandra made with Eris.

"I've still got eyes on Aeternaphiel's car," I say, glancing at the rearview mirror again. The SUV that appeared minutes after we left the gallery grand opening in pursuit of the archangel hasn't cleared the intersection yet.

I press down on the gas, glad I upgraded the engine. Even though the Jaguar F-Type came standard with a 5L V8, I wasn't satisfied until I'd installed a V12. It had taken a lot of work, not just to the engine but to the chassis too. As I smoothly race through traffic with a sniper's precision, the speedometer creeping closer to eighty, I can't help the savage grin that bares my fangs.

Even as a human, I was addicted to the adrenaline rush I'd get from risking my life. It only grew over my time as a vampire. Whether it was riding wild stallions bareback along the craggy mountainsides of central Europe, carriages at night in lightning storms, helicopters, planes, cars—it didn't matter. As technology advanced, all it meant to me was I had more ways to feel alive.

"Ashe..." Eris growls my name in warning, and I swear I hear Cassandra's voice in there. My heart races faster than the car, knowing she's so close to the surface. My wife never had the same need to feel the rush that only living a moment away from death brings.

Ignoring her warning, I tilt my head towards the glove box, then take a sharp left when our target does further ahead. I'm familiar with this city. He and his team aren't. "I'm going to cut them off. Use the rifle in there to take out the tires."

Eris frowns, no doubt questioning how the small compartment could hold anything like a rifle. When she opens it, she cackles—a dark chill running down my spine and reminding me of her true nature.

"Smart and rich," she says, pulling the matte black AR-15 from the compartment I'd extended into the front trunk space. Yeah, I'd insisted on the European design with the engine in the back. For this exact reason.

"Coming up," I warn her, and she rolls down her window. We're racing through a back alley, leaving a trail of destroyed trash bags behind us. Fortunately, there aren't any dumpsters, the buildings are too close for them.

The wind rushes inside, carrying the scent of refuse, piss, and death. Mixed in, though, is the woodsy, citrusy scent of my wife though it's tainted by sulfur. I fight the memories threatening to overwhelm me, needing to focus. If we capture this asshole today, I could have Cassandra back in my arms tonight.

I don't care who I have to kill to get my wife back. I'll burn this world to the ground if that's what it takes.

Sometimes I wonder if I'm more like Landon than I want to admit.

I shift gears, pushing the engine harder and we launch out of the alley onto a two-lane road. I press the button on the steering wheel that lowers my own window as I swing the back end out left. Then I draw the gun from my shoulder holster as I fight to keep us in control as people swerve around us. The black SUV is barreling down the road towards us, close enough I see the eyes of the startled driver go wide.

Eris pushes her upper half out of the passenger window, the semi-automatic rifle's butt tucked against her rifle. The rapid shots fill my ears, the smell of gunpowder and accelerant cloud my nostrils. The windshield of the SUV becomes a spiderwork of cracks. I slide my arm out of the window, aiming for the front tires without ever slowing. My hand is steady, and I hit both. Eris is still emptying the magazine with a hellish snarl.

Feet away from a head-on impact, I drop my gun in my lap and jerk the car to the right, the disabled SUV inches from my side mirror. The moment we're clear, I pull the hand brake and whip us around again. Eris grunts as her hip slams into the car door but she doesn't lose the gun or fly out the window.

From the moment we entered the alley to now, watching the SUV fishtail, jump the curve, and finally stop by slamming into a light pole was a matter of seconds. A minute at the most.

I don't stop until we're at the back of the SUV. Eris is already out of the car, abandoning the rifle for the celestial blade that'd been strapped to her thigh. I follow, wishing she wouldn't be so reckless with Cassandra's body.

Right now, though, with the gunmetal silk dress hugging her body before flaring out around her long legs, her dark hair tumbling chaotically around her neck and shoulders, I can believe Eris had once been an angel. One full of retribution and glory; a destroyer of anything in her path.

I've got my gun in hand again, releasing the clip and letting it clatter to the ground as I slam another one in.

Eris reaches for the back passenger door, a snarl twisting Cassandra's beautiful face.

Time stops as the door explodes open, brilliant white light searing my eyes. I throw my arm over my eyes even as I turn away, a primal hiss escaping me as my very essence begins to burn.

A sound—a scream from another world, reverberates and pummels my skull. I roar in challenge even as I slam my hands over my ears. The torturous light has disappeared and I whirl back, refusing to abandon my wife and Eris to whatever the fuck was in the back seat.

A dark-haired man—not a man, an archangel—is towering over Eris as her knees begin to buckle against the onslaught of whatever power he's pushing towards her. She bares her teeth in a vicious snarl, her face twisted in pain. Her dagger is on the sidewalk beside her, melting. Black, oily mist looks as if it's been forced from Cassandra's body, being pulled towards him.

He doesn't even pay attention to me.

He raises an arm, a golden light coming from his hand and forming into a damn sword.

I charge, pure fury and the need to protect my mate pushing me past the pain of his angelic radiance. I unload my handgun, each bullet slamming into the power around him. Not a single one reaches him. My vampire speed seems to slow to nothing as I watch in horror as he raises the fully formed blade then begins to bring it down on Cassandra.

I push harder, every part of my being screaming as if I'm burning away.

The point of his blade inches closer to where Eris and Cassandra are now kneeling on the sidewalk before him. His eyes are a bright blue ringed with silver and his face is a visage of satisfaction.

I never take my eyes from him as I sweep my hand down and grab the melting celestial blade. My skin chars but I grip it tighter. With a snarl, I slam it into his gut. His eyes turn to me with hatred as my blow pushes him back a step. The blade swings down, barely missing my wife's chest and sweeping down through the black mist.

Then Aeternaphiel laughs.

He drops the blade, and it dissipates. I'm caught in his powers, unable to move, my supernatural strength useless against his might.

He says something, a language only known by angels and demons. I'm helpless as he presses two fingers against my forehead. His smile is more twisted and evil than Eris's has ever been.

I don't care if I die. Not if it means I've kept Cassandra safe. The celestial blade is still in his stomach, and he finally looks down at the wound. My gaze follows his and he scowls as his own skin begins to flicker as if being burned by invisible flames.

He staggers back again, hitting the totaled SUV. He's far enough from me that his power is no longer holding me up. I fall to my knees, twisting to face Cassandra where she's collapsed. She looks distorted and too pale. Too still.

I croak as I try to say her name, reaching towards her with a weak arm. Whatever the asshole did to me, I have no strength left.

I don't care as another SUV pulls up and men in white cassocks rush around us to help Aeternaphiel. I have to get to Cassandra.

Someone kicks me in the shoulder, sending me to sprawl on my back.

The archangel is snarling down at me, his arms thrown over a justicar on either side of him. He hisses something and power slams into me. I fight against the darkness overwhelming my mind. I must keep her safe.

I can't fight it anymore when one of his assistants kicks me in the head, the darkness overwhelming me at once.

1865

Ashe

The house Ambrose had established our clan in was a recently finished sprawling, Greek Revival mansion. It was two stories, but larger than anything the people of Willow Creek had ever seen. We'd arrived in the moderately sized hamlet over a week ago, and the original intended occupants of this house, the Jamesons, had met with a swift, bloody end. The man who considered himself the appointed mayor of the town had a list of crimes against others and the townsfolk longer than a thoroughbred full stride. Ambrose had discovered the injustices perpetrated by every member of the family—even the sixteen-year-old daughter—and decided to make it the Nightshades' business.

The people of Willow Creek believed the Jamesons had left under the cover of darkness, the story supported by Malachi and me taking the family carriage and racing out through the main road. By the time Ambrose and the rest of us moved in, rumors had spread and done most of the work for us. Officially, Ambrose had announced that the Jamesons had fled from him because the man had been deep in debt to the Nightshades. Not that our true nature was advertised, of course.

The villagers were more than willing to believe the story, since the family hadn't paid their own debts to many in town. Their esteem for Ambrose and the rest of us rose when Ambrose paid the outstanding debts, including to the laborers who'd built the home we now occupied.

Unofficially... the Jameson family had been bled dry as we fed from them, ensuring they suffered every moment. They'd tormented countless people and had deserved the violent justice that they'd never face otherwise. The only one we did not harm was the youngest, a boy of four years old. The night I drove the carriage through the town, Malachi had held him close in the carriage. We delivered him to a family Ambrose trusted, ensuring he would be raised with love and care—and be taught to care for others.

The afternoon is becoming late as I guide the gorgeous black Saddlebred through the gate from the Nightshade estate and onto the road that'd take me to the center of Willow Creek. Wind rustles through the boughs of the trees which the area was named for, adding an earthy floral scent to the clean air. I take a deep breath, taking pleasure in the scents of plants, horseflesh, healthy soil, and wildlife. I prefer this to the city air clogged with smoke, metal, and sickness we left behind. While it had been easier to feed in a crowded city, those we fed on had blood as disgusting as their hearts. If it weren't for our vampiric abilities, we'd have taken ill just like the human filth we fed on.

Being here allowed me to do something I couldn't in the city, not properly at least.

"Ready, girl?" I murmur, patting the horse's silky neck. The stable boy told me her name was Lily Dancer, on account of her light gait. The mare's ears twist back at my words, and she sidesteps with excitement, proving her name. I've always had an affinity with horses. I grin at her eagerness. I cluck my tongue and touch my heels to her side. She doesn't need any other prompting. Lily Dancer launches forward, moving from a walk straight into a gallop with a toss of her head.

Grinning savagely, not needing to hide my fangs, I loosen my grip on the reins and give her head as I lean forward over her as we begin to fly.

Her black mane whips my face, her muscles working like a powerful industrial machine underneath me, and our hearts begin racing in time together. For a moment, I wish I'd foregone the saddle, but I couldn't risk the questions it'd raise among the humans. It was unseemly for someone of supposed wealth to ride bareback, never mind that when I was human, I was a stable boy and then a groomsman before being conscripted in the military.

A high-pitched shout cuts through the wind in my ears, quickly followed by a woman stumbling into the road ahead of us. I throw myself backwards, yanking Lily Dancer's head to the left as I pull back. There's no way we can stop in time, not with how fast we were going, but I can make sure we don't trample the woman.

"Whoa," I say. The instinct to calm and reassure the mare is second nature even as I crane my neck around as we pass the woman. Lily Dancer settles quickly, her sides heaving in breaths and she stomps her hooves in the dirt, sending dry dust into the air. I turn her back around, eyes moving from the woman struggling against her skirts to rise to the trees she came from. I can't hear anything pursuing her, either man or beast. There's a woven basket on its side, its contents of greenery spilling out pathetically.

By the time we've walked to her, the woman is finally back on her two feet. She's not too worse for the wear from her tumble, though her high-waisted green skirt is streaked with pale dirt and I spy a tear along one side. Her cream-colored, high-necked, long-sleeved blouse has come half untucked from her skirt, and if her black as night hair had ever been pulled back in an appropriate fashion, it was a mess now.

"Are you in distress, miss?" I ask, unable to take my eyes from the woman. Something is different about her. I breathe in, my nostrils flaring as I scent her. Heat coils in my gut and my fangs ache, lengthening on their own. Mine, the vampire in me growls from the depths of my heart.

She huffs, a sound of pure frustration, and shoves her wild tresses out of her face, finally turning her eyes upon me. Brilliant amber and hazel eyes lock on mine, and I swear I can no longer breathe. Her eyes are golden, but of a different nature than those of vampires. Ours are an unnatural gold, but hers are a gold that makes me think of fields of wheat and fresh, spring honey. Her skin is sun-kissed, with freckles dusting the rounds of her cheeks.

Her eyes widen, the black of her pupils expanding in apprehension. The scent of her changes, a hint of the tang of fear and more revealingly, the smell of witchcraft—the scent of ozone just before lightning strikes.

"Vampire," she breathes out even as I declare her a witch.

The witch raises her hands, as if to strike first, and only later will I understand what causes me to do what I do next. I dismount, and lower myself to a knee, bowing my head in respect. Something I've done for no one after Ambrose turned me.

Her power thickens the air around us; the horse neighs and shies away. I do not move, waiting to see if she will strike me down. I'm unsure if she knows how to kill a vampire, but my body refuses to obey me. I will not defend myself against her. I can't. The thought of harming this woman, this witch, is anathema to the vampire and man inside of me.

"What are you doing?" she finally asks, her beautiful voice reminding me of the babbling creeks in the area. Cool, crisp, and happy.

"I mean you no harm, witch," I say, finally daring to raise my head and meet her gaze. My heart pauses and then races faster than I'd just been galloping. She stands above me, like a goddess of the wilds. "By the gods, you're beautiful."

Her narrow brows frown before one lifts questioningly. She lowers her hands, until they are on her waist as she inspects me. "And you're unexpected. I knew that story about the Jamesons fleeing in the night was off. Suppose that was your folk then?"

I rise to my feet, careful to avoid spooking her again. "Aye," I answer. "We're the Nightshades, our sire is Ambrose d'Vil. We'd heard what the family had done to people in the city and here."

She snorts, and seeming to decide I was honest, marches with a limp across the road to where her basket lies. I go to the mare, collecting her reins, and watch the witch grumble as she shoves everything back into the woven basket.

"Never took vampires as the vigilante type," she says as she stands again, the basket now propped on her hip. "Well, I'll just be on my way then."

I blink rapidly, and then stride to her side—reins in hand, where she'd already begun walking towards town, the horse following behind. "You're injured. Were you being chased?"

The public had stopped hunting witches over two centuries before, but I know too well about the groups of humans who still sought to eradicate anything super-natural.

"No," she huffs, glancing at me before looking ahead at the road. "I'm just horribly clumsy. Always have been. Tripped over a root as I came out of the trees."

Her limp is getting worse, her gait lopsided. I couldn't abide it. I move in front of her, blocking her way and forcing her to halt.

"Let me give you a ride into town," I tell her,

inclining my head towards her foot. "You'll only make your ankle worse by walking on it."

Her hypnotizing eyes narrow suspiciously at me. "I'm not one to take rides from strangers, especially if they're vampires old enough to walk in the sun."

I can't let her go so easily. The idea of separating from her fills my chest with the buzz of bees. Thinking quickly, I hold out my hand. "My name is Ashe Halford."

I swear her mouth twitches as she fights a smile. She sighs dramatically and takes my hand, giving it a quick shake before saying. "I'm Cassandra O'Brien."

I smile, keeping my fangs hidden though as I squeeze her hand. "It's lovely to meet you, Ms. O'Brien. Now, as we are no longer strangers, may I please offer you a ride on my horse so you don't injure yourself worse?"

"Only if you never call me Ms. O'Brien again," Cassandra bargains, her eyes bright with amusement.

I bow deeply, my arm swinging out towards the horse. "As the lady wishes."

She shoves the basket in my chest as I straighten, a grin on her face. I take it hastily, not wishing to drop it. By the time I've got it securely in hand, Cassandra is mounting the mare with a scowl, yanking her skirts down around her legs as best as she can while riding astride. She sends me a look that dares me to say anything about the appropriateness of the scene, and I know better than to take it. Josephine would have my head if I made such a comment to a woman in need of help.

Cassandra gestures forward, commandingly. "Lead on, my unexpected vampire."

"Try not to fall off the horse," I tease, clucking my tongue as I begin walking the mare with the reins. "I'm fast, but I'm not sure I can save you from yourself."

The growl I get only makes me smile wider as we begin down the road again.

G oddess, my head hurts. What on earth did I drink last night? I groan and try to rub my temple but something heavy is draped over my chest. I grin, despite myself, recognizing Ashe's scent. When he sleeps, he might as well be a boulder rather than a vampire. If my head hurts this badly and he's out, no doubt that means Rhys and Ezra convinced us to do something crazy.

I pry open my eyes, squinting against the pale light only to immediately frown. I don't recognize the ceiling. This isn't our cottage. In fact, the plush bed under me is too soft to be the featherdown mattress Ambrose gifted us for our wedding.

"Cassandra," a soft familiar voice whispers my name, and I crane my neck to the right to find the speaker.

"What—" I croak out the question and Josephine shushes me before bringing a glass with a straw to my lips. I gulp down the tepid water eagerly before pulling away and trying again. "What happened? Where are we?"

Ashe still hasn't moved, a dead weight against me pinning me flat on my back. I can just make out Josephine's golden eyes in the shadows, and they're filled with concern.

"How much do you remember?" she asks and my brows furrows deeper.

What I remember. . . I try to think, the pounding in my head yet to lessen. I wrestle my arm from under Ashe's embrace and freeze as I see manicured nails filed into sharp points. With a gasp, memories flood my mind like hurricane waves barreling into a city.

The last hundred and fifty years of sharing my mind and body with Eris returns. More importantly, I remember Eris facing the archangel Aeternaphiel and her essence being sucked from me. I remember the pain as she dug her metaphysical claws into my own essence to hold on. I remember the mind-splitting pain as the angelic blade sliced through the revealed shadow form of Eris. It was as if the blade had tried to siphon my insides, sucking my very being from my body.

Except Ashe had defended me, pushing Aeternaphiel far enough back that the blade only struck Eris.

I struggle upwards, Josephine quickly helping shift Ashe's arm, until I'm sitting up against a gray headboard. I look down at my husband, but I don't have the enhanced eyesight that vampires do.

"Is he?" I can't finish the question, my eyes never leaving his relaxed face.

"He'll be okay," Josephine answers, moving his arm until it's draped over my lap and adjusting the plush blanket until Ashe is tucked back in. Josephine's fussing brings a small smile to my lips. Things change over time, but Josephine's need to fuss and take care of those around her never will.

"And you?"

Her question has my vision unfocusing as I search for Eris within me. I've never woken with full control of my body, so for her to not be shouting in my mind is concerning. Josephine is quiet while I search the recesses of my mind. It's as if I'm walking through an empty home, knowing someone is missing but not knowing where they went.

I search deeper, drawing on my experience as a witch to dive into the depths of my being. I cry out, Josephine's hands bracing my upper arms and I cling to her for support. If I'd been standing, I'm certain my knees would have given out.

"Cassandra?" The matronly vampire's voice is insistent.

"Something—something is wrong with Eris." I pry my eyes open and meet Josephine's worried gaze. "She's—" A gag cuts my words off and I turn to the side but nothing comes up. My stomach cramps as I heave again, my insides cramping as fire fills my stomach.

Strong hands grip my shoulders, an achingly familiar weight presses against my back. Ashe slides an arm around my chest, offering me a brace as my body struggles.

"I've got you." The steady tenor of his voice wraps around me like a warm blanket on a winter night. I grip his arm with one hand, anchoring myself to him while I'm tossed about in a torrent of pain.

"Ashe," I say when the pain finally retreats into the depths of my being.

"I'm here," he says again, with such heartbreaking tenderness tears slip down my cheeks. I turn my head towards him and then he's lifting and moving me until I'm cradled against his chest. He rubs my back and I tuck my head under his chin. "Do you know what's happening?"

Rigors shake my body, and he holds me tighter while I grip his white shirt in a tight fist, riding it out.

"Something is wrong with Eris," I manage to say. "With me."

Ashe is quiet for a long moment, and I focus on his slow heartbeat under my ear. If I can keep focused on the sound, the sheer wrongness at my core won't drag me under.

"What do you need?" he asks at last, his trust in me undeserving. Not after what I'd done. Guilt threatens to overwhelm me just as quickly as the pain and I grit my teeth, forcing my thoughts to clear. I think about everything I'd learned as a witch, then everything I'd seen while Eris possessed and controlled my body.

I find Josephine, now standing at the edge of the bed. "I need a sachet of lavender, salt, St. John's Wort, and white sage if you have it."

Josephine gives me a firm nod before hurrying from the room. I let out a breath as the pain continues to fade, wilting against Ashe.

Ashe. My husband. My mate. The man I've spent over a century and a half locked away from by my own decision. A decision that I'd make again and again, as long as it saved his life.

"Cassandra," he murmurs. "Tell me what's going on. Where's Eris?" A growl rumbles from his chest and through me. "I remember that bastard trying to stab you with a sword, but I got to him before he could. You still went down, though." His arms tighten around me, his fingers digging into me as fear colors his words. "Then they took me down. I had to wake up with Malachi's damn face in mine."

Ashe tries for levity and while it falls flat, my lips

curve in a sad smile. I match his tone; I don't have the energy to deal with the threat growing deep inside.

"Oh, such a horrible experience for you," I tease. My voice is still rough, and I'm jostled as Ashe reaches for the water Josephine left on the nightstand. He helps me hold it steady as I drink, managing the flimsy-feeling straw without too much awkwardness. When I've had enough, he returns it quickly. His hand goes to my thigh, gripping me as if afraid I'll disappear at any moment. To be fair, Eris never gave warning to when she'd return and take over once more.

"I don't know for sure," I admit, rolling my lips. I lean my head against his shoulder again, telling myself it's because I'm exhausted and not because I'm afraid to look my mate in the face. "But whatever that blade was, it hurt Eris. A part of her is missing." I rub the space over my heart with the heel of my palm.

Ashe is preternaturally still around me, practically holding his breath. "Does that mean..."

He trails off but I don't need him to finish the question. I take a deep breath, bracing myself. "The bargain is still there. There's enough of her within me that the bindings still tie us together."

Ashe hisses and drops his head against mine as he wrangles with his disappointment. I can't feel him through our mate bond, but I don't need to. It oozes from every pore. He'd locked the mate bond down when it was clear Eris had possessed me and hasn't opened it since.

I can hardly judge him for such a punishment. Not after I'd done the same the night I betrayed him.

I stroke the arm holding my legs to him, soothing both of us. I feel every soft hair on his arm, refamiliarizing myself with the strength of him as I ghost my fingers over him. For so long, I've lacked this freedom.

Eris, bound by the terms of our bargain, allowed me time in control to maintain the integrity of my mind and humanity. There was never consistency, though. I never knew when I'd have the opportunity to soak Ashe in, to remind him of my love, to apologize again, to steal anything that could keep me strong through the years of separation.

There'd been a time when Eris's frustrations with her failing hunt turned to doubt, which fed into my own. A demon would never willingly give up a bargain, and as much as Eris and I've shared together, Kasar is right when he said Eris knows nothing of compassion. Eris will never break the bargain.

Tendrils of shame and guilt creep into my thoughts and around my heart, making my breath stutter in my chest.

"I'm so sorry," I breathe out in a rush. It's the same lament, the same thing I say almost every chance I have. "I know you can never forgive me, but I couldn't let you die."

Ashe freezes and while he doesn't move, I practically feel him withdrawing from me.

"This isn't the time." His voice is firm, borderline sharp. "We need to figure out what Aeternaphiel did to you and Eris first. Then we'll find him again and finish this at last."

I open my mouth to protest, but what can I say? A foreboding grows in the pit of my stomach, my magic warning me that we don't have as much time as we hope. Something has happened to Eris, and it's hurting me too because of how entwined the demon and I are.

The door opens, preventing me from saying anything else. Josephine hurries in, sachet in hand. A flutter of warm and fondness fills me at the sight of the familiar satchel as she holds it out.

"I've kept all of your workroom supplies in pristine condition," she admits with a beaming smile, before it falters and her brow furrows. "Well, all those that survived the fire. Still." Josephine leans over the bed, straightening the blankets over us and plumping the pillow behind Ashe. "I always knew you'd need them when you returned to us."

"She wasn't on a vacation, Matka," a languid drawl came from the doorway. I tuck the sachet close to my chest and look at the platinum blond man leaning against the door frame, hands casually tucked into slacks.

"Landon." I purse my lips after saying his name. Then I raise a brow. "Still annoying as always?"

He cocks his head as if confused. "I believe you mean charming."

I smile sweetly, falling back into the familiar banter with ease. "As a snake, of course."

Ashe says nothing, and more than ever, I wish he'd open his side of the mate bond. I need to know he's okay.

Landon pushes off and straightens, cocking a brow. "Don't let my mate hear you," he starts before Josephine cuts her hand through the air with a chastising glare between the two of us.

"Do not start," she warns us with a pointed finger. "Cassandra has only just woken up and something still ails her. I do not have the patience for your childish squabbles."

There's always been something more intimidating about Josephine than the head of the Nightshades. Maybe it was the fact that she'd been turned when her hair was already silver, her mortal years lining her elegant face. Ambrose has always appeared in his thirties, a man in his prime. Josephine, between her gray Victorianesque dresses and her matronly manners, has always been able to bring even the most stubborn of vampires to heel.

To my genuine surprise, Lan moves to stand beside his mother. Something that could be concern—but more likely intrigue, softens his face. I practically gape, unfamiliar with this version of the vampire.

He gives me an exaggerated sarcastic smirk. "Don't be so surprised." His words are clipped as he studies me intently. He says nothing and his gaze goes over my head to Ashe. "What do you feel through the bond?"

I startle. I hadn't even considered asking Ashe to lower his mental block. I will never ask him to, even though I'm desperate to feel as close to him as we once were. I don't move as I wait for Ashe to say something, to do something—anything.

He tightens his hold and moves me until I'm on the bed beside him. Reflexively, I look at him but only catch a glint of his golden eyes as he slides out of the bed on the other side. He's wearing a white shirt that hugs his shoulders and is loose around his narrow waist, and soft charcoal gray sleep pants. Ashe runs a hand through his sandy-brown locks, pushing the strands back off his forehead.

He strides towards a door in the wall, pausing as he grabs the handle. He casts a look over his shoulder, but at Landon. I grip the covers, silently pleading for him to look at me. To give me something.

"Nothing. Like usual," he answers, his voice rough. He clears his throat. "I need to shower. I have work to do for Ambrose, and Cassandra doesn't need my help to determine what's wrong."

He slips into the en suite bathroom, closing the door solidly behind him. The soft tick of the lock makes me wince. Lan releases an amused huff and I quell him with a sharp glare. His lips twist up in a smirk and he spins back around towards the bedroom door.

"I'm off to kiss my mate," he informs us, the dig obvious.

Josephine sighs, the sound of an exasperated mother. I slump against the headboard, still holding the sachet against my chest. It offers a small barrier of protection against the foul darkness twisting through me but it's not a solution.

Josephine squeezes my shoulder, and I can't look at her. I can't see the pity in her eyes, or I'll lose it. Even now, I'm fighting back a torrent of tears building behind my eyes, the sorrow choking my heart.

"He'll come around," she assures me, like any good mother. "He just needs time. You both do."

I nod, unable to speak as I stare unfocused at the end of the bed. Josephine seems to know I don't want to talk, and she gives me another squeeze before heading out.

"I'll get you something to eat and I'm sure one of the ladies has something you can wear," she says, all pity replaced by the frank decisiveness she'd always run the household with.

When I'm alone, I let my head fall back with a clunk on the headboard. Josephine is right. Ashe and I both need time. Something that I may not have very much of.

1865

Cassandra

This vampire is certainly nothing like any others I've encountered. Warnings from my elders and my mother whisper in my mind. Vampires are creatures of death and the dark, never to be trusted. They are selfish, perverse, and delight in being cruel to others.

Yet this man, Ashe Halford, did not attack me when he sensed my true nature. In fact, when he thought I was no more than a human woman fallen to the ground, he'd turned his horse back to check on me.

Damn my clumsiness. I can't go more than an hour before tripping over something, even if it's simply my own feet. For years, my grandmother had thought spirits swirled around my feet and tried every charm and ward she could find. My mother had hoped I'd grow out of it. A daughter the age of ten and younger can be forgiven for such clumsiness, but once I'd begun bleeding and been declared a woman, it was an unforgivable trait in society's eyes.

Had my family been common tradesmen, perhaps I wouldn't have been considered such a disgrace. As it was, the O'Briens were an ancient lineage in the coven, and my father had been in line to lead the coven. I'd once explained it to a hedge witch I came across after leaving, that my father was basically the same rank as an earl in the human world. I was expected to be the perfect daughter, both in manners, grace, and spellcraft.

Instead, they got a daughter who preferred running through the forest with bare feet, dancing in storms, and playing with any fae creatures I could find. My magic is wild, something my family tried to overlook because of how much power I had.

But no punishment could break my wild heart and when I came of age, I made the choice to leave the coven. My mother, angry and ashamed of me, declared that if I left, I'd be erased from the family and could never return.

Better living in the wild, among the squirrels and deer, than dying in silks and jewels.

I'd stopped trying to force my magic to follow the stringent rules and rituals taught by my coven. I let my magic be free, allowed it to be as wild as the world I'd made my home.

I shushed the whispers of my past. Those voices had taught me so much I've already cast out. Why should this be any different?

"And we have arrived," Ashe says, halting the mare. He'd introduced her as Lily Dancer and my magic told me she loved the name. From her easy, lovely gait, I know it's an appropriate name. Before I can slide down, he grabs me by the waist and pulls me into his arms. My weight and, more surprisingly, my skirts don't hamper him as he braces one arm under my knees and the other around my shoulders.

"Put me down!" I yelp but put my arms around his neck instinctively. "This really isn't necessary."

I glare at him, and when he turns his face to me, my expression falters. We're so close, his golden eyes alive with mirth and his lips quirked in a grin. Long strands of brown hair have fallen across his brow and without thinking, I gently sweep them back.

Ashe isn't classically handsome. His face is oval, and he has a bump on the bridge of his nose suggesting he'd broken it once as a human. His eyes are a bit too close together, but his lips are envy worthy. His features combined should make him look homely and forgettable.

Instead, just like he'd ignored my protests earlier,

his features ignore expectation and create a face that's impossible to ignore.

"My mother will roll in her grave if I allow someone to further injure themselves when there's no need," he replies, and as if the matter is settled, he looks to Lily Dancer's reins, ensuring the mare won't become entangled, before turning towards my cottage.

I purse my lips. I'm loath to admit it, but my ankle does hurt something fierce. However, even on threat of death, I will never admit that I'm enjoying being held.

I've lived alone for years, necessary because I age so much slower than the average human. It meant companionship was few and far between, and I never let a partner get too close. Which ensured the relationships never lasted long either.

That's all this is, I decide. It's been so long since my last lover that it's only natural my stomach swoops with excitement as another waft of his scent fills my nose. It's pure masculine warmth and promises. Petrichor and amber with the green notes of a summer meadow. I barely resist tucking my face against his neck and breathing deep.

"I can sense the wards," he murmurs. I blink rapidly, coming back to the present. Right, wards. So creatures like him couldn't pass.

I sketch a sigil in the air, verdant green magic flowing from my fingers like ink. It fades from view the moment the sigil is complete, leaving an impression similar to a firework disappearing from the night sky.

"Thank you," Ashe says and continues forward. When we pass through the small wooden gate, he pauses again without being asked and I raise the ward once more.

"You'll be able to leave whenever you want," I assure him. "It only keeps things out."

He inclines his head, his eyes full of mischief. I narrow my own with suspicion but whatever the vampire was considering saying, he must have thought better of. With his long stride, we're across my small yard quickly and I fish my key from my pocket, blushing as I'm forced to wiggle against him.

It brings us into much too much contact, and it only makes me more frantic to free the iron key from its prison of cotton. Finally, I'm able to raise it triumphantly, as if I've completed a Trial of Heracles, and Ashe bends enough that I'm able to unlock the door.

He carries me across the threshold, and I point to the padded bench between my cluttered kitchen table and the stone hearth that divides my small cottage. He lowers me with unexpected gentleness, straightening my skirts so my modesty's preserved.

"A vampire gentleman," I tease without thought,

and my eyes go wide. My mouth has always been faster than my mind.

Ashe barks out a laugh. Thank the goddess he isn't offended. I may be powerful, especially in my own cottage, but with his unnatural speed, he could rip out my throat before my power ejected him from the wards. He looks around, clearly curious about my home.

"It's nothing as grand as I'm sure you're used to," I say, but not with shame. I'm proud of the life I've carved out here on my own.

My cottage had once belonged to Agnes, the elderly hedge witch and midwife of the area. She'd taken me in when I'd wandered through the area after leaving my coven. It was a modest size, with a sleeping loft accessible by a ladder. I'd slept downstairs, on the right side of the divided cottage, on a pallet near the double-sided hearth. That side of the cottage, Agnes had set up her small kitchen, round table with two chairs, and another more plush armchair angled towards the four-paned window on that side of the front door. The left side of the hearth was dedicated to her craft, and it doubled as a workspace for when the locals sought her medical assistance.

In exchange for room and board, Agnes taught me everything she knew about using wild magic, being a healer, and even her midwife and medical skills. When anyone asked, she told them I was a granddaughter who came to assist her since she was getting on in years. It always amused me when people thought she was approaching her eighth decade of life. In reality, Agnes was nearing two hundred.

She'd taught me everything she knew and within a year, we both knew I'd be taking over her duties when she made her way to the goddess. The night I'd lit her funeral pyre, I'd cried for the first time since I left my coven.

"It reminds me of my childhood home."

I cock my head at Ashe's words. "A humble beginning then?"

The vampire gestures to the wood pile and the banked coals in the hearth in silent question. When I nod, he crouches before the hearth and coaxes the fire back to life as he answers. "My father was a logger who died when I was five or so, leaving my seamstress mother with four of us to feed. My uncle was the stable master of the local lord, so I was sent off to him along with my two older brothers to work for him."

Satisfied with the fire, Ashe rises and brushes his hands off on his thighs as he turns to face me. He's grinning and my breath catches at the beauty of him.

"I slept in the hayloft with the other littles," he says without an ounce of shame. "To me, it might as well have been a palace. My bed was as comfortable as I chose to make it with the hay, and I had a pillow and blanket all to myself. Worked in the stables, learned to ride better than any noble. And I had a habit of sneaking into places I shouldn't be."

A grin twists my lips and I raise my brows at him. "Let me guess, like young ladies' beds?"

Ashe shoots me a rakish grin. He moves around to the other side of the table, taking a seat on the other bench. "When Lord Rivington took notice of my skills, I became a personal messenger." A shadow darkens his eyes, and he looks away before back at me, his expression back to easy joviality. "A minor war happened, Ambrose found me, and I've been with the Nightshades ever since."

There's pain hidden in his words, but I know better than to press. My stomach decides to remind me that lunch was hours ago. Loudly.

Before I can say anything, Ashe stands again. "How about this," he says, giving me no chance to speak. "Why don't you tell me what you need to fix that ankle of yours and, in return, I'll make you dinner."

I jerk my head back at the suggestion. "That is entirely unnecessary, and not even a fair trade. You get nothing out of it."

It sounded all too much like the type of deal my parents often sought.

Ashe cocks his head, a lock of sable hair falling across his forehead and my fingers twitch with the urge to push it back. The slow, lopsided grin he gives me offers a teasing point of a fang. "I don't consider the pleasure of your company nothing."

My cheeks flame; the heat quickly spreads to my ears before rushing down my entire body and pooling between my legs. I duck my head and straighten my skirts unnecessarily as I compose myself.

"Well then," I say after clearing my throat. I point towards a clay pot on one of the shelves along the far wall. "Please get me the salve labeled willow bark and arnica."

Chapter Three

ASHE

I'm avoiding my wife.

The hot water is near scalding as I stand under the rainfall shower head in the middle of a restored clawfoot iron tub. I have expensive taste when it comes to modern transportations, but when it comes to my private sanctuary, I crave the familiarity of ages past. Though once I experienced a rainfall shower head for the first time, I knew I could compromise to a degree.

Each of our suites in the Nightshade clan house are nearly identical when it comes to layout, but otherwise our rooms reflect our natures.

Unable to procrastinate any longer, I step out of the massive tub that's the centerpiece of the bathroom. A thick, square rug saves my feet from the cold slate tiles, and I snag the towel from the brass hanger, quickly drying myself before wrapping the towel around my waist. I pause, taking in the bathroom, unable to stop myself from wondering what Cassandra will think of it.

The sink mimics a bowl and ewer, set in dark cherrywood cabinets that stretch along one side. The walls are whitewashed—boring even. The only touch of color is the bouquet of dried wildflowers in a brown bottle vase tucked in the corner on the sink counter. I don't need to see my bedroom to know it's just as empty and void of much personality.

Like it's still waiting to be lived in.

I shake my head free of the thoughts and cock my head, extending my senses to see if Cassandra is still in the bedroom. I'd heard Josephine return while I showered, and it seems Cassandra left with her. She was always astute, knowing me better than I knew myself at times.

I've imagined a day like this countless times over the last century and a half. I thought of how it would feel to finally capture Cassandra, my Cassandra, in my arms and know that she won't be stolen from me again without warning. How I'd kiss her until we couldn't breathe, touch her until we were delirious with pleasure and need. How I'd claim her as my own once again even as I gave myself to her.

I never imagined how fucking furious I'd be.

Breathing through my nose, I swallow the anger down and re-enter the bedroom, forcing myself to get dressed by rote. It's torture to have her scent so strong in my rooms, taunting me.

A large king-sized four-poster bed dominates the center of my room. The bedspread, that's been remade neatly, is a rich chocolate brown, with several pillows arranged on it, and the frame a light mahogany. The room is masculine, with the color palette consisting of varying shades of brown and creams with accents of mahogany. Heavy cream-colored curtains are pulled back to reveal windows that span the length of the wall and overlook Ambrose's narrow gardens below.

A collection of old, handwoven rugs in faded various colors cover the hardwood floors. They are some of the only things I saved from our cottage after the attack. I think of Josephine returning with one of Cassandra's charmed sachets as I shrug on my black Armani suit jacket, shaking my head. Clearly, I wasn't the only one who saved things from Cassandra's and my old home.

I hadn't lied when I said I have duties to attend to for Ambrose today. I'm to oversee the retrieval and delivery of Rapture confiscated by the Knights of Hades. It's the final missing shipment after what the Hollands had stolen and began distributing. They'd bring it right to the door, but after the near war with demons decades ago, the truce prohibits them from entering the Barrows.

I make my way to his home office, pausing at the end of the hall as I pick up on enough heartbeats to know he isn't alone. I recognize each one of them. Eloise and Cassandra are in there with him.

Whatever I'm wrestling with about my wife can wait. I make sure my end of our mate bond is sealed just as tightly as when Eris first took possession of her. I can't bear the thought of Cassandra experiencing an onslaught of my confused emotions.

No matter what, I still love her with all of my being. I would—have killed for her, over and over. I'll kill again, if I need to. I'll die if that's what it takes to keep her safe.

Even if I want to rage at her for the pain of what she did to me.

Even if the sting of her betrayal has returned, as sharp and agonizing as the moment I realized what she'd done.

Cassandra's voice carries through the closed door to my ears, and I freeze, my hand nearly on the doorknob.

"I'll remind you, Ambrose." Cassandra emphasizes his name. "That I'm a witch, and am as such not bound by your decrees. That I am Ashe's mate does not make me one of your vampires."

I hold my breath, bracing for the vampire's response. It'd taken time for Cassandra and Ambrose to settle into an amicable association. I wouldn't say the witch and vampire had ever become friends, not with our kind's tumultuous history. The fact that Cassandra is bull-headed and rebellious while Ambrose is not used to people questioning his authority certainly doesn't help.

"Yet, because you are his mate, you have had the protection of my vampires since the day you accepted him," he replies steadily. "Even while Eris betrayed your mate. Even after you betrayed your mate. We've kept you protected as well as Eris would allow."

His words are barbed and meant to strike. I fight my instincts which demand I charge in, fangs bared, to protect my mate. Neither would take kindly to that. Ambrose no doubt knows that I am outside the door, but Cassandra and Eloise don't have our heightened senses. And with our mate bond closed off, Cassandra can't sense how close I am to her.

Cassandra is quiet for long enough I reach for the knob. I know my sire's words have done the damage he intended, and I can't fight my need to go to her. How many times over the years during our stolen moments has she apologized to me? Too many.

I ease the door open, but only Eloise looks towards me. She's standing at Ambrose's side behind the massive, centuries-old desk that he's towed across the globe as the clan moved. Ambrose's and Cassandra's gazes are locked on one another, staring each other down. Cassandra's body is lined with tension, even as she tries to hide it. I know her too well not to see the signs of her turmoil.

Since I left her in my bed, she'd changed out of the nightgown I'd dressed her in with Josephine's assistance the night before. She's wearing a dove gray, high-waisted skirt that reaches just above the floor that I recognize from Josephine's wardrobe. A long-sleeved, wine-colored blouse, most likely borrowed from Deidre, is tucked into the skirt. The mock high-neck collar is loosely tied closed above a modest V-neck trimmed in lace, a short line of small buttons end just above the skirt.

Together, along with the simple black flats I spy, the outfit is a modern version of what she wore when we first married.

It's also a stark difference to what Eloise wears, a woman born into the modern fashions of comfort.

When she lifts her chin a fraction, a pride I haven't felt in ages has my lips twitching upwards. She's never bowed to anyone since she left her family's coven. I slip into the study the rest of the way, silently closing the door behind me and standing just in front of it.

"I recognize that, Ambrose." Her voice is steady, even if her hand twitches as if she wants to clench a fist. "I would hope that you also recognize the service Eris provided and continues to provide the Nightshades. In addition, I remind you of the times you needed my assistance and Eris allowed me to provide it as necessary."

Ambrose is silent for one heartbeat, and then another. Then Eloise makes an exasperated sound beside him, drawing all our attention as she throws her hands up.

"For fuck's sake, Ambrose," she admonishes him with a glare and a poke. "What's with the third degree? Whatever happened to, 'Welcome home, Cassandra, we've missed you, especially your mate?'"

A chagrined expression flashes across Ambrose's face, much to Cassandra's obvious surprise. They both compose themselves, and Cassandra finally gives me a quick, tiniest of smiles before looking back at him. The other vampire captures Eloise's flailing hand in his own, bringing it to his lips and pressing a kiss to the center of her palm. "You are right, my lioness," he says before turning her hand and lacing his fingers through hers. He returns his gaze to my mate and nods.

"Despite my tone, your return is very welcome,

Cassandra," Ambrose says, his tone warmer than I'd ever heard before. "I agree that you must determine what Aeternaphiel did to Eris and how to fix it. You have the full support of the Nightshades behind you. Whatever you need for your research, you'll have it. Josephine would allow no less." He gives a sidelong glance at his mate, his lips curling up into a smirk. "Nor, would it seem, will my mate and queen."

He looks at me, his golden eyes seeming to pierce through me and read every secret I have. He inclines his head towards Cassandra, indicating that I join her at her side. I stand closer than I ever did with Eris, but the gap between us isn't missed by either the king or Eloise. While he gives no indication of his thoughts, Eloise frowns. She gives me a questioning look, tilting her head enough that the messy bun of her black hair threatens to topple and spill the few pencils she's stuffed in there.

I give her the slightest shake of my head, not wanting to deal with it right now; she gives me a look that promises an interrogation later. We've come a long way since I first delivered her to Ambrose from the small studio she and Deidre once shared. Typically, I consider myself fortunate to count Eloise as a friend. Now, though, I'm wondering how I can avoid her as well as Cassandra.

"Do you need a workspace to determine what is

draining you and Eris, or will her lab in the Rapture facility work?"

My head snaps to Cassandra. What the hell does that mean? She gives me a pained glance before clasping her hands together, bobbing her head as if between two thoughts. "I believe it will be if I have all the materials I may need. Josephine says she saved much of my tools from the cottage. Regardless, I will need to visit Darcelle at the coffee shop. If they don't have the books and grimoires I need, I will simply have to do my best."

"Are there any other covens that could help?" Eloise asks, earnest in her sincerity. "You're a witch, so don't you have a family coven?"

I jerk, fighting the instinct to wrap an arm around Cassandra at the mention of her family's coven. Cassandra, to her credit, gives her a soft smile and a small shake of her head. "My family coven has burned me from the family tree. Long before I mated and married a vampire."

"Oh." Eloise's mouth snaps closed and she shifts, clearly feeling awkward at bringing up unknown familial drama. "Well..."

I take pity on her and interrupt. "I'll take Cassandra to Darcelle's before my rendezvous with the Knights. The witch is fond of Eris, so I believe that they'll be eager to help."

Ambrose gives a commanding nod, a familiar dismissal. I grasp Cassandra above the elbow, keeping my touch light but insistent as I turn to guide us from the office. She follows after a brief resistance and the moment she does, I release her. We leave in silence, the house quiet enough that sounds of the Barrows filter in through the windows Josephine must have opened.

"Ashe—" Cassandra starts, her soft voice piercing my heart more painfully than any blade or bullet.

I swipe my hand through the air, cutting her off with a grunt. "Not here." I have no desire for any of the others to overhear whatever it is Cassandra is going to say. I stride towards the door that leads to the underground garage. The Jaguar is out of commission after the chase with Aeternaphiel, so I debate which vehicle in my collection to take. While a large portion of the vehicles parked in the garage are a part of the Nightshades' fleet, there are five I own personally.

As I push the heavy door open, the click of the door echoing in the silent concrete of the garage, I decide on my gold Mercedes-Benz GLC. I've reinforced the SUV's frame, replaced the windows with the highest grade of bullet-proof glass, coated the interior of the body with polymer before lining it with three layers of ballistic nylon, and installed military grade tires. To be fair, I've done the same to every vehicle the Nightshade vampires use as a clan. Kasar,

Malachi, and Lan have done their own personalizations to their vehicles, as has Ambrose.

I detour to the metal cabinets and shelves that run along the left side of the wall with the entrance. Motion-activated lights under the cabinets turn on and I press my thumb to the biometric scanner which secures the key vault. It's impossible to ignore the weight of Cassandra's silent present behind me, but I push past the warring emotions vying for my attention.

The metal mesh door to the key vault pops open and I snatch the appropriate key from the hook before relocking the vault. I jerk my head towards the gold SUV, remote starting it from the key fob. Cassandra startles, a small meep escaping her, and I turn to her before I can stop myself.

She looks chagrined and my heart is racing as I look for any threat, before realizing it was the SUV that startled her.

"Not used to this century's technology," she says, before seeming to steel herself to approach the SUV.

I snort, amused despite myself. "It's a car, not a wild animal."

Cassandra scowls at me before pointedly marching towards it, her spine rod straight. I smirk at her all-too familiar ire. The easiest way to get my wife to do anything was to annoy her. She can—and has—outstubborn and outspite Ambrose himself.

By habit, I follow her, picking up my pace until I reach the passenger door and open it for her. When she hesitates at the side of the tall vehicle, I offer her my hand. Just as I'd done so many times back in Willow Creek. She takes it without thought and gathers her skirt in her other hand before stepping up and settling into the front passenger seat. At least she recalls enough from Eris's experiences that she's able to figure out the seat belt by the time I'm in the driver's seat.

She's quiet as we drive away from the clan house and deeper into the Barrows. I practically hear the thoughts churning in her head. I'm impressed she's held her tongue this long. Cassandra isn't known for withholding her opinion, especially with me.

I take pity on her when we're halfway to Black Death Beanery, Darcelle's coffee shop.

"What did you mean when you said something is draining you and Eris?" I ask, my voice tightening with emotion by the end. By the time I finish, I can't fight the terror that's climbing around my ribs like a briar bush.

The silence between us grows thicker and darkness begins to yawn in my stomach, filling me with dread. When we come to a stoplight, I turn to look at her. She meets my gaze, sorrow and guilt filling her beautiful eyes. I want to reach out and swear I'll protect her no matter what, but I failed her when it mattered most. Because of that, she sacrificed herself to a demon.

"Whatever Aeternaphiel did to Eris," Cassandra says, her voice wavering. She swallows and continues. "Eris is dying. Which means I am too."

Chapter Four

CASSANDRA

The Black Death Beanery is Eris's favorite coffee shop. It's owned by Darcelle, an open-minded witch. Because of that, the coffee shop is always filled with different supernatural species. Darcelle has a tolerance policy for rivalries in their shop and the witch is powerful enough to enforce it. Eris had been drawn to Darcelle the moment Darcelle had cocked a brow at the demon before warning her to keep her talons to herself and before immediately asking what her order was.

Over the years, Eris and the witch had grown close, and that relationship is what I'm hoping to draw on. My magic has never been as structured as a witch within a coven and while Darcelle does not flaunt it, they are a high-ranking member within the Barrow's obscure coven. Ambrose has created a safe haven for supernatural creatures within the Barrows, including witches without covens. The coven is very insular, protecting its members from those who have grudges against covens.

Ashe follows me into the coffee shop, opening the door for me as if I'm just another duty he's forced to attend. I want to beg him, yell at him, go crazy and make a scene if that's what it takes to get him to actually look at me.

I spent so much time in the recesses of my body, trapped within my own mind, envisioning the day I'm able to be with Ashe again. I thought of all the different ways I could show him my love, my trust, and my sincere remorse at causing him so much pain. In every scenario, he'd listen to me—even if it meant releasing his carefully controlled temper. Never did I think he'd treat me with such indifference. Between the two of us in our relationship, I had always been the more reserved, the less willing to open myself to vulnerability.

The coffee shop is as eclectic as ever, with restored vintage and antique light fixtures, mismatched refurbished furniture, and bare brick walls. It should clash, with how everything is similar but not close enough to match, and yet just like the patrons sitting and working at the tables or booths, there's a harmony here. No one pays us any attention as we walk up to the counter. It's disconcerting, since the last time Ashe and I walked anywhere together, the townsfolk of Willow Creek couldn't avoid staring.

"What can I get for you?" the cheerful young man behind the counter asks. He takes me in, and his friendly smile turns flirtatious. "If you have any questions, I'm more than happy to help you with anything you need."

I blink rapidly, dumbfounded at the overt implication especially when he winks. And I'd thought Ashe had been scandalous when he would request me to allow him to see me safely home from the market. The young man—a shifter, if I read the natural predatorial glint in his eyes— leans forward, bracing his elbow on the modern cash register.

"I could tell you the things I like?" His voice is a rumble of a growl, and my cheeks go hot as my lips part in surprise.

Then he's slammed flat against the counter, Ashe's hand gripping the back of his neck as he snarls viciously.

"What the fuck!" the shifter shouts, his skin beginning to ripple as black fur sprouts.

"Ashe!" I say, shocked speechless at the encounter.

Ashe ignores me, tightening his grip on the shifter's neck, uncaring that the male is half-wolf by this point. As he leans closer to the male, I catch sight of his red-hazed eyes, his fangs long enough to be visible as he speaks.

"That is my mate you're flirting with." The wolf-shifter freezes at Ashe's words, delivered in a blood-chilling quiet. "Keep shifting, boy. Give me a reason to gut you."

"Enough!" A sharp voice cracks through the stunned crowd. Darcelle marches up behind the counter, their crimson red dress flowing around their legs and the heavy blue eyeshadow doing nothing to soften the anger in their eyes. They storm up to Ashe without fear and put their fists on their hips. Ashe still hasn't moved, snarling down at the shifter, who's begun to shake.

Darcelle looks at me, taking me in with narrowed eyes. Their eyes give me an up and down and their eyes flash with realization. They turn back to Ashe and their employee with a huff.

"Ashe, let the pup go. He's new and doesn't know when to keep his mouth shut," Darcelle snaps, tapping their foot on the hardwood floors.

The customers collectively hold their breath, waiting to see what the Nightshade vampire will do. The wolf-shifter has returned to his human form, his eyes squeezed shut with terror.

With an annoyed huff, Ashe shoves the man into the counter as he straightens and releases him. Ashe meets Darcelle's gaze with his own iron-filled eyes, the red retreating. "See that he learns quickly, witch." Ashe adjusts his suit jacket cuffs, as if he weren't just threatening to dismember someone seconds ago. "Cassandra and Eris have business with you. Take us to your office."

Darcelle's eyebrows shoot up at the order and I clear my throat, drawing the witch's attention before they decide to curse Ashe for his impertinence.

"Please forgive the commotion," I say, drawing on all the polite manners my parents and grandmother hammered into me. "It has been some time since I've been around other males, and so my mate is understandably on edge."

"Considering what I know of Eris, it's been a lot longer than some time." Darcelle cocks their head at me. "Something tells me that you've got a story to tell. You can come with me to my office."

They turn and I move to follow on the other side of the counter, going towards a narrow hall in the back. Ashe follows, but Darcelle stops at the hall entrance, whirling around with a pointed finger at the vampire. He stares down at them with a blank expression.

"Not you, vampire," Darcelle bites out. "Your clan might run this city, but no vampires are entering my office. Especially not after that display. You can wait in the car for your mate."

Ashe's lip curls up in a snarl and I grab his arm, squeezing to get his attention. He turns his glare to me and I raise my chin. He knows better than to growl and bluster with me.

"You know this is the witch's way," I remind him. "Don't you have a meeting to make? This will take some time, so go do your work for Ambrose. I'll stay here within the wards."

Ashe looks like he's going to argue with me, but he looks away and my shoulders relax. He glares at Darcelle, who doesn't back down. "If a single hair is harmed on her head, I will destroy this place brick by brick."

"Ashe!" I gasp as Darcelle says, "Acknowledged. Now leave my shop before I kick you out."

With one final pointed look at me, one filled with ice-rimmed flames, Ashe strides away. We watch him until he wrenches the front door open, the bells clanging as it slams into the wall. I wince at the display.

"I'm so sorry about him—" I begin to apologize and Darcelle lets out a low, deep laugh, waving away my concerns.

"I'm just proud of the boy for finally showing some emotion," they say before heading down into the wall. "I've always thought Ashe was too contained. It's not good on the stomach to bottle everything up like he does. Now, then, why don't you tell me what's going on?"

I roll my lips, considering Darcelle's words about my mate. While Eris is in control of my body, I'm not completely unaware of what is happening around us but what Darcelle is describing is not the Ashe I know. My Ashe is passionate and tender and always trying to coax a smile or laugh from me. To hear that he's now as bottled up as, say, Kasar makes my heart ache and guilt weighs down my shoulders.

Instead, I focus on explaining what I know happened when Eris and Ashe pursued the archangel Aeternaphiel from Wren's gallery. The witch listens without comment as they open the door and we cross into their office, the buzz of their wards rippling over my skin with comforting familiarity. I stop just over the threshold, struck by the eclectic mix before me. I shouldn't be, considering the decor of the coffee shop behind us.

An antique electric chandelier casts a warm glow over the space, the intricate designs juxtaposed against the exposed brick walls lined with shelves. The shelves themselves hold a dizzying collection of leather-bound tomes interspersed with modern plastic binders in different colors.

Aromas of freshly brewed coffee and exotic spices mingle in the air, drawing me deeper into the space. I close my eyes, breathing in the scents and feeling my own wild magic being soothed by the natural tones. I barely hear Darcelle shut the office door behind me before murmuring an incantation to ward the room from eavesdroppers.

They say nothing as my feet take me past the worn, wooden desk cluttered with papers, a computer, and a few empty white coffee mugs. I'm drawn to the heavy oak work bench pushed up against one wall, its surface meticulously clean compared to the desk.

A small standing shelf is atop it against the wall, and I trail my fingertips along the edge as I catalog the mortar and pestles, the small iron pots, glass vials and jars whose contents hum with wild magic.

"You're a wild witch," I breathe out, my heart fluttering. I think of my old mentor, Agnes—the witch who became my family when I left my coven behind. I blink back the tears as fond memories of the stern woman bring me back to that time. What I would give to have her counsel for my predicament. Not just with Eris and the archangel, but with Ashe as well.

She'd demand to know if I've gone soft over the years and forgotten that nearly every problem can be solved with good, hard work.

I clear my throat and turn back to Darcelle, who is watching me with sympathetic understanding. We consider each other for a long moment before Darcelle gestures for me to take the single wooden chair opposite their own in front of the desk. The witch mutters under their breath as they stack papers and shove them into a drawer before giving me an apologetic look as they move the empty coffee cups behind them onto a short filing cabinet that has different types of bagged coffee on top.

"Results of the trade," they say with a grin. "I'm always trying to find new blends of coffee to share, which means I have the horrible burden of personally taste testing them."

Remembering my own love of bitter teas, I share in their grin as I settle my skirts around my legs. "Oh, of course. I'm certain it must be a terrible strain on you."

Darcelle gives a bark of a laugh, shaking their head as they head towards one of the shelves, tapping their long blue nail against their bottom lip. "No one appreciates teas and coffees like us wild witches. My magic is what helps me find the best roasted beans for the shop. I refuse to serve anything I haven't fully tested. Ah!" They pluck a thin book off the shelf, the spine so thin to have nothing written on it. Darcelle returns to the desk, taking their own seat and setting the book down and flipping it open before I can try to read the gold script printed on the green cover. "Not too many books exist on angels, considering the opinions of humans in the world. This one is a copy of one of the earliest witch hunters clans, descending from the Beya clan from the Near East."

A chill trickles through my veins and I remind myself that there are no hunters in the streets preparing to burn down the building with us trapped inside.

Darcelle doesn't notice my struggles, scanning the page quickly before flipping to the next. "They believed all creatures of magic were to be eliminated, and certainly didn't believe angels were the soldiers of some deity. Fortunately, some of their collected writings were saved from being burned. I could have sworn I've read something similar to what you described back when the demons were causing a ruckus in the city and Ambrose needed to explore his options."

I snort at Darcelle's description of the war that nearly broke out between the Nightshades and demons. Eris refused to assist Ambrose, and after Ambrose exiled Ezra from the clan, I supported Eris's stance. Ezra had been one of the first Nightshades to accept me, seeing as he too was considered different. Ezra's father was a demon, and his mother was human. It was when a vampire turned the woman without realizing that she was pregnant, which resulted in Ezra's mixed natures. His duality always challenged him, pulled between different urges, yet he was always eager to destroy. I once accused Ambrose of only ever seeing Ezra as a weapon, and Ezra shocked me by claiming that's exactly what he was.

He'd never taken a mortal soul until the conflict a few decades ago, something Ambrose had explicitly forbidden within the boundaries of the Nightshade territory. I know Ezra. He wouldn't have given in to his demonic nature to bargain for a mortal's soul, but the male refused to name the human whose soul he'd taken. The punishment for the mortal was death, to force any bargain between them and the demon to be void. Ambrose had exiled Ezra, banished him from the clan and told the rest of us Ezra was fortunate to be alive. It had driven Eris away, which meant I left the Barrows too, for some time.

She had never trusted Ambrose, it wasn't in her nature. But from that moment, she never considered him anything more than an employer.

When we'd finally returned, I learned that not only did we lose Ezra but Rhys left as well. The vampire had considered Ezra closer than any brother or best friend, and to lose Ezra was a loss too great. Rhys hadn't abandoned the Nightshades, but instead begged Ambrose to allow him to wander until he was ready to return. Eris and I had both been surprised that Ambrose agreed, until we learned that the king of vampires had given Rhys the duty similar to a diplomat and spy. Ambrose is never altruistic. He saw the opportunity to expand his empire through Rhys and took full advantage.

Rhys has never returned to the Barrows, that I know of, since.

"Here we go," Darcelle says, yanking me from my contemplation. "From your description of the blade being summoned with bright light and Eris being essentially sucked out of you like a vacuum..." The witch trails off, their brow furrowing. They flip to the next page, then back again to reread it.

"What?" I jump up, coming around to Darcelle's side to read over their shoulder. Fortunately the copy was printed in English. I peer closer, rereading the passage. "This doesn't make sense. Why would an archangel use a blade to siphon the essence of a demon into them? I swear the idea isn't even familiar to anything in Eris's memory, and she was once an angelic soldier under direct command of Aeternaphiel. She would have known about this."

Darcelle looks up at me, a grave expression on their face. "You said Ashe stabbed him with Eris's celestial blade?"

I nod in confirmation. "It was melting, though, according to him. The archangel did something to it."

Darcelle turns the page to the one they'd consulted after trailing off, tapping a passage with a sparkly blue nail. My eyes follow theirs, and I narrow my eyes.

Darcelle speaks before I have a chance to comprehend what I read.

"Any being from the celestial realm would be immediately sent back from this plane if struck by a celestial blade. That was their main purpose here on Earth. Aeternaphiel should not have survived being struck." Darcelle leans back in their chair, blowing out a breath. As for me, I stare at them dumbly, my mind unable to see what the witch is suggesting.

Darcelle must see how stupefied I am and takes pity on me. "Here in the Barrows, we deal with many different creatures and magical beings. The blade this book suggests Aeternaphiel used is nearly identical to what a sorcerer or a warlock uses to add to their power. And there is only one way I know of to separate the soul from a body that allows the person to continue living."

I shake my head. "That can't be it. Why would an archangel need to become a lich? Why would he remove his soul from his body?"

Darcelle scrunches their lips and shakes their head. "I can't say why, but I do know that it means you're right. You and Eris are running out of time. Eris wasn't struck true by the blade, but enough has been cleaved from her that she's dying. Not just dying, but being consumed. And because of how enmeshed your souls are, you will be consumed too.

The only way to save either of you is to find the soul and destroy it."

I stagger back around the desk and collapse back onto the chair. I stare, wide-eyed, at Darcelle and utter something more appropriate for Eris.

"Well. Shit."

Chapter Five
ASHE

The dining room is silent as we each grapple with what Cassandra has revealed. Even forewarned, I struggle not to rage against the injustice of the situation. I have my mate back, we're closer than ever to fulfilling her demon bargain. Now we only have days to complete the task that's been nearly impossible for a hundred and fifty years. If we don't, my mate dies.

Ambrose, sitting at the head of the table with his chin resting on his steepled fingers, catches my eye. Silently commanding me to lock down the fury that must show on my face. It's more than fury. It's rage. It's pain. It's devastation. It's grief. It's terror. A gods-damned hurricane inside me, threatening to rip me a part at my very seems.

I curl my fingers into fists, my knuckles going white

as my nails dig into my skin. My jaw locks and I glare down at the dark oak table and struggle to control my breathing.

Cassandra hadn't stayed quiet during the drive back from Black Death Beanery. Instead, she told me everything she'd discussed with Darcelle. I almost wish she hadn't, but I'm glad she didn't try to hide it.

As soon as we'd arrived, I'd told Ambrose that we needed to speak—all of us. While he called in the inner circle, Cassandra gave him the explanation. He'd said nothing, his face cryptically still.

I've admired his talent to maintain composure in the worst of situations but watching him take in the fact that Cassandra will die in a matter of days without blinking has me wanting to lash out. If it were Eloise in danger, he wouldn't be this calm.

Eloise sits to his left, and Kasar across from her. Cassandra sits beside him next to me, and Deidre and Malachi across from us. Lan and his mother, Josephine, take two of the remaining seats at the side of the table, leaving the end vacant. Wren didn't join her savage mate, tending to their daughter, Emily, at their home.

When I'm certain the hurricane is suppressed, I scan the faces of my fellow Nightshades. Every male here has known Cassandra since we met in Willow Creek. She saved every single male here with her actions that night, even if she betrayed me.

That icy fact hardens my resolve and I plant a hand on the table, pressing down and meeting every golden gaze at the table before speaking.

"If it weren't for Cassandra, none of you would be here today," I intone, the silence growing more profound as their attention is riveted to me. "We owe her this help." I meet Ambrose's hard golden gaze, knowing my own golden eyes holds just as much of a challenge. "You owe her."

Eloise and Deidre frown, with Kasar giving his mate a slight shake of his head. Her frown turns to a scowl. Deidre has never liked secrets, which is why she excels as an investigative journalist. Eloise opens her mouth to say something, but Ambrose cuts her off.

"I agree."

I jerk my head back as if slapped, so shocked I am at his frank words.

Josephine reaches out, laying her hand over mine and squeezing gently, drawing my gaze. Hers are golden orbs shimmering with the threat of tears while filled with understanding and compassion. I turn my hand under hers, grasping her in a quiet display of need. Josephine may only be Landon's blood mother and she may be the one vampire we dare not cross even more than Ambrose, but it is because she holds us all in her heart.

Her husband's love was matched with abuse, but

despite that, she has made sure to shower those in her family real love. Unconditionally and without doubt.

Ambrose and Eloise may be the king and queen of the vampires, but Josephine? Josephine is the mother of us Nightshades. There is nothing we will not do for her. And not a single time has she abused that power. Not even when we could have punished her husband, brutally and violently, for laying his hands on her.

"Of course we will help Cassandra," Josephine says, a gentle chiding in her tone. She reaches out with her other hand, beckoning my wife to take it. When Cassandra does, she smiles at us both. "Cassandra, you are one of us. You have been from the moment you became Ashe's mate. Eris may have her conflicts with us, but she too has become one of us. To lose either of you would be too great a loss."

My throat thickens at her words and I have to swallow back the emotions she's conjured. Her soothing compassion and love for us dampens the acidic rage inside me, making it easier for me to think.

As if she knows what she's done, she draws away after one last squeeze. She stands, sweeping her hands down her black skirt to smooth out any creases. She directs her next words to Ambrose.

"I will have tea, coffee, and food brought," she announces. "No doubt this will be a long night if you are to plan how to save our witch."

Ambrose inclines his head, an indulgent look in his eyes. He may appear in his late thirties and Josephine in her sixth or seventh decade, but he's always considered her his daughter.

The moment she's swept from the dining room deeper in the house, Lan rises as well. Before anyone can speak, Lan's calling out to Deidre. "Grab your laptop and I'll get mine. We need more information on this archangel. He was at the Memento Mori gallery opening, so he has a social presence in Topside. By the time we're done, we'll know what underwear he prefers."

Deidre scoffs, but rises. "I'll leave you to his underwear preferences." She follows the blond vampire, the two of them already bouncing ideas on how to track the man's movements and locations down.

Malachi coughs, a bad attempt at covering up a laugh. He shoots Kasar an amused look. "If he wasn't mated, I'd warn you that Lan might steal your girl."

Rather than react as explosively as he may have in the past, Kasar leans the dining chair onto its back legs, crossing his arms over his chest with a devilish smirk. The man's jacket is a credit to his tailor with how the fabric strains against his muscles but doesn't burst at the seams. "Even if he was, the way she rode my cock this morning—"

"Gah!" Eloise interrupts him, her face turning beet

red. Kasar's smirk grows. "Shush. I don't need to hear about my best friend's sex life from you."

The table snickers and not even I can suppress a slight smile. Eloise is no prude; no woman could be when mated to Ambrose d'Vil. It makes it all the more amusing to scandalize her. Malachi, especially, enjoys teasing her — so long as Ambrose isn't around. Unfortunately for Malachi, Eloise makes him her primary target when trying to antagonize her mate. More than once, I've seen him hightailing it from the clan house to avoid the ire of a mated male. Malachi might lean towards good-natured teasing, but when it comes to getting a rise out of the king of vampires, he's not stupid.

Personally, I'm convinced Eloise thinks it's hilarious to see the general of the Nightshades' force speed walk away. Speed walk, since of course no vampire male as old as Malachi would admit to running.

"Besides, we need to start planning how to save Cassandra and Eris," Eloise continues, pushing past her embarrassment. She looks at Ambrose. "We won't be able to actually plan something until Lan and Deidre get back, but there's got to be something we can do in the meantime."

Ambrose inclines his head towards her. "Indeed." He studies us all, the calculations he's running clear in his eyes. After a long moment, his attention snaps to

Kasar as he stands. "We'll need to get Aeternaphiel in a known location, which, if he is maintaining some sort of position in Topside's social circles, shouldn't be too difficult. Call in Rhys. We'll need him."

Malachi and I share stunned looks, and Ambrose doesn't miss them. "He will come." His tone is hard as steel.

"Yes, sire," Malachi and I both murmur.

Rhys hasn't been in the Barrows since Ambrose cast Ezra out during the difficulties with demons. They'd both been orphans in their own way, forming a tight bond of brotherhood that went beyond sharing the same vampire clan. I doubt Rhys has forgiven Ambrose for what he sees as a betrayal of both Ezra and himself.

"Malachi," Ambrose carries on as Kasar removes himself from the room. Even if Rhys will come, I don't envy Kasar's job to getting in contact with him. The vampire is constantly on the move, having adopted the persona of a rock star of all fucking things. Ambrose allowed it, using it as an opportunity to use Rhys as a sort of paranormal diplomat. "I want you to have our people on the streets keeping their ears out for any word of this man and his movements. Whatever Lan and Deidre can't find, I expect you to know."

"Sire," Malachi says with a nod, pushing back from the table. He gives me a nod then Cassandra a small smile. "We'll get the bastard. Eris never let us help before. Now it's not just her looking. We protect our own." Then he's out the door in Kasar's wake, leaving Cassandra, myself, Eloise, and Ambrose at the table.

"What can I do?" Eloise asks, eager to help.

Ambrose hesitates and I can sympathize. The planning won't be dangerous, but whatever we decide to do —there will be danger. Eloise still hasn't given in to being turned, though I think she's getting more used to the idea. I also know that Eloise will refuse to be left out. She might not go behind Ambrose's back right into danger, but she refuses to be kept safe at home like Ambrose would prefer. She gives him a hard look, clearly reminding him of her stubborn nature.

"Get ahold of Tara, mon lion," he says at last. "She has taken over Mr. Tailor's, and we will need to be ready for a social event. Her skills will be key to our success."

"On it." She's already pulling out her cellphone, fingers flying across the screen as she texts.

Ambrose directs his attention to us. "Cassandra, ready yourself however you think is necessary. We'll need your skills as a witch, I'm sure. Ashe, make sure our cars are in top form. Meet back here in two hours, no later. Otherwise, we will be in my office."

With the final command given, Ambrose takes Eloise's hand and sweeps her from the room.

Cassandra stifles a yawn. I get up and offer a hand to her. She quickly hides the flash of her surprise but it still churns the ire bubbling inside. She takes it and I help pull the chair back as she stands. I let go of her but don't increase the space between us.

"You don't need to act surprised every time I touch you," I mutter. I can't fully hide the bitterness escaping.

Cassandra stills, clearly taken aback, and my jaw clenches. I incline my head towards the open doorway. "You should rest."

Cassandra's eyes fill with a familiar stubborn glint. She meets my gaze, her lips pressed into a firm line before speaking. "We have things to discuss first, Ashe."

There's no use in arguing with Cassandra when she gets like this. Easier to hear her out or let her do whatever it is she's set on. I consider arguing anyways; this isn't a topic I'm sure I'm ready for. Then, as if a phantom hourglass haunts me just out of the corner of my eye, I hear the sands of time passing. A stark reminder that we may only have a few days left.

"Upstairs, then."

She follows at my side as we head to my—our suite. How many times since we've claimed this residence have I walked beside Eris. Always on edge, never fully trusting her. Now I'm on edge for an entirely different reason. It's as if I'm bracing myself, expecting an explosion or a gunshot, anything that will have me ducking for cover. Except I'd be protecting the dark, withered organ of my heart.

Shit, Malachi's addiction to *Married at First Sight* is getting to me if I'm psychoanalyzing my feelings.

"This is certainly different than our cottage back in Willow Creek." Her voice is soft, a soothing siren's call I've never been able to resist for long. I'd never wanted to before. She pauses before the stairs that lead to the higher levels, taking in the built-in shelves filled with a combination of books and antiques or trinkets from the Nightshades' past. They tend to be items we've set down carelessly and Josephine has saved, displaying them just so in the clan home.

A brass astrolabe Malachi used for years, both during his travels at sea and his own casual study in astronomy. A curved dagger, with a pure silver hilt embossed with geometric patterns and a large ruby set as the pommel, Kasar was gifted by a grateful Allamah after saving her family after a ghul took on the guise of her husband. A framed, intricately embroidered linen handkerchief depicting a bouquet of wildflowers a young woman infatuated with Ezra had gifted him. There's even Rhy's almost ancient, at this point, fiddle; a Chinese jade teapot of Lan's; and gilded music box, long silenced, purchased by Ambrose when he lived in Naples.

The dark stained shelves polished until they reflect the warm light from sleek, modern table lamps make this room look more like a home than a museum of curios.

Cassandra slowly walks along the cases, a fond expression on her face as she occasionally touches items she's seen before. When she's completed the room, her brows are pinched together.

"I don't see anything of yours here," she says, but the look in her eyes makes it a question. "Even Ezra's life is on display."

I shrug a shoulder, sliding my hands into my pants pockets. "I just don't leave my shit around for Josephine to pick up and put on display." I turn and head up the stairs, escaping the conversation before I tell her the entire truth. "Didn't you want to talk?"

I can never hide anything from Cassandra for long. I've never been able to; especially if she turns her innocent, soft-looking eyes at me and asks me in a voice as warm as a summer's day.

Cassandra has always been the siren to my lonely sailor. Except now I'm clinging to the safety rope, terrified that if I embrace her only to lose her again, I won't ever recover.

The truth is, I've saved more than a few items from

our shared past. I simply hoard them away from the clan house. I've created a private sanctuary that I can retreat to when Eris gets too much. Only Ambrose knows about it, though I'm sure the rest suspect. They're respectful enough not to pry.

Cassandra says nothing until the bedroom door is closed behind us. I shouldn't be surprised when she speaks a lyrical phrase, one I dredge the purpose of from my memory. Warding and silencing the rooms from any listeners. A bomb could go off now in this room, and it wouldn't be heard outside of the wards.

Nervousness, anxiety, irritation, anticipation—whatever emotion is buzzing under my skin makes it impossible to sit down. I stalk to the windows, the curtains secured back, and stare vacantly out onto the street in front of the house. The sun is sinking, traffic increases as people head home from work. An entire world that moves on without a care that I might lose my mate forever in a matter of days.

The silence draws out, strangling my nerves along with it. Her heart races, the rapid thump-thump clear to my vampire hearing.

"I'm sorry, Ashe."

Fury at Cassandra's words floods me, so swiftly I can't contain it. It's all-consuming, breaking free after festering over a fucking century. I whirl on her, snarling, my fangs long and bared.

"I'm so fucking sick of you telling me you're gods-damned sorry, Cassandra."

In an instant, I'm in front of her. I grip her throat with one hand, forcing her to look up at me, while I pin her wrists to the small of her back with the other. My nails threaten to turn sharp and press into the soft, thin skin, on the verge of drawing blood. Her pulse flutters against my palm like a caged bird, but I'd moved too fast for her to react.

Her nostrils flare and her pupils widen. The scent of her fills me but does nothing to quell the beast I've become.

I crush my mouth to hers, biting sharply at her lower lip until she gasps. I consume her, pressing my tongue into her, tasting her with a frenzy of a starved man. Just as quickly, I pull back. My chest heaves as my gaze clouds red, reveling in Cassandra's dazed expression.

I force her head to the side. Then I'm burying my fangs in her neck. Right on top of her siren song of her pulse, ready to drown.

1865

Ashe

If I didn't know any better, I'd think you were following me, Mr. Halford."

I close the short distance between me and the black-haired beauty I haven't been able to stop thinking about since I met her a week ago. I keep my hands in my pockets, otherwise I'm afraid I'd reach out just to feel her skin against mine. The memory of her in my arms, her warmth against my chest, her scent in my nose, has haunted my nights. Even now my fangs tingle with the need to sink into her, to drink her heart's blood and claim her as mine.

"Can a man not look through the wares of the market without being accused of such?" I ask, my tone teasing. The village square is lined with stalls, many vendors already packing up for the evening. Malachi and Kasar are speaking with the gunsmith of the town, and I nod when Kasar looks over at me. Josephine is chatting animatedly with the baker's wife as the woman wraps up the large order Josephine had placed the day before.

Cassandra smirks, amber and hazel eyes flashing with amusement. Today, her black hair is braided in a crown around her head, tendrils already escaping to frame her face. She wears a yellow blouse with a white pinafore apron tied around her waist. "Considering you've never come to town before now?"

I shrug, unable to take my eyes from her. Cassandra raises a brow, the smirk shifting to a knowing smile. It's true. Usually, I don't bother coming into town, preferring duties that take me in the woods. My siblings are the ones who tend to handle the trips into Willow Creek.

Cassandra tilts her head, studying me. "Have you had dinner yet, Mr. Halford?"

I incline my head. "I have not." No doubt she means the food a witch or human eat. But my heart races and my fangs and cock throb at the idea of her arching her neck and offering me her blood.

She hums, her smile widening. "Would you care to have some with me tonight then?"

A woman walking by gasps, no doubt at the audacity of a woman asking a man to dinner. Even here in such a small, secluded town, modern rules of society reign. What would the woman think if she were born in my time, when men and women worked side by side? Or when sex was nothing but what a male and female did to find pleasure and procreate? There was no taboo in pleasure, but now, heavens forbid a woman own her desires.

I eye Cassandra. No doubt the witch wouldn't ascribe to modern beliefs when it comes to passion. She would not simply lie on her back, her legs spread, and allow her body to be used for the sake of a man. No, my witch would be demanding, the fire in her eyes would spread throughout her body and she'd command her own blaze.

I long for her to burn me.

"I would be honored, Cassandra," I reply. I'd love to see her eyes flare with anger and perhaps even a hint of arousal at my use of her given name in a public setting.

Her smile softens, her expression full of a feminine confidence that draws me in. "Good," she declares and turns, gesturing for me to walk beside her.

I fall in step with her, enjoying the way she doesn't match her pace to mine. Instead, Cassandra keeps a brisk pace, her skirts swishing around her ankles with her movements.

"No Lily Dancer today?" she asks as we grow further away from the main square. I could race to her house in less than a minute with my enhanced speed, but that would reveal my true nature to the humans behind us and threaten the Nightshades' place here in Willow Creek. If I'm honest, though, I want as much time as possible with this woman. I'd walk slower if I didn't think she'd tell me to hurry up.

"Why? Are you worried you'll trip again?" I tease, remembering how she'd tumbled into the road. Before she can do more than gasp in outrage, I duck my head down towards her ear and whisper, "Don't worry, I'll catch you before you fall. Or, perhaps, I'll let you fall just to have an excuse to have you in my arms again."

I straighten, amusement flooding through me as I continue to amble down the dirt road towards the forest path she lives down. Cassandra is still frozen in place, and when I chance a look back at her, she's gaping at me. When our eyes meet, she turns the most becoming shade of red.

Cassandra huffs and begins marching towards me again. "Don't tease a witch," she warns, her tone a mix of playful and serious. "Or I'll turn you into a toad."

I cock a brow, grinning. "A toad? Why not something more creative? Like a frog?"

She stops beside me, her arms crossed, and she narrows her eyes at me. "Are frogs and toads not the same thing?"

"Most definitely not," I insist. "Though I can see why a witch from New York would be confused."

Cassandra scowls, her expression promising retribution, and I laugh. The witch marches ahead, but I hear her muttering about toads and frogs and I can't stop my grin.

I hadn't laughed so much in decades, not since Josephine and Kasar found me, and it felt wonderful. Cassandra brings lightness and joy I'd long since forgotten existed.

I'd had lovers, of both the vampire and human variety, but none had sparked this fire within me. The idea of her tripping again so I can catch her and have her in my arms, the idea of her threatening me, fills me with more joy than feeding from a corrupt, abusive soul.

Cassandra halts at the path towards her cottage, narrowing her eyes suspiciously at me. "Did you not think I was serious?"

I blink innocently, raising a hand over my heart. "About the toad? Of course, I take your threats very seriously, Cassandra."

Her scowl returns and she points down the path. "Follow me, vampire, so I can prove to you that frogs and toads are the same thing."

She spins and marches down the path, her steps purposeful. I follow her, keeping a normal human pace. The path is narrow, the trees overhead intertwining their branches in an archway, and the shadows grow the deeper we go. Cassandra's skirts and hair bounce with her steps and I smile.

My fangs tingle and my cock begins to harden, imagining Cassandra bouncing in another way. With me inside of her as she rides me, her breasts bare and her head thrown back. My cock jerks, imagining her breasts would be generous enough for me to fill my hands.

Cassandra stops suddenly, and I nearly run into her. She turns, her eyes narrowed again, and I force my fangs to retract. Her amber and hazel eyes flash with the light of the full moon beginning to rise and I can't resist.

I crowd her, my hand rising to cup her jaw. Cassandra's eyes widen, and a spark of something more than suspicion fills her eyes. Desire, sharp and heady, fills her scent and it's all I can do not to bare my fangs.

I trace my thumb across her bottom lip, and Cassandra's lips part on a soft breath. Her pupils expand, and I can no longer resist.

"May I kiss you, Cassandra?" I ask, needing to hear the words from her. I wouldn't cross the line until she gave me permission.

Cassandra's pupils expand even more, until only the barest rim of her iris remains. "Yes."

I swoop in, claiming her mouth. Cassandra's gasp

gives me access and I deepen the kiss, exploring her mouth. My tongue finds hers, and Cassandra grips my forearms, holding on as I devour her.

My fangs elongate, wanting to taste her, to bite her and claim her as mine. Cassandra moans, and the sound is all I can take.

I break the kiss, pressing a final, chaste kiss to her swollen lips. Cassandra blinks, her eyes glazed and unfocused. Her lips are red and kiss-swollen, and she's never looked more beautiful.

Cassandra blinks again, coming back to the present. Her cheeks flush and her heart races.

Before she can reply, I sweep her into my arms, racing the rest of the way to her cottage.

Chapter Six

CASSANDRA

Ashe's bite is brutal. A pure animalistic attack that reminds me I am nothing but I am flesh and bone against his vampire nature. He is the predator and I'm the prey; and I'm at his mercy.

I relish it, relish him.

Tilting my head into his grip, I offer my throat willingly. The growl of approval that rumbles from him blisters my skin and coils into tight arousal. Each tug of his, drawing my life force into his mouth, churns my magic as much as it fans my desire.

He doesn't release my hands, keeping them pinned at my lower back.

His fangs are deeply embedded in my throat, his tongue rasping over the wounds. The sharp, aching pleasure of the bite is heightened by the lack of his touch.

Ashe's free hand cups my breast, kneading and shaping me through the fabric of my shirt. I moan his name, wanting him to touch me, skin to skin. He growls, his thumb and forefinger tweaking the hardening point of my nipple.

It's a shock, jolting through my bloodstream to center between my legs. My knees weaken, leaving me to hang suspended from the grip Ashe has on my wrists.

Magic, vampire, and primal need combine into a heady concoction that clouds my thoughts. All I want is more. More of him. More of us. More of the pleasure that is building with each passing second.

My shirt tears, the sound of ripping fabric sharp and loud. Ashe releases my breast only to rip away the bra covering my chest. His palm is hot against my skin as he grips my naked flesh once more.

My nipples harden further, aching for more than the light touches and teasing pinching.

Ashe bites harder, my blood spilling over his lips to stain his chin.

I struggle against his hold, gasping out, "I need to touch you." I whimper as he licks a long path up the column of my throat until he bites my lower lip. "Please."

"You need to earn it, my dear wife," he murmurs against my lips. His golden eyes are bright with lust, his words ghosting across my flesh with a dark, hedonistic promise.

"Tell me," I whisper, nipping at his chin. The coppery tang of my blood teases my taste buds.

Ashe's smile is sinful, his talon-tipped nails slicing through the remainder of my clothing. The silk of my blouse and my long skirt flutter to the floor around my feet. The bra I'd been given is already hanging from my shoulders, and with a heat-inducing bite, he snaps the straps, leaving me in the shockingly small underwear Josephine assured me was the standard. According to her, there are more revealing underwear, and I can't imagine such a thing.

But if Ashe continues to look at me the way he is, I will happily wear whatever scantily covering items he wants. Under his gaze, I feel like the rabbit cornered by a wolf—the wolf fully intent on devouring me as an act of worship.

He holds my gaze, my chest rising and falling as my heart races, while he slowly—so damn slowly—traces a talon-tipped finger down from the hollow of my throat. Down between my breasts, making my nipples tighten, down the soft curve of my stomach before hooking it underneath the elastic of my underwear. I shiver, but it has nothing to do with being cold.

This, right now, is nothing like the first time we came together when I accepted I was his mate. That had been a thing of love and beauty.

This is darkness and promises violence. The claiming between two wild animals.

With a twist of his wrist, he tears the fabric from me, leaving me fully bared before him. I'm revealed to him, while he drinks me in like a dying man.

I struggle once more, wanting him as bare as me. I want him to feel what I'm feeling. What he's done to me.

He tsks, the sound a low, sensual purr. "Impatient little mate."

I bare my teeth at him, but the effect is less than I'd hope when his lips are slick with my blood. My magic crackles around us, traveling under my skin, desperate to join with him.

"Release me, Ashe," I hiss.

"Are you begging me, Cassandra?"

"Yes," I whisper.

As soon as the word leaves my lips, Ashe has me pressed against the wall.

"No," he growls. He pins my hand above my head. "Do not move your hands, witch."

"And if I do?"

The dark flash across his face has me tempted to disobey.

"Then I'll punish you," Ashe confirms. His lips twist up in a beautiful smirk. "But the real punishment won't be the spanking. It'll be taking what I want from you without ever letting you come."

I groan, bereft at the idea of him withholding my pleasure. "Okay," I whisper, dropping my head back against the wall to stare up at the ceiling. He releases my hands and I look back at him. He steps away, sliding off his black jacket and laying it neatly on top of the dresser along the wall. My mouth goes dry as he turns to face me after slipping his feet from his shoes and removing his socks.

In black trim trousers and a white button-down, seeing him shed his clothing feels more like he's shedding his armor.

When Ashe unbuttons his shirt, revealing a triangle of beautiful skin dusted in fine hair, I begin to reach for him without realizing. His pointed growl has me flattening my palms against the wall above my head.

"This is torture," I groan.

He shakes his head once in rebuke, before sliding the shirt off and laying it over his jacket. He meets my gaze as his hands go to his belt, unfastening it. "No. Torture is seeing your mate every day and never being able to touch her. Never able to taste her. Never sleep beside her at night and wake up every morning with her."

He pauses, his belt dangling open. I watch as Ashe swallows, his throat working as his jaw tightens. "Torture is seeing the one person you thought would be beside you forever disappear from you. To have their body possessed by a demon." Ashe's eyes bleed crimson, the color seeping from the outer rim of his irises to spread towards his pupil. "Torture is wondering every single day if it's worth continuing to live since your reason for living was gone."

My heart cracks, splitting open as Ashe strips bare before me. Emotion clogs my throat, tears pricking the corners of my eyes.

"Ashe," I whisper, choking on the guilt and pain that flood me. I'm drowning, unable to breathe as his pain becomes my own. "Ashe, I'm so sorry."

Ashe stalks forward, naked and glorious, his arousal thick and heavy between his thighs. He grasps my neck, the side clear of blood. This time his touch is gentler, an anchor to ground me. "What did I say about you saying that?"

I swallow, lowering my eyes. There are no words to truly express the remorse for the pain I caused him. I don't regret it, though. I will never regret saving his life.

"Cassandra," Ashe murmurs, dipping his head to capture my attention. His free hand trails down my side, leaving goosebumps in its wake. When he reaches my hip, his fingers dig in and he jerks me forward. My gasp is lost as he kisses me, this one tender, coaxing, and filled with love.

The stark difference between this kiss and the one from before leaves me dizzy.

His tongue tangles with mine, his fangs nipping and teasing. He doesn't draw blood again, though. Instead, Ashe drops his hands to the back of my thighs and lifts me. Instinctively, I wrap my legs around his waist and wind my arms around his neck, holding him close.

"I love you," Ashe whispers against my lips. "I hate you." Ashe's voice breaks. "I need you." His chest brushes against my nipples as he takes a deep breath. "I miss you." He slides one arm free from supporting me and I'm pinned tighter against the wall as Ashe cups the back of my head. "I'm so gods-damned angry at you, Cassandra," he grinds out.

"I know," I manage. His emotions are pouring into me. I absorb them, welcoming the pain and the anger because I deserve it. I welcome it because it's a sign Ashe is finally opening the bond between us.

"I'm so gods-damned angry, Cassandra," Ashe repeats, resting his forehead against my own. "I'm so scared, mate."

The last word is a broken plea.

"I'm here," I answer, cupping his face and smoothing my thumbs over his cheeks. "Ashe, I'm here. I'm not going anywhere. I swear it. We will figure this out. This time it's not just Eris. It's all of us."

Ashe shudders, his breath leaving him in a rush. "I can't lose you again."

"You won't," I promise him.

"You don't know that," he growls. Then he crushes his lips to mine.

This kiss is punishing, all teeth and fangs and blood. Ashe consumes me, his free hand sliding up the inside of my thigh until his fingers find my core. His groan is low and deep as his fingers slide between my folds and discover my arousal.

"Cassandra," Ashe growls, sliding his fingers free and gripping my hips. He rocks his hips forward, his length sliding through my center. I shudder, a whimper escaping my lips as Ashe's fangs scrape down the column of my throat.

"Ashe," I plead. "Ashe, please."

"Please what, Cassandra," he murmurs.

I lift my hips, tilting my pelvis to find the tip of Ashe's erection.

His groan is ragged, his arms tightening around me.

"Ashe, please."

"Gods, Cassandra."

He captures my lips as he thrusts up and inside of

me. My gasp is swallowed by his kiss. My magic crackles in the air, the purple wisps curling around Ashe and me. My nails dig into his shoulders as Ashe withdraws and slams back into me.

This is violent and primal. It's the reunion of two souls who've been separated for too long.

Ashe is relentless. His movements are hard, driving into me with a force that threatens to splinter the wall at my back.

"Cassandra," Ashe mutters over and over, his forehead against my own. Our gazes are locked, and I can't tear mine from his.

"Ashe," I answer. Magic flows freely from me, wrapping around us both, twining us together. Ashe's emotions pour into me. Love. Anger. Pain. Longing. Hope. Desire.

"Cassandra," Ashe whispers, slowing his thrusts. He pulls back, cradling my cheek with a gentleness that shatters me. "Cassandra," he murmurs again, like a prayer, kissing me.

I melt against him, tears trailing down my cheeks. I had never allowed myself to admit how much I missed this connection with him. I wouldn't have been able to survive all these years being possessed by a demon otherwise.

Ashe's pace changes, his thrusts slow and deep, his grip on my hips gentle as he helps me lift and lower my hips. My magic curls around us both, strengthening the bond and our connection.

Ashe groans, burying his face into the crook of my neck.

"Ashe," I gasp, my core tightening. Pleasure winds tighter and tighter, each brush of his body against my clit heightens the tension.

Ashe growls my name again, biting my throat. He drinks, his thrusts growing faster, harder.

I shatter, crying out his name as I find my release. Wave after wave of bliss crests over me, leaving me floating. I'm weightless, lost in Ashe's arms and his love.

Ashe shouts my name, his hips stuttering as he finds his own release.

We remain entangled, my magic dissipating as my breathing calms and my heart slows. Ashe's weight presses against me, and I welcome it, running my hands down his back.

After a few minutes, Ashe carefully withdraws and carries us to the bed.

We lay wrapped in each other's embrace, our bodies touching, our gazes locked.

"I love you, Cassandra," Ashe whispers, tracing a finger down my cheek.

"I love you, Ashe," I answer, smoothing the pads of my fingers over his cheek and down his neck.

Ashe's lips twitch in a small smile. He leans forward, brushing his lips against mine.

I answer his smile, kissing him before tucking myself against his chest.

"Rest," Ashe murmurs. "I'll wake you up when it's time to meet with everyone again."

I hum in agreement; I know he has his own tasks to perform before the meeting but I want to cling to him and this moment a little bit longer.

I trace whirls on his chest, refamiliarizing myself with every aspect of my mate. A quiet trepidation intrudes on this peace, one that I can't hold back.

"Are we going to be okay?" I whisper, barely hearing myself but knowing Ashe can anyways.

He's still under me, his arm holding me to him tightening. My head lifts and falls as he lets out a deep sigh. My eyes flutter closed, readying myself for rejection. I'd deserve it. Just because we had sex doesn't mean he's forgiven me or ready to be mates again. I'd understand if he says he needs more time.

He presses a kiss to the top of my head and relief sends a shudder through me. "We will be," Ashe answers, his voice filled with tentative hope. "We'll figure it out. Together."

I shift until my chin is on his chest and I'm looking into his golden eyes. "Together," I vow.

There won't be any more decisions made only by

me. If Ashe says no to something, I won't do it. We're mates, and because of the newly reopened bond between us, I can feel his hesitancy to trust. I swear to the goddess I will earn his trust once more. I will repair the damage I've done. Even if I can't be saved and only have days left to live.

1865

Cassandra

The celebration is beautiful, strings of lanterns stretching between buildings across the square. Some enterprising women have swathed the fountain in evergreen boughs and wildflowers, and the husbands had hauled many tables and benches out for the platters of food their wives had cooked.

A wedding always brings Willow Creek together, and I smile as I raise my mug in a cheer as another villager makes a toast to the happy young couple.

They look blissfully happy, with flushed faces and their hands clasped together as they speak with others. Young, naive, and full of dreams and desires.

My smile becomes wistful and I take a sip of the ale, wrinkling my nose. Humans love the bitter drink, but I've always preferred wine.

Someone sits beside me, and I turn, ready to welcome them. My smile becomes genuine as Ashe Halford smirks at me, his golden eyes alight with mischief.

"There you are," I tease. I look beyond him to see the rest of the Nightshades making their way into the celebration. Josephine goes immediately to the young couple, pressing a large basket full of gifts into their hands before wrapping them both in a genial embrace.

Unlike the Jamesons, Ambrose never treated the villagers as lesser creatures. In return, the humans were loyal and welcoming to them. I'd worried the humans would question their nature, especially since each vampire boasts distinctive golden eyes. But whatever questions they had were soon forgotten by having a leader who sees to the needs of the town.

Ambrose is speaking with the father of the bride, a smile on his handsome face as the older human speaks. Malachi, Ezra, Landon, and Rhys disappear into the crowd, but not before Josephine shoots a look at Ashe.

"Josephine will have your hide if you disappear," I warn, nudging Ashe with my shoulder.

The vampire grins, the sight making my heart skip a beat. I take another sip of ale, needing to cool the heat that's been growing in me ever since we kissed.

Ever since Ashe stole kisses, teased me, and made me long for more. I've never reacted to a man like this.

I'd had a couple lovers, but because of my witch nature, I never kept them for long. I'd never considered taking a vampire lover before. My slow aging would mean nothing to a nearly immortal being. Something is still holding me back, though, from letting go and giving myself to him.

I'd been betrayed by loved ones before, hurt by those who were supposed to protect me. I don't know if I can open myself again to that pain.

Ashe leans in, his lips brushing the shell of my ear and I shiver. "I can steal you away, Cassandra," he murmurs, and his warm breath against my skin has me clenching my thighs together.

Ashe chuckles, no doubt scenting my arousal, and I scowl at him. He straightens, his hand settling on my knee and his thumb rubs soothing circles through the fabric.

My eyes dart around, trying to see if anyone else notices the too familiar touch. It's quite inappropriate for Ashe to be touching me like this, especially in public, but I can't bring myself to pull away from him.

No one seems to notice, and I take another sip of ale. Rhys is sitting with two other villagers, opening the case of his fiddle and setting it to his shoulder with a grin at the others. One has a hand drum and the other has a well-worn guitar. As the music starts, the groom leads the bride into a small clearing while the rest of the people gather around them, clapping in time with the music.

I frown when I see an unfamiliar man leaning against the post of the general store's perch. He's half in the shadows, but I'm certain I've never seen him here before.

I jump, almost spilling my ale, when Ashe's lips brush my ear again.

"Dance with me," Ashe cajoles before stealing my mug of ale and downing it with a roguish smirk. He stands and I shake my head, laughter building in my chest.

"Oh, no, I don't dance," I tell him and half-heartedly pull back when he grabs my hand. "I trip over my feet enough walking!"

Ashe doesn't relent, his eyes sparkling with amusement. My heart is helpless against his grin. "It'll be fine, trust me."

I narrow my eyes at him, allowing him to pull me to my feet. "If you let me fall, vampire, I'm cursing you."

Ashe laughs, the sound causing warmth to blossom in my chest. "If I let you fall, Cassandra, I'd deserve it."

We join the villagers already dancing, and Ashe pulls me closer with a hand on my waist. I allow him, not bothering to hide my pleased smile when I wrap my hand in his. The music is a quick reel, and sure enough I trip as soon as Ashe starts us spinning along with the rest of the dancers around the area. True to his word though, he keeps me upright, holding me against his chest in the most indecent fashion. My feet barely touch the ground as we continue to dance, both of us breathless with laughter.

Ashe twirls me, and I laugh again, my head thrown back. I meet the eyes of the unfamiliar man and I stumble, losing my balance.

Ashe catches me, pulling me against his chest. His golden eyes are serious, his mouth a hard line. "Cassandra?"

I shake my head, nodding towards the stranger. "There's someone I've never seen in Willow Creek before."

Ashe's head whips towards where the man had been, his brows furrowing. The man is gone, and Ashe turns back to me, his expression concerned.

"Are you sure?" he asks, his hands gentle on my arms.

"Of course I'm sure," I say, frowning. Then I shake my head, laughing again. "Come on, I'm desperate for a drink after that."

He leads me through the dancers and the gathered crowd towards the table with refreshments. A few of the unmarried young women eye me with envy at Ashe's attention and my cheeks heat. With how small Willow Creek is, there aren't many options for marriage, and Ashe is attractive and well situated. If he were human, he'd been an ideal husband for any of these women.

A thrill goes through me when I meet his gaze as he presses a new cup into my hands. Ashe has never once looked at another woman around me, even though I'm certainly not the most beautiful one here. I take a cautious sip, then drink greedily of the perfectly tart and cold lemonade.

"Better?" he asks when I finish, a sigh of contentment slipping from my lips.

"Much." I look at the dancers and confess, "I don't think I'm up for anymore dancing, though."

When I look back at Ashe, the hunger in his eyes steals my breath and has heat rushing between my thighs. My core throbs and I swallow roughly, my heart pounding.

Ashe doesn't speak, taking my empty cup and setting it on the refreshment table.

"Come with me?" he asks, but he's already leading me away into the shadows. We pass Lan and Ezra chatting with two younger women, and Ezra winks at me.

Such strange company I'm finding myself in since the Nightshades came to town. I never thought I'd meet a half-vampire, half-demon in my life. I never thought they could exist.

Ashe leads me down the narrow lane towards the

edge of Willow Creek, and when we pass the last lantern, he sweeps me into his arms. My startled squeak turns to a laugh, my arms going around his neck.

Ashe's grin flashes in the moonlight, his golden eyes glowing, and I'm struck again by how beautiful he is. How beautiful they all are.

Vampires have always been creatures of the night, the dark their home. Yet Ashe's pale skin and sable hair seem to glow, as if the moon herself has blessed him.

I trace my fingers along his cheek and Ashe turns his face, pressing a kiss to the sensitive skin of the inside of my wrist. My heart skips a beat, and my core pulses again with need.

Ashe's lips curve, and his eyes flash brighter. "Cassandra," he murmurs, his lips brushing my skin with each syllable.

I'm helpless against his pull, drawn to him like the flowers towards the sun. My lips brush his, and Ashe groans, his hand tightening on my waist.

Ashe turns and presses me against the rough bark of a tree, his lips devouring mine. I moan, my hands threading through his silky hair.

His hips pin mine, and I gasp at the press of his hard length against my thigh. Ashe growls, his fangs grazing the curve of my neck.

I tilt my head, pleasure rushing through me at the

idea of his fangs piercing my flesh. Ashe groans, his lips blazing a trail along the column of my neck, his tongue tracing the lines of my pulse.

My hands fall to his shoulders, and I whimper when his fangs graze the top swell of my breast. Ashe growls again, the primal sound vibrating through me.

I know he must drink blood to maintain his supernatural power, and the witch in me revolts at the idea of letting him pierce my skin. It goes against everything I was taught by my old coven.

After leaving them, though, I've learned magic and our world seeks balance. Giving my blood to Ashe, letting him give me pleasure in return—that feels right. It feels natural and magical and intimate.

Ashe's fangs skate lower, his hands cupping my breasts through my clothing. Pleasure rushes through me and I moan, my head falling back against the tree trunk.

Ashe groans, his tongue tracing the curves of my breasts. "Gods, I've dreamt of these breasts," he speaks against me. "What spell have you put me under, witch?"

I gasp, my hips thrusting against his. Ashe growls, and the sound goes straight to my core. My body knows what it wants, what it needs.

"Cassandra."

"Yes," I gasp, my hands gripping his shoulders.

"Take my blood, Ashe. Drink from me."

He stills against me and I squirm, desperate to continue feeding the pleasure he's begun. I look down, meeting his glowing eyes—a serious expression in his eyes.

"Are you certain?" His voice is a smoky rasp. His entire body is taut, on the verge of losing control. His determination to respect my choice only confirms my decision.

"Yes," I say, moving my hands to his hair and guiding him closer to my neck. "Please, Ashe."

He doesn't strike right away, languidly dragging his tongue against my pulse. My head falls back against the tree, my back arching against him.

When his fangs do sink into my flesh, it's not pain —it's pure pleasure. My fingers tighten in his hair, holding him to me as Ashe's fangs sink deeper into my neck.

Blood wells and Ashe groans, drinking from me. I moan, pleasure rushing through me, and my core throbs.

One of Ashe's hands cups the back of my head, protecting me as he continues to feed. His other slips beneath my skirts, his hand hot against my thigh.

Ashe's fingers brush against the wetness soaking my undergarments and we both moan. He traces the edge of the silk, his fingers dipping beneath the edge.

I bite my lips to hold back the moan choking me, my hips bucking into his touch. Ashe drinks, his fingers finding the sensitive nub of my core. I cry out, pleasure rushing through me.

Ashe circles his thumb, and I writhe against him, my hands skating over him, grabbing him in any way I can as my body is pushed closer to that edge.

Ashe retracts his fangs, his tongue sweeping across the wound to seal it. My blood drips from his fangs and the sight is so erotic I cry out.

Ashe claims my lips, his tongue thrusting into my mouth. He tastes of my blood and I moan, the coppery, rich taste intoxicating.

Ashe breaks the kiss, his other hand sliding beneath the other side of my skirts and gripping my bottom, lifting me higher against the tree.

I wrap my legs around his waist, my core grinding against the hard bulge straining against Ashe's trousers.

"Cassandra," Ashe growls against my lips. He continues to circle my sensitive core and I'm helpless against the rush of pleasure.

I cry out, my release crashing over me. My fingers dig into Ashe's shoulders, my hips grinding against his.

Ashe groans, his lips trailing kisses along my jaw and down the other side of my neck. He licks the spot he drank from, his fangs grazing the sensitive skin.

He continues to circle my sensitive core, drawing

out my pleasure. I gasp, pleasure rushing through me again as my core pulses with need.

"You're perfect," he murmurs the praise so quietly I barely hear it over my pounding heart. "Such a perfect mate for me."

I still, uncertain I'd heard him correctly. Clarity sweeps across my mind like a gust of winter wind and I struggle to look at him. He lifts his head enough to look at me, his pupils blown wide with need, the hardness against my core ever present.

"What did you say?" I rasp out, needing him to say it again.

He blinks rapidly and then a slow smirk slants across his bloodied lips. "You're my mate, Cassandra." He brushes a whisper of a kiss across my lips. "I knew it the moment I saw you that day you tumbled into the road."

I shake my head, thoughts racing through my head so fast I can't catch any of them. "No," I finally choke out. I push at his chest and he lets me go, stepping away as I frantically straighten my skirts. "It's impossible," I say again. I don't know if I'm talking to him or me or the universe.

"Cass—"

"I need to go," I interrupt him. Then I flee.

Chapter Seven

CASSANDRA

H ands come down over my eyes, blocking my view of the book I'd been reading, hidden alone in the room. I frown, confusion and annoyance at being interrupted. While I'd been present with Eris throughout the time I'd been possessed, I still missed so much of the world as it changed. Eloise had found me a modern history book, while Deidre had told me about a pop culture documentary. Wren offered to tell me about technology, but that seemed much too overwhelming.

Not to mention, this all might not even be worth the effort if we can't pull this off.

Still, I'd always loved to disappear into books, and reading about things I'd only gleaned is fascinating. I'm reading about the interspecies politics between the paranormal world and the human world after the

Second World War made pretending we didn't exist impossible.

"Guess who, little witchy?" A smooth baritone voice croons against my left ear. The words are filled with mischief, identifying the speaker immediately. My heart practically erupts as I shriek and push his hands away. The book falls from my lap to the floor with a hard slap as I leap up but I ignore it to whirl around, a smile stretching across my face.

"Rhys!"

I fling myself at him, stepping up onto the club chair I'd been lounging in, and wrapping my arms around his shoulders. His bellow of laughter fills a place that had been missing since I returned. I adore Ashe, and the rest of the Nightshades, but Rhys and Ezra were the two vampires who truly became my dear friends.

He hugs me just as tight before releasing me when I pull back. I'm still standing on the chair, which I'm sure would cause Ambrose to wrinkle his nose if he saw. I hold Rhys by the shoulders, pushing him back until he's at arm's length.

"Let me look at you!"

Rhys' golden eyes sparkle as his lopsided grin appears. His dark hair is cut short, practically shaved on the sides, while the top is long enough to flow back in a small wave. Rhys looks like the supposed rock stars in Deidre's movie. He's got the lean, muscular frame, the slightly tanned skin, the leather jacket, and the cocky swagger. His golden eyes are rimmed in a slight red, but I'm not worried he's about to sink his fangs into my throat and feed. While he might not be the model citizen, he's not a mindless monster.

"Cassie," Rhys breathes my name like a prayer, his smile softening into something more genuine. He pulls me into another hug, and I laugh. Rhys is an affectionate creature, and I missed that. Ezra, his pseudo brother, is the same way.

"You know I hate that name," I growl in jest. He holds me tight against his chest and pulls me over the back of the chair. He only releases me when I'm steady on my feet.

"Wouldn't want Ambrose to exile you for dirtying his furniture." Rhys' tone is teasing, but his eyes dull. It's enough for me to know that Rhys still holds resentment and hurt from Ambrose's decision.

Ezra had done the one thing Ambrose explicitly forbid all demons within the Barrows. Decades ago, the demons had been stirring up trouble in the Barrows—something Eris found amusing though stayed neutral in. Back then, the demons wanted to take the souls of humans, their new leader believing it was their due. Ambrose has only ever allowed bargaining and only on the strictest of terms. It nearly came to a civil war, the Nightshades against the demons. But Ambrose had been able to negotiate a truce. It helped that the upstart leader had been killed by his own supporters.

The night before the agreement was signed, Ezra violated the agreement. He claimed a soul. Rhys had begged Ezra to reveal who it was, but Ezra refused to allow them to be punished along with him. Ambrose, furious, exiled Ezra out of the city—a Nightshade no longer. Rhys intended to follow him, but Kasar and Malachi had stopped him. I still don't know how.

I gentle my voice. "Still no sign of him?"

Rhys shakes his head in a pained jerk. "It's like he's not even on Earth anymore, let alone in the country."

Rhys gives me and Kasar a pleading look, and both of us shrug. Rhys awkwardly pats his side, asking to be let down. Malachi doesn't let him go once he's back on his feet. Instead he grips one shoulder and the back of Rhys' nape. The commander of the Nightshade vampire's soldier's face is grim; grim enough for worry to lift its head.

"Everyone around me is mated, Rhys," Malachi intones. I let out a breath and roll my eyes. "Even Josephine is having a romance with Wren's driver! Though—truth be told, I don't think they're mates." Malachi grimaces and shakes his head. "That's like picturing your mom having sex."

He grips Rhys tighter, almost shaking him. Humor replaces my worry at the vampire's antics.

"Seriously, though. I am the only unmated vampire in this house. It's disgusting. They're all so in love! I can't escape the sickly stench of lust and heart eyes."

Rhys tugs free of Malachi, whose eyes go wide with dawning horror. "Oh, fuck. Not you too, Rhys. Tell me you don't have a mate."

Rhys barks a laugh and shakes his head, which makes Malachi wilt in relief. "No, not mate for me. Too busy touring and sampling women across the country."

Malachi slaps his palms together as if in prayer, his head tilted back as he looks to the ceiling. "Thank you; someone who still gets his dick wet."

I cough, covering my mouth with a fist as I try to hide my laugh even though my cheeks flame. They are all so much more . . . explicit than I'm used to.

A rumble of a growl comes from beside me and Malachi rolls his eyes dramatically as he looks at Kasar. He cocks a brow, egging the Lion of the Barrow on. Malachi is on his own with this one, I think as I step away with a wry grin.

"If my dick is dry, it's only because it's being milked daily."

Oh, goddesses. I slap my hands over my ears, my face flaming even brighter. Something I thought impossible. Thankfully, I'm saved.

"I'm sure you aren't talking about our sex life," Deidre says as she strides into the room, a tablet in her hand and Lan behind her with his own. She gives Rhys a once-over before quickly dismissing him. As if she hadn't just reprimanded her mate, Deidre walks up to Kasar and boldly grabs the messy hair he'd tied back and yanks his head down for a kiss. A kiss that is entirely too inappropriate in public.

"Malachi is simply envious he isn't having as much sex as the rest of us," Lan drawls, making Malachi sputter and try to claim he's having plenty of sex.

My blood has been replaced by sheer mortification at this point and I'm ready to melt into the floor. I do - not- remember these males being so open in conversation. If Eris knew this was happening, I'm sure she'd be rolling on the floor, cackling at me.

Ashe appears at my side, his hand on my lower back as he looks down at me with concern.

"Cassandra?"

Without thought, I bury my face in his chest, thankfully hiding against my mate. His arms come up around me, and along with his warm, campfire scent, I can smell grease and gasoline. He'd been working with the cars as Ambrose had asked earlier.

More voices join the din and, somehow, my mortification grows at my display of nerves and clearly being a woman new to this time. Ashe cups the back of my head, coaxing me to look up at him.

There's some amusement in his face and I scowl pointedly.

"I believe you all owe me," Josephine announces and the room goes silent. We all turn to look at her, even Ambrose and Eloise, who I hadn't realized joined us. Josephine looks smug, like the cat who got the cream and the canary. She inclines her head towards us before casting her gaze around the room. "Did I not say they'd come back together within the day?"

My eyes go wide and my throat dries enough to choke me as her meaning hits me. Even Ashe stiffens before chuckling lightly and moving me until I'm tucked against his side.

Everyone—Malachi, Lan, Kasar, Ambrose—and even the women, Eloise, Deidre, and Wren nod, different expressions across the group.

"You couldn't have held out one more day," Deidre grumbles accusingly at my mate as she slaps a fifty into Josephine's outstretched palm.

It takes a moment, but then a shocked expression takes over my face—one that probably makes me look like a squeezed frog. "You all placed wagers on Ashe and me?!" My voice was a shriek by the end, making Ashe wince. I glared around the room and no one had the grace to look chastised. Only Rhys holds up his hands as if surrendering.

"I didn't know about this," he quickly defends.

Kasar rolls his eyes. "Which is the only reason why you didn't have money in the pool."

Rhys drops his hands and his grin tells me Kasar is absolutely right.

I ball my fists, irritation replacing humiliation. I want to stomp my foot but I refuse to give in to such a childish urge.

"To be fair, the topic of you and Ashe's reunion has come up sometimes," Eloise says from where she's beside an amused-looking Ambrose. I'll admit they make an adorable pair, not that I'd ever say that to the vampire king's face. He is tall and regal, wearing a tailored black suit that oozes wealth, and dominates the room as a quiet promise of death and power. Eloise only comes up to his shoulder because of the mess of black hair bundled on top of her head, and wears what I recognize as leggings and, if I'm not mistaken, one of Ambrose's button-down shirts. She's not thin, but thick and soft with curves—the perfect opposite of Ambrose's hard cut lines. With her, he's more expressive than I've ever seen. He's looking down at her like she's a sweet morsel he wants to devour. It's enough to make my stomach twist, the need for my own vampire to hunt me down growing.

"And with how Eris liked to taunt Ashe, some of us thought he'd hold out to be sure it wasn't just another joke on him," Malachi added, in a way that made it clear he was one of those.

"Oh, leave the poor mates alone," Josephine tuts even as she tucks the folded bills discreetly into a pocket. She looks at me, giving me an understanding yet beseeching look. "Unlike the rest of these fools, I remember how devoted you two have always been to one another. I knew that your love would pull you together, no matter the reasons why either of you tried to resist."

Before we can discuss anything else, Ambrose clears his throat, taking control of the room. "I believe we have much to discuss and organize. I suggest we move to the dining room."

"Food, tea, and coffee will be out as soon as you are all settled," Josephine says over her shoulder as she leads the way. Ashe holds me back, pressing his nose against my temple and breathing in deeply. My eyes flutter shut, my heart becoming a warm spring, soothing my irritation away. I lean into him, the slightest pressure, and let him ground me to the earth and my body. I release a shuddering breath and straighten, smoothing down my linen blouse and skirts out of habit.

"Thank you," I murmur, turning just enough to

press a kiss to his lips. I meant it to be brief, but Ashe lingers. He sups at my lips, never deepening them, never pulling me tighter. It's a gentle worship, an adoration, and it turns me to a puddle quicker than snow falling on a fire.

"Are we fucking or are we planning to kill an angel?"

Lan's shout ruins the moment. Well, not entirely, as we pull apart. The bond between us is still open, something I thought would take me more time than we had to earn back.

"Ready?" Ashe asks, lacing his fingers through mine.

"Together," I reply, squeezing his hand.

He grins, the one that captured my heart the first day I met him. I beam back. "Then let's go figure out how to kill this angel."

Chapter Eight

ASHE

A mbrose stands at the end of the table, both palms flat on either side of the digital blueprint currently being projected from Lan's computer. Almost all of the chairs have been pushed to the walls or out of the way. Only Deidre and Eloise sit at the table, both of them focused on their individual laptops.

Even Wren has joined us, though she paces the room as she cradles her and Lan's daughter, Emily. The sight of the young child makes my stomach clench with envy, something I never thought I'd feel in relation to Landon. Cassandra has—had?—always wanted children, and until her, I'd never believed it possible for me to be a father. When I lost her to Eris, it was as if I lost my future too. I look across the table at my mate, who watches Wren with a fond expression.

I couldn't fight for our future then; I sure as hell will fight for it now. I won't lose her again, not when she's in my arms.

"Rhys, you're good to go to replace the band at the gala," Eloise says with a fist pump and looks up to the estranged Nightshade vampire. He saunters over to her, looking over her shoulder while resting his hand on the back of her chair. He can't help that he naturally oozes sensual confidence; no doubt the time traveling as a lauded rock star has only made it worse. If it weren't for the utterly serious expression on the vampire's face, Ambrose would be doing more than gritting his teeth.

While Eloise and Rhys work out signing and faxing the contract, I drag my attention back to Ambrose, Kasar, Lan, Wren, and Cassandra. Malachi left earlier, ensuring that the event's contracted musicians found themselves suddenly unable to perform.

"It'll be better if I'm there," Wren repeats while bouncing Emily gently and letting the infant chew on her knuckle. "I know you don't like it, but it's not like I'll be doing anything more than I would at a normal charity dinner. Fostering HopeTech has already purchased two tickets as a courtesy and it won't be an issue to get two more even the day before."

Lan gives his mate a look that's frozen men and monsters. Wren raises a brow, as if challenging him to deny the truth of her words.

"Agreed," Ambrose says, effectively overriding Lan, no matter how much his instinct to protect his mate rears up. He taps the table where a back entrance is of the venue. "Eloise and I will also be in attendance. With our presence, there will be enough attention on the room that no one will notice when Kasar and Malachi slip in."

Cassandra leans over the table, inspecting the ballroom layout where we'll be. "And you're sure there won't be any wards that stop illusions? Otherwise Giuliani will recognize us."

Kasar snorts but shakes his head. "Too many of these people use magic for their appearance. Not that they'd ever admit it. Small magics like this are fine. I won't be surprised if this guy isn't using his own."

"Okay," Ambrose interrupts, his expression as serious as when he'd planned battles. In a sense, this is one. "This Benevolent or Aeternaphiel, whatever he goes by, won't be there tonight in spite of sponsoring the event. Which means Giuliani, who owns the venue and is his personal rep, is the key to the invite for the private event the following day. We need him to get in..."

———

"WE'RE IN PLACE." Kasar's gravelly voice is clear in my ear as Cassandra and I follow Wren and Lan towards Alfonso. Alfonso Giuliani is surrounded by a bevy of beauties, all of them hanging on to his every word as if they can't bear to be more than a foot away. I grip Cassandra's hand tightly, reminding myself that this is our cover, and Giuliani is our target. We need him to get access to Aeternaphiel's estate with a private luncheon tomorrow. Which means Cassandra needs to capture Giuliani's attention enough to provide the invitation.

Wren and Lan are our introduction, the two of them wearing contact lenses to disguise the distinct golden eyes of vampires. As for Cassandra and me, we both are disguised with a minor illusion spell to conceal our identity entirely.

Wren, experienced at navigating the upper echelons of society, seamlessly inserts our small group before Giuliani.

"Ms. Foster!" The man himself greets, bringing her close, and she allows him to kiss her cheek. Lan, to my surprise, appears as utterly unbothered. "I was so sorry to hear about your father."

"Thank you," Wren says graciously. It's not public knowledge that Oberon Benoit was slaughtered by Lan after the man attempted to ritualistically sacrifice her in a bid for immortality. She gestures towards Cassandra and me. "I wanted to introduce you to my friends, Elana and Timothy Farr. I believe you may find their projects inspiring and I convinced them to come simply so Elana could meet you."

Alfonso gives Cassandra a lascivious once-over that has my blood boiling. A part of me can't blame him though.

Cassandra wears a floor-length gown that's a dark, deep teal. The dress is held up by two delicate straps, leaving her shoulders and chest bare, including the faint marks I left on her earlier. A primal satisfaction fills me with my obvious claim, even if our identities are disguised by magic.

The skirt of the dress is loose and flowing, the silk fabric rippling around her legs as she moves. The bodice, however, is fitted around her waist and torso, the silk fabric shimmering against her skin. Her breasts are pushed together, creating a slight valley of cleavage that Giuliani can't keep his eyes off.

Her illusioned white-blonde hair is styled in a loose bun, with soft tendrils framing her face. The makeup she's chosen makes her look like a fresh-faced goddess, with dark, smoky eyes, a subtle, natural lipstick that's supposed to make her lips look flushed. Her natural mist blue eyes have been darkened to hazel, and her magic has softened her features. She's soft and rounded, like a fertility goddess ready to be worshipped.

Her different face unsettles me, but my body

knows it's Cassandra. A selfish, savage part of me is glad Giuliani doesn't get to see the real woman.

Giuliani takes Cassandra's offered hand and brings it to his mouth, kissing her knuckles. "Enchantée, Elana—I can call you Elana, right?"

Cassandra titters, a sound that grates my nerves, but sparks a look of glee in Giuliani. "Of course. Wren has told me so much about you. I've been dying to meet you."

Literally. I barely suppress rolling my eyes. Clearing my throat, I put my hand out in clear expectation. I channel the suave attitude of Malachi and smile at the man. Hopefully, my mate's magic is strong enough to disguise my desire to rip the man's hand off for touching her.

"Timothy," I use the false name we've adopted. Giuliani reluctantly lets go of Cassandra's hand to shake mine. He gives me an assessing look; it's nowhere near as suggestive. I know what he sees. Black slicked-back hair with tanned skin, and a soft face and jaw suggesting I spend more time at my desk than the gym. Magic can do nothing about height, which means I'm still a few inches taller than Giuliani, to my petty satisfaction. Where he's wearing a classic black tuxedo, Tara—the Nightshades' new tailor after Mr. Carter retired, put me in a navy-blue velvet suit jacket with black lapels along with a crisp white shirt, navy blue bow tie, and black slacks.

"Easy," Kasar says, humor in his voice. "We need him alive."

"Do we though?" Malachi replies. "We really just need access to the computers here for the security codes at the estate."

Giuliani shakes my hand, and I force myself to ignore my brothers' running commentary in my ear. Giuliani grips my hand hard, satisfied to think he's won this round of a pissing contest. He doesn't say anything, just offers me a polite smile. I'm far from offended at the obvious dismissal.

Kasar is right, though. Giuliani's offices may be on the top floor here at the Verdant Pavilion, but getting into Aeternaphiel's estate will be much less complicated if Cassandra and I can walk in through the front door.

"I insist you let my wife tell you about our recent ventures," I say, laying on the charm while purposefully directing his attention back to Cassandra. I place my hand on her lower back, my fingers pressing hard in the only display of possession I allow myself. Lan catches my eye from the other side of Wren. To my surprise, there's a look of understanding. Considering what I know of Lan and how Wren must circulate in these shark-infested waters, I should be more surprised he hasn't turned the streets of Topside into rivers of blood.

The event coordinator announces that dinner is ready and, reluctantly, I release Cassandra when Giuliani offers his arm to escort her to our table. Wren, with her connections as the CEO of Benoit Tech, was able to secure the four of us seating at the round table with Giuliani. A few people send us disgruntled looks, no doubt the ones who were bumped from the highly sought-after table.

Giuliani dominates the conversation while a lavish six-course meal is served. He sits on Cassandra's right, while I sit on her left beside Lan. Lan leans back in the seat, always in an arrogant repose. Even wearing the blue contacts he uses to hide his vampire nature in Wren's circles, there's something that unsettles the mortals around us. No doubt it delights him. When I catch the faint scent of arousal, I cough to hide a laugh before I shoot him a look. His expression gives nothing away, but Wren is incredibly focused on the meal in front of her.

I'm too tense to really notice the food, eating mechanically. It's a new brand of torture to listen to Cassandra flirt with Giuliani and do nothing about it. My comfort is knowing this tittering socialite is not the real Cassandra. She knows how to speak with men like Giuliani because of her family's coven. It doesn't matter if she hasn't been active in the world since the Victorian era; the maneuvers of high society never change.

Ambrose catches my eye towards the end of the dinner service while dessert is being brought out. Like he'd predicted, his and Eloise's appearance had caused a ripple throughout the guests. I'd overheard more than a few people expressing concern about their safety, while there were even more whispers about what it would be like to be fed from by a vampire. Nerves settled when Michael Garner introduced him as a personal business acquaintance. How would people react if they knew Garner is under a compulsion to obey the powerful vampire? He gives an idle nod, one that could easily be passed as a response to the conversation at his table. I clear my throat and gratefully set my napkin on the table.

"If you'll excuse me," I say, and Cassandra looks up, as if annoyed.

"You'll be back for dancing, right?" Her tone suggests a long-running irritation and I play into it as we'd discussed.

"Yeah, yeah," I grumble, matching her irritation. Then, as if the idea comes to me, I look over her head to Giuliani. "My wife loves to dance and I can't think of anything else I like less. Maybe you can take one—or two for me? As a favor?"

Giuliani guffaws loudly enough to draw attention, his rotund belly bouncing before he stands and claps me on the shoulder. "If you won't dance with this beautiful woman, I will be glad to."

I pat him on the shoulder, keeping it light by sheer force of will. Otherwise, I'd send him crashing into the table like a buffoon. I lean closer to whisper, "Distract her, yeah? There's a hot piece of ass I spied at the bar earlier that I need to introduce myself to."

When I pull back, Giuliani's eyes gleam with satisfaction. The seed that he's free to pursuit Cassandra has been planted. Now it's up to my mate to secure the invitation to tomorrow's event while I go let Kasar and Malachi in through the back.

Excusing myself again, each step away from Cassandra is pure agony. Every instinct is telling me to turn around, to protect my mate from the male I've left her with. The only thing that makes it possible for me to leave is the affection and reassurance Cassandra sends to me through our bond. I breathe easier; I'd gone so long without our connection open that I'd forgotten how much I'd needed it.

I head towards the bathroom, nodding politely at the security guards posted in discreet locations. Each one is human; Lan's research said as much but with the unexpected attendance of Ambrose, there was always a chance the company would bring in some sort of supernatural guard.

I slap my hand against the bathroom door, shoving it open. I act as if I'm about to enter, timing my move until any guard or camera surveillance will be sure I did. Then I'm running, using my vampiric speed to travel from the bathroom door to the back hall without notice. Seconds later, I'm pushing the back service door's bar, opening it knowing Malachi or Kasar would have disabled the alarm.

Two Nightshade vampires slip in, dressed in their own suits in the event a guest sees them. Malachi turns when the door clicks shut, pulling out a phone with a short cord attached. He puts it next to the security box on the wall, tapping at the screen.

"Giuliani?" Kasar's question has me turning to him.

"Enthralled by Cassandra," I bite out.

"Sensitive, are we?" Malachi asks, still doing something to the alarm system.

"Shut it," Kasar orders, and I snap my mouth closed on the retort threatening. Kasar's known as the Lion, a moniker he earned long before the Barrows grew under Ambrose's hand. He outranks both of us and isn't afraid to remind us. His golden gaze burrows into mine, questioning me. "Can you keep it together to finish the job?"

I don't hesitate. "Yes."

He gives a terse nod, then jerks his head down the hall. "Go on," he says. "We're good here."

I don't question him. When working with a team, you have to trust that they'll do their part just like they're trusting you to do yours. The rest of my night, the goal is to make sure I don't rip Giuliani's head off and ruin the whole plan.

I make my way back towards the ballroom, but I head to the bar like I'd told Giuliani I would. A slim woman leans casually against the bar top, talking with the clearly enraptured young bartender. She's wearing a steel gray backless dress that turns transparent just under her ass, putting her shapely legs on full display. Her mahogany curls are pinned flat on one side, while the rest of the curls fall free around her shoulders.

With a sly grin, I join her, ordering a whiskey neat and a second drink for her. When the drinks are served, she takes the martini glass and raises it in thanks before sliding the olive off the toothpick with her lips.

"Does Kasar know what you're wearing?" I ask, refusing to look towards the ballroom where the first notes of music are beginning.

Deidre snorts inelegantly, finishing the olive before replying. "He knows he gets to tear it off me later tonight," she says before taking a sip of her martini. She keeps her voice low, eyes on me instead of the ballroom where our cohorts are doing their parts. "That bad, eh?" She gives my drink and white-knuckled grip a pointed look.

I knock half of it back, not giving a fuck about the rouse at the moment. I'm grateful for the familiar smooth burn, even if the alcohol does almost nothing for vampires.

"Yup," I admit, knowing I can be free with the woman. She might be Kasar's mate, but she's someone who won't judge anyone for their emotions.

"Bummer."

I snort, but that's Deidre for you. I finish the rest of my drink before finally letting myself look at the ballroom. Immediately, I find Cassandra in the crowd. She's got a fake smile plastered on her face while Giuliani holds her too close for my comfort. She glances my way, and our eyes find each other for a heartbeat. Then he's spinning her, stealing her away from me.

Except he isn't, not really. Not when she is bound to me for eternity, our souls connected. Not when I can feel her love through that bond.

"Another one?" Deidre asks, pulling my attention away but my eyes don't leave the dance floor. I nod and vaguely hear her hail the bartender.

Kasar and Malachi should be entering Giuliani's

office by now, accessing the blueprints for Aeterna-phiel's residence estate. When a flare of discomfort hits me, I narrow my eyes. Giuliani has pulled Cassandra flush against him and I snarl.

Deidre pushes the tall boy of whiskey into my hand and I toss it back in one go.

Malachi might have a point. We don't necessarily need Alfonso Giuliani alive. If he doesn't let my mate go soon, he might not survive the night.

Chapter Nine

CASSANDRA

W e know that Aeternaphiel a.k.a. the Benevolent a.k.a. William Egress to most of Topside lives here." Lan pulls up surveillance photos and what I vaguely understand as drone images. It's a sprawling estate three hours northwest of here, tucked away off any main road, surrounded by dogwoods and white oaks. "Everything we've been able to uncover suggests Aeternaphiel's soul is being protected here."

I curl my lips between my teeth, uncertainty threatening to rear its ugly head. I can't not think about the ticking clock counting down until Eris and I are completely drained away. I know Ashe is fighting the same war. At least I can shield him from the growing weakness within me. If he truly knew how quickly I feel I'm being siphoned away, my mate would do something drastic. I have to trust that we're going to win. That we're going to make it into this archangel's fortress and destroy his soul. Even still, I refuse to spend what could be my final days spent in worry and fear.

"Malachi and Kasar will get the blueprints to the estate and anything else they can grab from Giuliani's office while," Lan points to me, "you do your best to flirt and secure a personal invitation. The archangel has to maintain a specific image, which means inviting a select few people to his estate every quarter to offer potential investments. It's convenient he's hosting one. Otherwise getting in would be a lot more difficult."

"What do we do once we get in?" Ashe asks, his arms crossed as he stands at my side. He shows no signs of being tired, none of the vampires do, as they stand around the dining table that's become our war-board. "He's got security, and with so few people invited, we'll have eyes on us at all times."

Kasar's the one who nods. "You and Cassandra need to slip away. Little witch, only use magic if absolutely necessary. This place won't be like the Verdant Pavilion. Your disguise should be fine, but anything else?" He shakes his head before giving a pointed look between Ashe and me. "You'll need to go back to basics until you get to the vault with the soul."

Ambrose studies the images as he flips through the slides. He finally looks at Lan, his brows furrowing.

"And the rumors about a creature bound to the room as another measure of security?"

Lan frowns, clearly frustrated that he doesn't have an answer. *"Rumors only. If it's true, then Cassandra and Ashe are going to have to think on their feet."*

The room is quiet as all the Nightshade vampire males, Rhys included, are considering his words.

"I don't like it," Rhys announces at last. *"I'm going in with them."*

"Rhys..."

———

THE DOGWOOD TREES that fill the estate are bare of leaves and flowers as Ashe drives us along the winding asphalt private driveway to house. Rhys sprawls in the back of the Mercedes, one shoulder against the door and a leg stretched along the backseat. The guards weren't too happy with Rhys's presence, since access to the billionaire they know as William Egress is supposed to be limited. As always, though, Rhys put on the charm and with a few selfies, autographs, and a promise to leave tickets to his next concert in town had the guards waving us through.

As we drive further, the sprawling house known as the Haven appears.

It's a massive antebellum-style mansion, with two

sweeping colonnades along the front. There are two stories of windows, all lit with a warm glow from within. We pass beneath the colonnades and Ashe pulls to a stop, allowing a butler to open the door. The man's professionalism is on display at the unexpected additional guest, and I've no doubt the guards called ahead to warn them.

Ashe hands the keys off to a uniformed carhop, giving the younger man a smirk that suggests a familiarity with the process. It's strange to think of Ashe as a man of wealth, stature and power when while we met, he always downplayed his position in the Nightshades and often passed for a stable master. In Willow Creek, the other villagers had thought it odd that Ambrose maintained familiarity with his supposed staff. Now, Ashe carries the confidence of a powerful male sure of his position as easily as a falcon weaves through the air.

In the exact opposite of Rhy's casual look of rugged, low-slung jeans and a dark long-sleeved top, Ashe is polished without looking stiff. He strides around the car with natural elegance, dressed in white linen pants and a sky-blue button-down that's untucked and the sleeves pushed up past his elbows.

Tara really has outdone herself when it came to outfitting us for this party. The loose fabric on Ashe disguises the gun he's got tucked in a holster at his lower back, along with a blade along his lower leg, and the slender tool kit we'll need to get through Aeterna-phiel's security systems.

As for my own outfit, I thought I'd be uncomfortable with a dress so revealing compared to what I wore in the late 1800s. Instead, the white, breezy wrap dress with a blue floral print and short sleeves has me craving to run barefoot through the trees. The wrap style covers enough of my decolletage to give me a sense of modesty. That modesty is obliterated by the fact that each time I move, the dress slips around me enough to reveal my leg up to the middle of my thigh. I almost demanded a different dress from Tara, but then Ashe saw the dress. The combination of hunger and adoration in my mate's eyes changed my mind.

"Welcome!" Alfonso Giuliani's voice booms towards us as he strolls out of the open double-entry doors. His eyes drink me in and I fight the urge to hide behind Ashe. Sensing my discomfort, Ashe steps ahead of me, reaching his hands out to shake Giuliani's.

"Thanks for having us," Ashe says smoothly, before turning and tucking his arm around my shoulder, effectively cutting off any chance Giuliani would have to touch me. He jerks a thumb behind us towards Rhys and says, "Sorry about the plus one. You don't really say no to -the- Rhys, vampire rock star. Might end up as his next meal, you know?"

Giuliani's eyes darken for a moment as Rhys laughs

loudly and saunters up to us. Then Giuliani's expression brightens to a more welcoming one.

"Of course," Giuliani says, almost friendly enough to hide his displeasure. "My daughter loves your music."

"Oh?" Rhys says, arching a brow and pointedly looking over Giuliani's shoulder into the house. "Is she here by chance? I love getting to know my fans." The purr shifts Rhy's innocent words into something more salacious. If he wasn't supposed to be creating a disturbance, I would elbow him.

"No." Giuliani's sharp reply has me fighting to look at Rhys, but our host invites us inside the house before Rhys can make any more waves in these hot waters. "Come, let me introduce you to the other guests for our luncheon."

We follow along, and my eyes go wide at the display of wealth within the house. There are crystal chandeliers, marble floors, and artwork I recognize as originals. There's a mix of modern and classic furnishings, with plush furniture and low tables in the formal rooms we walk past. I'm so busy taking in the rooms that Giuliani's introduction catches me off guard.

Fortunately Ashe is paying attention. Beyond us, there are six other people. I vaguely recognize all of them from the event last night, but even now I can't recall their names. Four are men and the other two are women who don't appear to be with anyone. One of them, a shrewd-looking blonde, glares at me when Giuliani lingers too close to me. She seems appeased when I tuck myself against Ashe's side, making it clear I have no interest in the much older man.

Rhys's presence causes a stir, just as we'd hoped. Rhys is known for being hard to pin down, which means he's built an air of mystery around himself and his personality as a modern day rock star. From fuzzy memories, I know that half of his fans doubt his claim of being a vampire while the other half obsess over it.

"When will William be joining us?" one of the men asks as he settles back on a plush couch and crosses his ankle over his knee. His miffed expression makes it clear his opinion on Rhys monopolizing the second woman's attention.

Ashe and I do our best to keep our expressions at an appropriate level of interest, but my stomach twists. Soon, the same being that betrayed Eris and is currently the cause of her and myself dying will be in the same room as me. I send a quick prayer to the goddess that the illusions I cast over Ashe and me will hold and we won't fail so early on.

"I am here now," a new voice says, drawing the room's attention. Giuliani moves to stand beside Aeternaphiel—or William Egress as he's known by. He claps Giuliani on the shoulder, and the man adopts the fawning expression of a beloved hound. "Introduce me to my guests, my friend. I must know how I can be of help to you all."

How about handing over the container you've stored your soul in, so we can hurry up and kill you and I don't have to be more nervous than I already am?

Because the moment I see him, his perfectly coiffed hair, strong jaw, sun-kissed skin, and lean figure, the nerves I've been ignoring burst into the forefront of my mind. Ashe rubs my shoulder where his hand rests and waves of calm radiate down our bond. By the time Giuliani reaches us, I worry I'm going to ruin everything by puking. No amount of social etiquette lectures my family gave me could prepare me for facing an archangel who is directly responsible for my impending death.

"Mrs. Farr, how lovely to meet you," Aeternaphiel says, clasping my hand in both of his. His hands are unexpectedly rough, and images from Eris's memories ricochet through my mind. Aeternaphiel leading a charge against demons; Aeternaphiel training Eris in multiple weapons; Aeternaphiel seducing Eris the night before he betrayed her. His blue eyes narrow and he tilts his head, a slight smile on his face. "Have we met before?"

Magic prods against my mind, testing my illusions for weaknesses. If I were a high magic user like my family was, he'd be able to see the threads of magic holding the spell together. As a wild magic user, though, the illusion becomes a part of the person or object disguised. He'll be able to tell we have something hidden behind illusions, but Ashe and Ambrose assured me that it's the norm now for wealthy humans to use magic as regularly as they do makeup. The archangel has enough power that he could break our disguises, but the goal is to avoid giving him a reason to.

I force a bright smile onto my face before shaking my head. "I think I'd remember meeting someone like you," I say, managing to keep my voice steady. "Wren Foster is a friend of mine, if you've met her. She was kind enough to introduce me to Alfonso last night."

Aeternaphiel's eyes brighten as the suspicion melts away at Wren's name. "Ah. What a shame about her father," he says before flicking his gaze to Ashe and Rhys. I did my best to mask Ashe's vampire scent. Hopefully, between my efforts and Rhys flaunting his presence, Aeternaphiel will dismiss my mate. The archangel looks back to me. "He never seemed to accept he was mortal."

I startle before covering it with a nervous laugh. "Don't all billionaires forget that?"

Does Aeternaphiel know the true circumstances around Oberon's death? If so, how?

Ashe saves me, pulling the archangel's attention to

him by shaking his hand. "Timothy Farr. Wren Foster said you might be able to point us in the direction for investments. Alfonso was kind enough to invite us, but I'm hoping to find some advice."

Aeternaphiel releases my hand before shaking Ashe's, and my shoulders relax. We've passed the first test. My mate and Rhys have our backs. "Of course," Aeternaphiel says warmly before stepping away from Ashe and me. "Everyone, why don't we move this to the back patio? I have arranged a wonderful lunch for us while we discuss the various projects you are all passionate about. Perhaps our unexpected musical guest can provide some entertainment?"

Ashe gives me a subtle nod. Rhys's presence is certainly helping keep the attention off of us. We linger, taking up the rear of the small procession through the house. As we pass through a drawing room, the sudden presence of magic makes my breath catch.

"What is it?" Ashe whispers, looking ahead to be sure no one has noticed we've stopped.

"Wards," I reply distantly. I peer around the room looking for anything. The dark hardwood floors are polished to the point they reflect the warm light coming through the windows, and the sleek, angular sofa seems intentionally placed to direct attention away from the fireplace against the wall. The fireplace itself is clean, without even decorative candles to fill it. The mantle matches the dark floor, but unlike the rest of the surfaces in the room, there's nothing atop it.

It feels too obvious.

Shaking my head, I give Ashe a tight smile. "I can't pinpoint it, but there's something close."

Ashe's expression is hard, his eyes full of determination. "Then it's time for Rhys to up his ante and give us that distraction."

1865

Ashe

The forest surrounding Willow Creek was a tapestry of darkness. The shadows were deep and the moon was a silver coin high above, casting a soft, pale light over the leaves and grass. The trees were thick, towering giants that cast their own shadows, and the ground was soft with moss and ferns.

The silence was absolute, and I inhaled the earthy scents, relishing in the coolness of the air. Nights like this, with the full moon rising and the stars winking, reminded me of my human years. Of the nights I would sneak from the stables and lie in the field, staring up at the sky and dreaming of adventure.

Cassandra had fled from me a week ago, her eyes wide with shock even as her cheeks were flushed from pleasure. According to Rhys and Malachi, I've been in a "mood" since. They both have an opinion on what I should do to fix the issue. Rhys thinks I need to send her chocolates from the city and letters full of heartfelt prose. Malachi, on the other hand, thinks I should toss her over my shoulder and take her to bed.

I know my little witch, though. If I chase her, she won't run. She'll raise her defenses, and not just emotional ones. Cassandra will have no issue using her magic to keep me away.

So I've waited, as painful as it's been. The taste of her pleasure is my addiction, more than any high I get from racing stallions along the edge of cliffs or guiding a raft down rapids. I crave her, not just her blood or her body. I crave her in my arms. I long for her soft laughter. I'm desperate to feel the weight of her head on my shoulder, the warmth of her fingers entwined in mine.

Even if she won't like it, I've made sure to keep watch—my instincts allowing no less. I've kept my distance from her cottage at night, staying high in the trees instead as a silent guardian.

Ambrose had noticed the strange man that Cassandra had. Ambrose had Malachi follow the man after he left the wedding celebration. Malachi had returned, reporting nothing suspicious. Ambrose was still concerned, though, and I didn't disagree.

Something about the man's scent had been wrong —off. I hadn't wanted to worry Cassandra that night, and if I'm honest, I was thinking more about stealing my beautiful mate away for kisses than any potential danger. Something that could have ended in disaster. Something I won't let happen again.

I circle the village twice before allowing my feet to take me to Cassandra's cottage. Rather than climb the tree that's become my self-imposed post, I lean against it. The night air has a bite of chill to it, the early whispers of changing seasons. It doesn't matter, though. A blizzard could storm around me and I wouldn't abandon Cassandra.

The windows on either side of the door glow behind the curtains with warm yellow light. A beacon of sanctuary amidst the dark of the night.

She's alone, and has been each night. I have to believe she feels the same pull towards me as I do her.

I lose myself in thought, my eyes wandering the darkness as the nocturnal creatures begin their night. I'm not sure how much time has passed when the cottage door opens. I push off the tree, standing upright, my sharp eyesight drinking in Cassandra's silhouetted face.

"I can feel you brooding and I'm tired of it," Cassandra calls, her voice a sultry rasp.

I smirk, prowling towards her. "Is that so?" I tease, stopping just outside her wards. I know my brothers would advise me to not reveal how eager I am to have her attention once more. Fuck them, though. When they've found their mates, they'll understand the futility of that.

Cassandra crosses her arms and stares. The breeze captures her scent and wraps it around me, both a torture and delight. Her black hair is loose and wild, and her eyes gleam in the moonlight. Cassandra wears a simple gown, her curves soft and tempting in the light spilling from the doorway.

"Come inside," she orders and turns, her skirts swishing around her ankles as she disappears into the cottage.

I cross her wards, the faint sting of magic passing over my skin. Cassandra leaves the door open and I enter, closing the door behind me. The wards settle with a snap, and I glance around, taking in the familiar one room cottage with relish.

Cassandra is at the hearth, the flames already crackling. A kettle hangs on a hook, and the scent of an herbal tea fills the cottage. My witch glances over her shoulder at me, her lips curving in a smirk.

"Tea?" she offers.

I prowl towards her, and Cassandra stands, turning to face me. She raises her hand, stopping me with the gentle touch of her fingertips.

"We need to talk," she says, and I swallow the urge

to gather her into my arms. Cassandra searches my eyes, her hand rising to cup my jaw.

"Of course." I cover her hand with mine, turning my face to press a kiss into her palm.

"Sit," she orders, gesturing with her other hand. Cassandra slips past me, grabbing a kettle and pouring the boiling water into a clay teapot.

I obey, taking the same bench I sat on a week ago. The table is cleared of the herbs she'd been drying, the bundles and baskets stored away.

Cassandra joins me, her skirts swirling as she takes the other bench. She sets a wooden tray down and two cups, pouring tea for us both.

"You've been avoiding me," I begin when she seems reluctant to speak. Cassandra meets my eyes, her expression calm.

"I have," she admits, taking a sip of tea. The firelight casts shadows and highlights across her face, her eyes gleaming. "I needed time to think."

I nod, mirroring her and taking a sip. The tea is floral, and Cassandra smiles when I wrinkle my nose.

"What have you thought about?" I set my cup down and lean forward, propping my elbows on the table. Cassandra's fingers are wrapped around her cup, the steam curling around her hands.

"Us," she answers, her honey eyes flashing with vulnerability. "Mates. My family."

I lean back, keeping silent. She doesn't look at me when she starts talking again.

"My family's coven controls Boston. They have for generations." She looks at me, as if trying to weigh my reaction. I keep my expression relaxed and open. This is nothing I don't know. In fact, I likely know more than she realizes, given Ambrose's investigation of her history. Something I didn't know about until after the fact, else I'd have tried to stop him. Everything I learn about Cassandra, I want to hear it from her with trust.

She takes another sip of tea. "I hated the high society of the coven and I could never quite meet my family's standards. The night of my twentieth birthday, my parents hosted a dinner party—something they hadn't done in years. It seems, in their infinite wisdom, that my father had arranged for me to be married. When confronted after, he'd told me I should be grateful to have secured a good marriage. That, even if I struggled to perform magic and be the perfect daughter, I carried the family blood and could have powerful children."

A visceral rage threatens to overwhelm me at the thought of another man touching my little witch, mating her, filling her with their child. Her gaze goes to my balled fists and I force them flat on the table and release a long breath. She is here now with me, even if she hasn't accepted that we're mates.

She clears her throat, and her voice takes on a note of anger. "When I tried to reason with my mother and grandmother, both of them said there was no point in arguing and that I would willingly marry the man or they'd cast me from the coven and disown me. They said that my womb was the only thing I had worth offering."

I can't stay still at that. I lean forward and wrap my fingers around her wrist. My grip is gentle, as if cradling a butterfly in my palm. When her eyes meet mine, I speak, "They're wrong."

Cassandra gives me a pained smile and pats my hand. I release her reluctantly. "Oh, I know. It still hurts all the same." She visibly recomposes herself. "I pretended to accept their decision. When everyone was asleep that night, I left. When I was far enough away, I sent them a letter. Rather than marry, I did them the favor of leaving. I disowned and disavowed them. It gave me petty satisfaction, even if I'm sure they told the coven otherwise."

Silence falls between us, but it's not strained. She's working through her thoughts and I reach for the tea, needing to do something with my hands so I don't try to touch her. The drink is much cooler now, but I don't complain. I'd rather have tepid tea than interrupt her thoughts.

When I set the cup down again, she meets my gaze

head-on. There is fire in her eyes, a fire I've fallen in love with. There's also fear, hidden deep within the spark. One that I silently vow to do anything to appease.

"When you said I was the perfect mate, all I could think was how that was impossible—no, wait, let me finish." She stops me with a raised hand and I hadn't realized I was moving towards her. I sink back down, my entire body protesting. Everything screams to convince her that she is perfect already.

"Every criticism they gave me came roaring back. I know running was wrong, but how could I consider dragging someone as amazing as you down? It killed me to leave you, but I couldn't stay. All I could hear was my parents telling me that you'd realize your mistake and leave." She reaches out and I knock over my cup in the rush to clasp her hand in both of mine, but we both ignore it. "Losing you would break me, Ashe. Break me so badly I don't think I'd ever recover."

Her name escapes me in a broken croak and she smiles again. This time there's joy in the quirk of her lips.

"I love you," I declare, holding her hand tightly. "You are my mate—every poisonous thing they said about you? I'll gladly, eagerly, spend the rest of our lives proving them wrong. There is nothing you can do that will ever stop me loving you."

She laughs, a watery sound but goddamn it, it fills the cracks in my soul. I'll do whatever it takes to hear that laugh every day for eternity.

"Over the last week, I've done a lot of thinking," she says, halting any other potential romantic overtures. "I realized I've been an idiot. I've let people who hurt me, who I haven't seen for decades, take you away from me. I won't let them ruin us, Ashe."

Hope lights up my chest. "Does that mean—" I clear the sudden ball in my throat. "You feel it, too? The mate bond forming between us? You accept it?"

Cassandra's eyes shine brighter than the moon and stars combined. "Yes, Ashe," she says, her tone leaving no room for doubt. "I am your mate, just as you are mine."

A growl of satisfaction tears from my chest and I move, using every bit of my vampire speed to round the table and sweep her into my arms. A squeak comes from her lips, a fraction of a second before I kiss her. Then I'm at the foot of her bed in the loft, her hair waving gently from the speed.

I toss her onto the bed, crawling over her, my eyes drinking in every inch of her. When I reach her gaze, I see my own need reflected there. "I'm going to claim you, little witch." My voice is an unrecognizable rumble, pure savagery and primal instincts. "Mark you and fill you, so every male knows who you belong to."

Cassandra wraps her arms around my neck, her own lip twisting into a possessive smirk. "I plan to claim you too, vampire. So that every woman knows you're mine."

"Take off your clothes, witch." I pull her upright and Cassandra leans back on her hands. She looks up at me, her cheeks flushed, and her lips kiss-swollen.

Cassandra raises an eyebrow. "Only if you take yours off, vampire."

I growl, shrugging off my coat and tossing it aside. Cassandra bites her lip, her eyes hungry as I unbutton my shirt and shrug it off.

Cassandra undoes the buttons of her dress, and my fingers itch to do it myself. She moves slowly, torturously, and I rip my belt free, the metal clanging.

She laughs, shimmying from the bodice. I groan, her breasts bared to me, the tips hardened and begging for my touch. Cassandra lies back again, and I yank my boots off.

Cassandra sits up, her fingers reaching for me, and I growl. "Off," I repeat, gesturing to her skirts.

She obeys, her fingers deft and sure, and I shove my trousers down, kicking them away. Cassandra gasps, her gaze heating even more, and I'm naked before her.

I prowl towards her and Cassandra scoots back, her skirts pooling around her. I crawl over her once more, settling my hips between her thighs. Her core is hot and wet against my aching cock, and I groan, pressing closer.

Cassandra moans, her hips thrusting up. I grab her wrists and pin them above her head. She gasps, her eyes flashing with challenge.

"Mine," I growl, and Cassandra bares her teeth at me.

"Yours," she vows, and my control snaps.

I capture her lips, swallowing her cries as I thrust inside her. Cassandra moans, her core stretching and throbbing around me. I couldn't wait and from how she soaks my cock, neither could she.

I release her wrists and her hands skate down my back, her nails digging into the skin. I growl, thrusting deeper.

Cassandra's back arches, her head thrown back and I trail kisses along her jaw, her pulse pounding beneath my lips.

I sink my fangs into the bold vein above her breast, the one that will bind her to me, and Cassandra cries out. Pleasure rushes through me, and Cassandra clings to me, her core pulsing and throbbing with her release.

I release her neck, licking the wound closed. Cassandra's eyes are hazy with pleasure and her cheeks are flushed. Her blood is richer than wine on my tongue, yet I pull back and drag a nail deep across my own heart vein. My blood wells up and some of the haze clears from her eyes. I cup the back of her head and bring her lips to my chest.

"Claim me, my love." My voice is haggard. She doesn't hesitate, pressing her lips against the bleeding cut and sucking hard. I nearly come from that alone.

Cassandra releases her hold, her tongue sweeping across the cut as if savoring every drop. I roll us, and Cassandra gasps, sitting upright. She braces her palms against my chest, her core clenching around me.

"Ride your mate, little witch." I cup her hips, my thumbs rubbing against the soft skin.

Cassandra bites her lip, her eyes fluttering shut as she begins to move. My mate is a temptress, a goddess of temptation. A goddess I plan to worship daily. Her hips swirl, her nails scraping down my chest.

I growl, thrusting my hips up. Cassandra moans, her core throbbing.

"Ashe," she cries, her hips circling again. Her breasts bounce with her movements, and I reach up, cupping them and rolling her tight nipples. Cassandra throws her head back, her hips rising and falling, grinding against me.

I sit up, my hands guiding her hips. Cassandra wraps her arms around my neck, her nails digging into my shoulders.

I kiss her, swallowing her cries as I meet her thrust

for thrust. Pleasure builds at the base of my spine, and Cassandra's core throbs and pulses.

"Cassandra," I growl, breaking the kiss and burying my face against her neck. I'm close but I refuse to give in without feeling her coming on my cock. I sink my fangs into her neck.

Cassandra screams, her core throbbing as pleasure catapults her over the edge. Her orgasm pulls me with her, my release exploding through me.

I release her neck, licking the wounds closed. Cassandra slumps against me, her heart beating in time with mine.

I roll us again, cradling my mate against my chest. Cassandra sighs, her leg sliding between mine, her fingers tracing patterns along my chest.

"I love you," she murmurs, her words slurred and sleep heavy.

I kiss her forehead, her hair a waterfall against my skin. "I love you, Cassandra. My mate. My witch."

My mate sighs, her breathing evening out. I listen as her heart beats a love song. My little witch is asleep, and I pull the blankets over us, cocooning us against the world.

Nothing will tear Cassandra from my arms, no matter how strong or persistent the threat may be.

I swear it.

Chapter Ten

ASHE

I navigate us to the patio, my senses heightened, every nerve tingling with anticipation. The midday sun casts dappled shadows through the grand windows, bathing the estate in a soft, ethereal glow. Around me, the chatter of the luncheon guests fills the air, a symphony of polite conversation and tinkling laughter that belies the tension simmering beneath the surface.

Cassandra walks beside me, her presence a comforting anchor amidst the swirling currents of tension rising in me. I clamp it down, making sure she doesn't sense any of it through our bond. She's already nervous enough. At least she isn't the only one obviously nervous, since the rest of the guests are fluttering around the area like anxious hens. Except these hens both crave and fear the attention of the fox.

Rhys, to Giuliani's chagrin, is holding court on the far side of the long, stone dining table set for lunch. It doesn't seem to bother Aeternaphiel, as he drifts through the guests. The archangel moves amongst his guests with the effortless grace of a predator stalking its prey. His eyes, sharp and calculating, sweep over the assembled company, missing nothing as he holds court with the ease of a man accustomed to command. Yet he gives up their attention to Rhys, seeming unperturbed that he is not everyone's focus.

He reminds me of a wolf searching for the weakest of the herd.

Alfonso Giuliani, his human representative, stands at the edge of the group, a sycophantic smile plastered across his face as he plays the role of the gracious host. He gestures towards the array of delicacies laid out on a wicker buffet, his words honeyed with flattery as he extols the virtues of his employer's hospitality.

Every word makes me sick, but I force myself to smile and nod as Timothy Farr would.

Beside me, Cassandra's hand brushes against mine, a silent reassurance that bolsters my resolve. I hate that she's at risk here. If I could do this without her, I'd lock her in our suite at the clan house.

Instead, I follow her to the side and follow her example in making a plate for myself. I hardly notice what I'm choosing. It's not as if I'm here to actually

have lunch. Another couple splits from Rhys's enthrall-
ment to file in behind us, chatting quietly with each
other.

"Here," I say, nudging Cassandra with an elbow to
suggest sitting at the middle of the table but still far
enough from where Aeternaphiel has set his drink to
prevent much attention, hopefully.

The moment we sit, Alfonso comes to stand beside
Cassandra, sculpting his wrinkled face into something
he thinks passes as charm. As much charm as a snake.

"Enjoying yourself, Mrs. Farr?" Alfonso Giuliani's
slick, oily voice makes my lip twitch, but Cassandra
remains steady, smiling politely.

"It's wonderful," Cassandra replies, and I can feel
her brittle nerves through the mate bond.

"And you, Mr. Farr?" Alfonso's beady eyes settle
on me, and I resist the urge to punch him.

"The spread is wonderful," I say, mimicking the
conspiratorial tone I used with him the night before.
"The company as well."

Alfonso preens at the praise, oblivious to the lie.
Beside me, Cassandra barely swallows a snort, and her
amusement eases the tension churning within me.

"Alfonso, thank you for such a wonderful surprise.
I didn't expect you to remember, let alone invite my
favorite musician today!"

It's a woman's voice, a shrill, annoying pitch that

sets my teeth on edge. Alfonso turns towards the speaker, his smile slipping. Cassandra and I share a look, and I can't help the smirk tugging at the corner of my mouth. I steal a glance at Rhys. Somehow the male has conjured a guitar out of thin air, his fingers strumming idle notes while he deploys his signature charming smile at the small audience. Not even Aeternaphiel seems immune.

"Susana, what a pleasure. Let me introduce you—"

"We met last night," the woman snaps, her voice dripping with irritation. She glares at my wife and I'm hard-pressed to not growl at her. She turns her attention back to Alfonso, her bright smile returning. "Come, I insist we sit together during the performance."

Unwilling to surrender the credit the attractive woman is giving him, Alfonso's demeanor shifts. He gives Cassandra an apologetic look. "We'll talk more later, my dear."

Susana tugs him away, a smug look on her face, and Cassandra chokes back a laugh. I meet her eyes, a smirk twitching at my lips. She leans against me, her mouth going next to my ear. I breathe in her scent, wrapping it around me. I ignore the pang of fear when I notice the sulfuric scent of Eris has grown more faint.

"It seems Rhys hasn't lost his ability to charm crowds," she murmurs, her lips caressing the shell of my ear. I lay my arm across the back of her chain, brushing my knuckles against her shoulders.

"If anything, giving him permission to get on stage in front of thousands of people has only made him worse," I reply, amused. Rhys may have left the Barrows in anger, but letting him travel and hone his musical talents has let my friend grow in ways he would never have otherwise. "Are you ready to explore?"

She nods and straightens. I let my eyes drift over the area with a pleasant expression, as if enjoying the company. I make note of the server near the buffet, keeping the food area tidy; the server keeping track of the carafes of water and fresh fruit juices; the discreet human security guard in a white polo and khaki slacks at the end of the patio. Cassandra grabs her water glass and, just before she brings it to her mouth, fumbles it, dropping it all over herself.

To be entirely honest, my mate is clumsy enough I have absolutely no idea if it was on purpose or not.

The two servers rush over as Cassandra and I stand, Cassandra apologizing repeatedly. Alfonso looks over his shoulder at me, a frown adding more wrinkles to his forehead. I wave him off, rolling my eyes at Cassandra pointedly. He gives me one of the good ole boys looks of sympathy before letting Susana and Rhys take his attention once more.

"Come on," I grunt out, gripping Cassandra's upper arm. I give the uniformed woman trying to help Cassandra clean up a glare. "Where's the bathroom?"

The brunette woman stutters under my focus and points back to the door we came through. "Inside, the second door on the left in the main hall."

I don't bother thanking her and she doesn't seem to expect me to. She takes a hurried step back, letting me practically drag Cassandra inside. The moment we're out of sight, I drop my hand to hers and give her a wry grin.

"Really? Spilling water all over yourself?" I tease. I slip the small earpiece out of my pocket with my other hand and press the discreet piece of technology into place.

Cassandra grumbles, her face bright red. It only adds weight to my suspicion it wasn't planned and I smile wider.

"Do you read?" I whisper under my breath, conscientious of potential security measures.

"Copy," Malachi's voice comes through clearly. "Lan was in control of the security programming before you reached the front doors."

The earpiece picks up Lan's voice but not clearly. The derisive tone tells me his opinions of the security well enough.

"Keep an eye on Rhys. Let us know if he goes overboard."

Malachi scoffs in my ear. "When doesn't the man?"

Cassandra and I slip through an open doorway into the aforementioned main hall. Just as she said, another door is ajar so the bathroom is obvious. Towards the entrance foyer are stairs up to the next floor. Places like this often don't have basements because of frequent flooding, but if there is an old root cellar, it'll be harder to get to.

"Which way?" I ask my wife, listening to all the heartbeats in the area. Being considerably younger than Ambrose and Kasar, I can't hear as far. I'm powerful enough to track the few staff in the busy kitchen, the fellow guests we've left behind and the security detail posted outside the front door. There's even a cat sleeping soundly a few rooms away. We might be alone now, but we can't linger.

Cassandra closes her eyes and, in spite of the situation, I wish she looked like herself. Part of me gnashes my fangs that she doesn't look like my mate, that if she has only days left, she shouldn't be disguised. I shut those thoughts down, refusing to consider we might fail.

The small frown smooths from her forehead a moment before her eyes flutter open and meet mine. "Upstairs, definitely."

"Mal?" I ask. Using the main stairway in the front of the estate is too high of a risk, one I want to avoid if possible.

A moment of silence and then Mal reveals a narrow stairway just outside of the kitchen entrance. It's closer to people, but the staff have no reason to be on guard. They're too busy focusing on feeding the entitled sycophants.

I grab Cassandra's hand, keeping my touch gentle, and lead her down the stairs. My steps are silent, a skill mastered over the years working for Ambrose. Cassandra sneaks as quietly as she can, wincing when one of the floorboards creaks under her toes. I have to bite my cheek to stop the smile at her frustration. She hates it when I'm better at something than her.

"How did you get so sneaky?" she hisses accusatorially when I reach the service stairwell. Its entrance is disguised in the wall, the paint and edging flowing almost seamlessly together. The wealthy never want to be reminded of their staff, no matter the era.

Double doors three feet away are closed but the sounds of the busy kitchen and staff talking are loud enough for even Cassandra to hear. Any minute one of them could walk out and find us here. A lie is already prepared on my tongue; we wanted a recipe or we got lost looking for the bathroom. My heart beats steadily but my nerves are on edge.

Experience with this style of house has me pressing my fingertips lightly to the middle right. A click sounds like a bullet in the quiet hallway as the hidden door swings inward and we both freeze. I wait for someone to come out of the kitchen or one of the guards out front to walk in. It goes unnoticed, and I push the door the rest of the way open and guide Cassandra inside. I don't answer her question until I've eased the wall panel shut again.

"I've learned a lot of new things over the years." I give her a grin and raised brow.

Even in the soft lighting of the service stairwell and under her glamour, I see her cheeks redden. The side of my lip climbs higher and my fangs tingle as the blush travels down her chest. The scent of her arousal is sharp and sweet. I crowd her against the white-washed walls, bracing my forearms beside her head. Dipping my head, I trail my nose along her delectable neck. It'd be so easy, so sweet, to sink my fangs into her.

"I know it's been awhile, but if you two could keep it in your pants for a bit longer, I'd appreciate it," Malachi says with a drawl. "Then again, I don't mind listening if you don't."

I bite back a growl, glad Cassandra can't hear Malachi's commentary. He's right, though. We don't have time for this.

I touch a knuckle under my mate's chin and brush

my thumb over her parted lips before stepping back. I tilt my head towards the stairs, and my will is tested when her pretty pink tongue darts out to wet her lips. The thought of that tongue of hers on my cock—no, I need to focus. I don't need an erection while skulking through an archangel's mansion.

I take the lead again, the stairs so narrow my shoulders almost brush the walls. At the first landing, I look over my shoulder in question. She purses her lips before shaking her head and pointing upwards. Nodding, I keep climbing.

We're almost to the next landing when Cassandra pauses and presses a hand to the wall.

"What's on the other side of the wall?" I ask while she focuses. This time it's Lan who answers.

"It should be a mezzanine balcony."

"Cassandra's got a lead," I say after she gives me a nod. I try to hear past the wall, but whatever is there may as well be ten feet of concrete. "We'll check it out."

"Copy," Lan says. "Wait thirty seconds before exiting. You've got a guard bored at his post wandering around."

I send my senses out opposite the silent void and, sure enough, there's a single heartbeat moving aimlessly nearby. I hold a hand up to Cassandra, and she waits obediently as I creep the rest of the way to the landing. If only she was as obedient all the time. Then again, she wouldn't be the witch I love if that was the case.

The stairwell is quiet, the air hardly moving around us and the midday heat making it stuffy. But I don't move, tracking the guard's heartbeat with single-minded focus. The guard finally reaches the end of the hall, his pace never faltering as he begins to explore another wing.

"We won't have much time," I warn Cassandra before I open the panel door. "We assess the situation quickly and retreat to plan."

"Got it," she says, her face hard with determination. Her nerves radiate down our bond and I'm damn proud of my mate as she refuses to hesitate.

I move to open the door, freezing when she's suddenly beside me gripping my wrist.

"What?" I murmur, flicking my gaze towards the wall as if I can see through it.

"I don't know," she answers just as quietly. "I thought I felt something, but now..." she trails off, uncertainty eroding her determination.

"Lan?" I ask. She's close enough to me for him to have heard.

"Scans show nothing," he confirmed. "Same with thermal. It's an empty hall."

Conflict wrestles with my instincts. I want to make

Cassandra stay here, to stay safe from any potential threat. Except I want—need to save her, which means I need her beside me. She must sense the internal battle I'm waging with myself. Her small hand touches the back of my shoulder, pulling me back to her.

"Together," she whispers.

She's right. Together. Like it's always been.

Resolved, I ease the door open, this one swinging out into the hall. The hall is empty and we leave the stairwell.

I look in the direction the guard went then towards where Cassandra is heading. Whatever balcony was there before, it isn't now.

"There's an addition," I tell Lan, wanting to curse. Of course there is. Why wouldn't there be an unmarked room?

Cassandra stops before the plain wooden door, no different in appearance than the two others in the hall. She raises her palms, hovering them a few inches from the door, and closes her eyes.

The air shimmers behind her. Then a figure just fucking appears out of nowhere. It grabs Cassandra by the throat and lifts her off the floor.

1866

Cassandra

I'm happier than I have ever been.

We've had spent the winter in a state of bliss, waking up each morning next to the vampire I loved. Ashe Halford is the man I never dreamed of finding, but somehow, I had been lucky enough to stumble into. Quite literally, I think with a chagrin smile and take another sip of the herbal contraceptive tea. A touch of magic ensures that I won't create a child until we're ready.

I'm selfish enough that I want my mate all to myself for some time. And now that we're mated, my life expectancy has extended to Ashe's. As a witch, I already expected to live close to two hundred years. Now, though, Ashe and I have centuries to spend together. A child can wait.

The tea room of the southern mansion is redolent

with New World wealth. When I first came to the mansion, the home Ambrose and the other Nightshades had claimed reminded me too much of my family's home back east. The magnificent chandelier in the foyer with white marble floors; the sweeping staircase carpeted in brilliant red; polished mahogany furniture and Turkish rugs atop gleaming white oak floors. In my childhood home, my family's wealth and standing in the coven was on constant display. It was never a home.

Somehow, though, Josephine and the Nightshades make the mansion feel cozy. Not as cozy as my cottage, of course. Gentle scents of jasmine blend with something sweet from the kitchens, combining to create a tempting invitation to sit in one of the overstuffed wingback chairs and stay for a while.

Laughter echoes through the rooms, growing closer, and I finish the last bit of my tea before pouring myself a fresh cup of assam tea from the delicate porcelain teapot gilded in golden filigree. I pour another two cups, placing the teapot back down on the tray just as Ezra and Ashe walk in.

My heart flies into my throat, beating against me like a hummingbird. Even after spending most of the winter tucked away in my—now our— cottage, the sight of Ashe's crooked smile fills me with elation. I feel like a young girl with her first crush, not a married woman who's memorized her husband's body.

"Hello, my beautiful mate," Ashe says just before dropping a kiss to my offered cheek. "How was your visit in town?"

My mood dips, my earlier concerns rearing up. I gesture to the two teas, inviting them to drink. Both vampires accept the offer, with Ezra sinking onto the white sofa with a happy sigh. I wrinkle my nose, holding back the urge to admonish Ezra for sitting when he and Ashe had clearly just come from the stables and their clothing had a fine layer of dust. Ezra's gold and red eyes sparkle with charm as he met my gaze. He knows exactly what I'm thinking. My grandmother would be appalled with me as I stick my tongue out at him.

The Nightshades have become my family, my friends. I never fit with my coven, craving freedom from their strict expectations and practices of magic. Even before Ashe and I mated, the Nightshades welcomed me with warmth. Only Ambrose holds himself aloof and, at times, we exchange terse words, but Josephine and even Kasar assure me that is simply how their sire is. It's hard not to take it personally, sometimes.

"Charity will deliver any day now." I start with something simple. Jane was the main reason I traveled today, checking on her progression as our doctor is traveling back from the coast. "Dr. Herschel may not arrive in time to deliver. I promised her and Johnathan that I will be ready to help at a moment's notice."

Her baby wouldn't be the first one I've helped in the small town, nor, I doubt, the last, regardless of Dr. Herschel's clear disdain for my "pagan" practices. I chew on the inside of my lip, thinking about the group of men I'd seen in the square as I left.

"Cassandra?"

Ashe's voice has me giving him a forced smile and I set my tea cup back on the table. A look at Ezra shows the half-demon, half-vampire mirrors my husband's concern.

"There are more men in town," I answer at last, my gaze darting between the two males. "Not travelers, either. Charity told me they've been asking questions around town. About Ambrose."

In spite of the mass witch hunts ending centuries ago, small cells of hunters have continued what they believe is a divine calling. They've killed as many innocent humans as they have anyone with paranormal blood.

Ashe squeezes my shoulder, a grim look clouds his face. "Ambrose knows," he tells me. My heart lurches. If Ambrose is looking into it, I fear the threat might be real. "He sent Rhys and Malachi to see what they can discover."

He moves to crouch in front of me, his still full tea

cup abandoned on the table beside mine. He takes my hands in his and presses a kiss to the backs of my fingers. "You're safe, my love," he promises, his vow adamant. "If they seek to hurt us, they will fail. They won't be the first to try."

Ezra snorts. "Not the last either," he says before grinning savagely at me. "We'll slaughter them like we always do."

Maybe it's because I haven't been with the Nightshades for long enough to share their history and victories, but I'm still unsettled.

I grip Ashe's hands, my brow furrowing. "All my childhood, I was told the stories of witch hunts as warnings. Humans, especially the overly religious ones, murdered so many of us. We were never allowed to interact with human society because of that fear." I huff a laugh through my nose wryly. "Well, that and my coven believed humans are beneath them."

Ezra snorts and shakes his head. I don't blame him. My family and their coven were entrenched in disgusting beliefs and, while I haven't sought them out in the last few decades, I doubt they've changed.

"We'll get through this," Ashe tells me again before rising. He cups my face, his thumb brushing gently over my cheek. "Together."

"Besides," Ezra interjects, "if all else fails, we'll just leave. No way any human can keep up with us."

My gut seizes at the thought of abandoning the cottage I'd inherited from Agnes, the one that Ashe and I are transforming into a home.

Someone pounds at the entrance door, hard enough for even my ears to hear. Ezra's and Ashe's heads snap towards the open doorway with the keen attention of a greyhound. It's almost enough to make me laugh at them.

Someone, like Josephine, must open the door because then a frantic voice grows louder as they approach.

A wild-eyed Johnathan charges into the room with Josephine on his heels. He's got his flat cap crushed in his hands as he stumbles to a halt. I'm already on my feet, all concerns forgotten.

"Johnathan?" I ask, striding towards him. "What's wrong? Is it Charity?"

He dips his head in answer. "Yes, misses. She says the babe is coming but she thinks something's wrong. Said to get you fast as I could."

I grasp the man's arms, locking my eyes on his. Johnathan doesn't need my magic to calm down, just good old-fashioned confidence from a midwife.

"It's going to be fine," I assure him. "My husband will take you and a carriage back home. I'll head to my cottage and get what I need before heading over.

Charity needs you to be strong now. Keep her comfortable until I'm there."

Johnathan sputters his thanks as I step aside. Ashe is already moving towards us, and he drops another kiss to my forehead. "Ezra will escort you home," he murmurs and I nod in agreement. By escort, Ashe truly means Ezra will carry me and use his supernatural speed to get me to the cottage. If Charity's instincts are saying something is wrong, then I need to be prepared. I've never assisted in a birth where the mother's instincts were incorrect.

Ashe claps Johnathan on the shoulder and guides the man out of the room. Ezra's up and collecting the tea tray for Josephine.

The gray-haired vampire tilts her head in question. "Do you need help, dear?"

Instinctively, I almost decline but I make myself take a moment and consider. I give a single decisive nod. "Can you catch up with Ashe and return with them to their home? As good of a man as Johnathan is, this is their first time. He's likely to stress the poor girl out more than help. Do what you can until I can get there."

"Of course," Josephine answers and waves Ezra away from the tea tray. "Leave it. We'll deal with it later. We've got a baby to help bring into the world!"

————

CHARITY'S ROOM IS QUIET, the young woman too exhausted to even whimper. Josephine is a godsend, having kept Charity wiped down with a cool cloth the entire time, relaying requests to Ashe and Johnathan, and seeming to predict my or Charity's needs.

Charity's sweaty hair clings to her forehead, her eyes squeezed tight as another contraction rips through her.

Josephine's soothing murmurs wash over me, her words a constant presence in the room.

Ashe paces the hall, his footsteps heavy.

Johnathan's frantic prayers float up the stairs.

Sharing a concerned look with Josephine, we both know the truth. If something doesn't change quickly, we'll lose both the mother and the babe. Charity has lost so much blood.

I close my eyes, laying my hands over Charity's womb, my magic wrapping around the babe. The little one's heartbeat is slowing.

"Cassandra," Josephine's voice is a warning. "We can't lose them both."

"I know," I answer, my magic sinking deeper, caressing the babe's tiny body. The babe is stuck, its head turned the wrong way, and Charity's blood loss weakens her body. Opening my eyes, I look to the young woman who's become close since she started coming to me for her pregnancy ailments. She's pale, her eyes glazed and wild.

"Save my baby," she whispers, her voice hoarse. "Whatever you have to do. Save my baby."

I curl my lips, thinking. I've avoided using magic directly with those who've come to me for aid, but no spelled tincture or medicine will help at this point. When Charity's belly contracts again, the scent of fresh blood filling my nostrils, I make my decision.

Unlike my family's magic, which requires strict structures and specific language to cast the spells, my magic is fluid. It comes from within me, keeping a balance between the natural world and the spiritual world. My magic guides me, and once more I cup Charity's swollen belly in my hands. I fall into myself, seeking the center of my core where I'm most connected to my magic.

Ancient words in a dead language spill from my lips. I cannot say what was spoken, not understanding the language of earth and magic. My heart guides my intention, the intention creating the words. Magic thrums to life in my veins, a buzzing static building underneath my palms. The world around me disappears until all that remains is myself, Charity's dimming soul, and the new soul of her babe.

The smell of blood intensifies, and I chant harder,

more desperate. Someone cries out, and the magic pulsates between us in a spiritual trinity. Pressure builds and builds and builds, my head threatening to explode but still, I push on. I refuse to let this new family be torn apart by death.

My head snaps back, my eyes unseeing as I stare up heavenward. My throat is raw as the words are drawn from me in a shout.

Then, the building lightning storm between my palms is sucked away. The magic is gone, leaving a staggering vacuum in its place. I look down, in time to see the babe's head. My hands are there, then, catching the babe as it slides without friction from Charity. The babe breaks the strained silence with a loud scream and there are no words for the joy and relief I feel. I bring the babe to Charity's chest, the young woman watching in wonder. She's crying now, cradling the little boy to her breast. Josephine, ever stalwart, is there, helping the new baby latch.

I step away, overcome with exhaustion. I lean against the bedroom wall, sliding down to the floor when my legs refuse to hold me.

The door bursts in. Johnathan is even more frantic than earlier, but when his eyes land on his wife and new baby, he's transformed.

I blink, and when I open my eyes, I'm in Ashe's arms as he carries me from the room.

Another blink and he's setting me on the seat of the carriage, brushing the damp hair from my forehead.

Another blink and a snarl. It's startling enough that I cling to consciousness. Ashe is staring down four men. They're making holy symbols and shouting. My blood turns cold as I meet one of their gazes. There is death promised in those eyes.

"Witch," he says and spits at the wagon.

Ashe says something, the coach launching into motion. Those damning gazes follow me into the dark of unconsciousness.

Chapter Eleven

CASSANDRA

My scream is captured in my throat as a massive hand curls around it and lifts me off the floor. My instincts were right. Something had been lying in wait for any would-be thieves. The creature turns me to face it, a beast's snarl sending goosebumps rippling across my skin. The most primal part of me quakes in terror, knowing I'm in the claws of a dangerous predator.

I grasp its wrist, thoughts blanking out as I meet familiar red-tinted golden eyes. I'm becoming light-headed, his grip too tight to allow even the smallest of breaths. A part of me rebels at who has me in his grip, while the logical part of me knows I'm not so light-headed to be imagining things.

Aeternaphiel's rumored guardian is a male I've considered one of my best friends, a chosen brother.

Ashe's snarl tears through my confused, blank thoughts a moment before he slams into the half-demon, half-vampire.

Ezra releases me and I collapse on the floor, my hand going to my bruised throat. I blink back the tears burning my eyes, coughing as I try to gulp in desperate lungfuls of air. I'm still struck dumb, unable to do anything but watch Ashe fight a male who should be a brother. Ezra had been a Nightshade, and even though I wasn't there when it happened, I know the demon vampire had been banished after taking the soul of a mortal.

Eris had tried to find him in the months following Ambrose's declaration but could never find a trace of him.

This Ezra is nothing like the male I knew.

In place of Ezra's easy smile is a savage baring of fangs; his once short black hair now reaches his shoulders in an unkempt mess of tangles. His striking face is gaunt and hollow, his cheekbones too prominent, his jaw too sharp. His skin is pale, pale enough to see the blue veins spiderwebbing underneath. He wears nothing except pants that are ragged and faded with age, the waistband hanging precariously from bony hips.

The ferocity that Ezra battles with against Ashe belies his emaciated appearance. His red-gold eyes have nearly no pupil, the black so small to almost be unseen. Even a human could tell Ezra isn't right.

"Ezra!" I try to shout, wincing as my bruised throat protests. It comes out more as a croak, but neither vampire seems to notice. I push up off my knees and get to my feet, my dress tangling between my knees. "Ashe, something's wrong with him!"

"No shit," my mate snarls in response, grappling with Ezra. I don't take offense to the sharp tone and take a step forward, as if to try to do something— anything to get them to separate. Ashe whips his head towards me, his golden eyes ringed thick with the red of rage. "Stay back!"

The warning cost my mate his advantage, and Ezra takes him to the floor with a resounding crash. There's no way the guards didn't hear that.

Goddess, I wish I'd insisted on getting one of those earpieces Ashe had. We need backup, but I've got no way to contact Malachi or Rhys.

I leap out of the way as Ashe rolls with Ezra, and I realize Ashe isn't trying to kill the former Nightshade vampire. Ezra, though, isn't holding back. He fights Ashe with a viciousness that terrifies me, a part of me afraid Ezra will kill my mate.

"Ezra, it's me. Cassandra," I call, forcing my voice louder. Pain laces my vocal cords, but I shove it aside. I have to get through to him. I have to. "You're my brother. Please, snap out of it! Remember, Ez?"

The nickname slips out, and the moment it does, Ashe freezes. His eyes flick towards me, wide with a realization I miss. Ezra doesn't hesitate and takes the opening to flip Ashe and slam a fist into the side of Ashe's temple.

"Ashe!" I scream. Ezra wraps an arm around Ashe's neck and starts to squeeze. I move forward, a spell already forming on my tongue. Using magic will alert Aeternaphiel if he hasn't realized something was wrong by now. It's a risk I'm willing to take.

Ashe bucks his hips, sending Ezra off of him and flying into a side table with a floral arrangement. The porcelain vase shatters and water splashes against the wall while flowers tumble around the demon vampire.

My mate is on his feet in an instant, gliding between me and the male we once considered a brother, a snarl on his face.

"No point in subtlety," Ashe says, never taking his eyes off the slowly rising Ezra. The demon vampire flicks out his arms to shake off the water dripping down him. His eyes find me over Ashe's shoulder. Instinctively, I fall back a step. There is no recognition in those eyes, no familiar intelligence.

Horror echoes through me. "What have they done to him?"

"Cassandra!" Ashe's sharp tone breaks me from my frozen thoughts. "Get in the damn room. Reinforcements are coming."

Goddess! I whirl towards the door, concentration furrowing my brows as I slap my hands against the warded door. The air stirs around me a moment before I hear Rhys' familiar deep tenor cursing. I don't let myself get distracted. If I stop to think about how Rhys must feel to see his brother in this condition, I'll be the reason this mission fails.

I close my eyes, forcing everything around me to disappear until only the pulsating magical barrier is clear.

It's rigid; the magic reminds me of the strict architecture and diagrams my family and old coven revolved around. The side of my lip curls up in a satisfied smirk and I curl my fingers as if I can grip the very wards themselves. If I'd wrestled my magic into the inflexible obedience like my family had wanted, I'd despair at the complexity before me.

According to their beliefs, I would need to locate the source of each ward spell and dismantle it piece by piece. It'd take hours—hours we don't have.

Instead, I let my wild magic free. In my mind's eye, my magic twists and writhes as it flows from my fingertips. My magic morphs between snakes and briar vines as it ignores the wards entirely. Instead, my magic wends between the wards, slipping between the infinitesimal spaces. In the eternity between heartbeats, my magic encases and penetrates the established wards.

It's crass, uncontrolled, a maelstrom of chaos that electrifies me as I command the magic to destroy the wards. The fine hairs on my nape raise; my fingers vibrate with energy; the smell of ozone fills my nose.

I curl my fingers, imagining taking fistfuls of the latticework wards and my own strangling magic. I wrench my hands down and back, tearing the wards apart and down. The magic doesn't stand a chance. Not against mine which is as wild and overwhelming as nature always intended. The dissipation of the wards crackle in my mind as well as in my ears.

I keep tearing at the magic, my own vines gripping the failing wards in a vice.

When the door is finally clear, the wards spark and flutter in my mind's eye. I shudder, my head falling back, as I pull my magic back within my skin. It curls around my bones, settling down with its own sense of satisfaction.

The wall explodes next to the door, and I drop into a crouch, my arms thrown over my head.

Looking back over my shoulder, I struggle against the fear threatening to paralyze me. Rhys is struggling against a berserking Ezra; he's holding back, but Ezra has no such restraint. My mate is facing off with five human guards, each of them with a gun in hand. Somewhere, Ashe has gotten his own gun, and there are a few bodies on the floor behind the standing guards.

Then Aeternaphiel appears at the end of the hall, fury twisting his angelic face into something monstrous.

"Stop them!" he bellows, and more guards charge towards Ashe.

As if reading my thoughts, Ashe and Rhys both snarl at me. I pull my magic back from where it'd drifted towards them before I realized it.

"We've got this," Rhys grits out, dodging another blow from Ezra. "Get inside and kill the damn soul so we can get the fuck out of here."

I choke on a sob as Ashe jerks awkwardly. Blood blooms on his left shoulder but my mate leaps forward and sinks his fangs into the guard who'd shot him. I throw myself against the door, shocked that it's unlocked. Apparently, Aeternaphiel believed the wards and Ezra were security enough. Shoving door open, I stumble into the room. A furious roar shakes the walls around me, and I slam the door closed before ordering my magic to wrap around the door and keep it sealed. Only Ashe or Rhys will be able to open it through the magic.

The part of me Eris clings to whispers caution.

Aeternaphiel is powerful enough to tear through my wards like parchment.

Moreso, she urges me forward. The vessel is here. We both sense it. The room around me is overwhelming.

The room is a treasure trove, and my magic churns at the magical artifacts and riches scattered throughout the space. Ancient tomes, large jewels, and brilliant weapons are polished and arranged tastefully. I can't help but pause, my fingers trailing reverently over a book older than my coven, older than the modern languages.

But Eris pushes me forward. The vessel is here.

At the back of the room, a dark cabinet is tucked into the corner. It's simple, elegant lines and dark wood blending into the shadows. I'm drawn to it, my pulse racing, as I cross the room.

With sure hands, I open the double doors at chest height, not breathing. There, nestled in a bed of plush evergreen velvet, is a box no larger than a jewelry box. It's gold, the ambient light reflecting off the latticed sides. On the top, two angels are carved on opposite sides, their wings outstretched towards one another.

I snort, the sound catching and scratching the back of my throat. Even Eris, whose presence is the strongest it's been since we were attacked days ago, can't help her humor.

Aeternaphiel, in all his hubris, has stored his soul in a damn replica of the Ark of the Covenant.

A boom against the warded door as me sobering. Eris pushes me, her presence frantic. This is what we've been searching for. This is where the archangel's soul is kept, the angel who was her mentor and lover before using her and casting her out of the heavens.

My hands are steady as I remove the box. It's heavy and I stagger forward as my breath is pulled from my chest. No, not my breath—my very essence, and Eris as well. This close to the soul, it's as if we've been plunked down into a river only feet away from the edge of a massive waterfall.

Eris, unable to speak directly to me, is furious and is shoving and pushing at me. She doesn't need to tell me to do something. My own need to survive has me moving.

I wrench the gold lid from the box, discarding it on the plush carpets without care. The pull is stronger now. There, inside the box, is a heart. Everything about it screams corruption, mottled with sickly purples and greens. It beats with stolen strength.

I hurry to the closest weapon, something I don't even have a name for. It doesn't matter though. It's a blade and Eris assures me it will work. Box in one hand, I grip the ornate weapon, nearly dropping it in pain as it sears my palm.

The door shudders again, loud and brutal. My magic cries out as it's stretched and torn. It won't hold much longer.

I don't hesitate, bringing the blade down and piercing the organ. At least I try to. It's as if I've struck unforgiving steel. Light sears my eyes and I close them against the flash. I keep pushing, believing Eris's fervent reassurances that it will give, so long as I don't relent.

Pain replaces each part of my being even as I feel the soul consuming Eris and my essence.

Then, with an elastic sensation, the blade sinks into the flesh before being repelled and ripped from my hand. I fall to the floor, black spots across my vision.

Eris is gone.

Completely and utterly gone.

The door is still under assault. The blade I used is somewhere, fallen behind another treasure. I climb to my hands and knees, collecting the box and staring inside. I look for any sign that it worked, but the heart beats on and the infected appearance hasn't changed.

My magic wails in warning, and I bolt upright, refusing to give into my spinning head. I retrieve the lid of the box, slamming it closed at the same moment the door bursts open.

I clutch the box to my chest, my heart leaping into my throat.

A furious archangel floods the room with golden light, his wrath-filled eyes focused on me.

He throws Ashe to the ground between us. He's too still, blood splattered all over him, oozing onto the floor below him. I cry out, taking a step towards him.

A warning sound, one more ancient than this world, stops me in my tracks. I lift my eyes to the archangel.

In this moment, it doesn't matter that I failed to destroy his soul. There's no way I can defeat him on my own, even if he became mortal. I know this in my very being. This is a creature not from this realm, not from my world.

He pulls the light within him, tugging at the hem of his shirt and sleeves, straightening himself. He curls a lip in irritation at the sight of blood on one of his arms before appearing to dismiss it.

"You and your vampires have caused me no end of trouble," he says. His tone is even, perhaps mildly irritated, as if we're nothing more than an inconvenience. "This one," he steps forward and kicks Ashe's leg, pulling a groan from my mate, "was an idiot and stayed when the others ran. They even took my favorite playtoy with them."

I lift my chin defiantly. "You are evil. Ezra is not a toy!"

Aeternaphiel cocks his head, his expression considering. He snorts. "Do you know I'd forgotten his name? Ambrose made such a mistake, letting a creature as unique as him out of his possession."

"Cassandra." Ashe's voice is weak, and it takes every ounce of my fragile control to not go to my mate.

"Oh, I see," Aeternaphiel says, looking down at Ashe. The vampire rolls to his front, pain contorting his face as he gets his hands and knees under him. "You two are mates. No wonder why he wouldn't leave you."

"Let him go," I demand. I thrust the box out at him, meeting his blank gaze with my own fierce one. "This is what you wanted, right? Take it. We'll leave."

Aeternaphiel swipes the box from my hand, not bothering to inspect it. That only confirms to me that I failed to destroy the soul and turn him mortal. "Why on Earth would I allow you to leave after you've caused such a ruckus? Do you know how many minds I'll have to wipe downstairs after this? Not that they have much in those minds, as it is, but it is so absolutely tedious."

I ball my fists, desperately searching for anything I can use to keep us alive. Where are Malachi and Lan? Why haven't the Nightshades rushed the estate?

As if following the directions of my thoughts, Aeternaphiel gives me a pitying look before setting the gold box on top of an antique table holding a stack of manuscripts. "Did you all really expect me to not recognize your mate's true nature? That I wouldn't recognize yours?" Aeternaphiel shakes his head, tsking. "The moment you entered my estate, I raised wards to keep any more of your kind out."

"Then why did you wait so long?"

"I was interested in seeing what your merry little band of thieves intended," he admits. "Though I'd expected you to be spies for that so-called king of yours. Or something more mundane, like jewelry thieves."

Ashe begins to rise and Aeternaphiel shoves him in the side with a foot, sending him skidding across the floor and crashing into the wall. He turns his attention back to me, but all I can do is look at the male I love. His chest is rising and falling rapidly, his breathing loud enough for me to hear the wet rattle.

Aeternaphiel snaps his fingers and I look back at him. "Indulge me for a moment. Why did you come here, seeking this of all things?"

I swallow back my first response. If Eris is gone, does it really matter if I tell him? "I made a bargain with a demon. She saved us and in return, I promised to help her seek vengeance against you."

Aeternaphiel looks at me for a long moment, a bit slack-jawed. Then he tosses his head back, laughing. He even slaps his thigh. "Oh, I'd wondered what happened to Eris after she was sent to the bowels of the celestial realm. So, she survived that little clash we had." Dawning understanding lights his face up and my stomach lurches when he looks back at Ashe. "You're the little bastard that stabbed me."

"She's gone!" I blurt out, hoping to distract him from Ashe. "Whatever you did to her, she didn't survive it. If you don't believe me, search my essence. I've been possessed by her for the last hundred and fifty years."

Aeternaphiel considers me for a long moment, then he waves my request away. "I don't need to, witch. I thought I could smell the stench of a second demon earlier. Seeing as it's entirely gone now, it means I've finally dealt with that loose end."

Charged silence fills the room. My heart is a war drum in my ears, drowning out everything. Aeternaphiel stands there, hands in his front pockets, looking at Ashe with consideration. It isn't long before I break.

"What are you going to do with us?"

Aeternaphiel startles, as if he'd entirely forgotten about my presence. "You?" At my nod, he shrugs dismissively and waves at the door. "You were nothing but an innocent pawn in the schemes of Eris. Well, perhaps not entirely innocent as you bargained with a demon. But that is neither here nor there."

My nostrils flare and foreboding scratches the back of my mind.

"And him?" I force out.

Aeternaphiel's gaze returns to Ashe, who's beginning to prop himself up against the wall. Ashe's golden eyes, bloodshot and swollen, meet mine under his lashes. He's too weak to even lift his head up. Tears burn at my eyes.

"Him?" Aeternaphiel's tone turns gleeful. "Well, seeing as I've lost one pet because of him, it seems only fitting for him to take Ezra's place."

"No!" I protest, staggering forward, heart ripping in two.

Aeternaphiel turns an icy gaze to me. "No?" He drawls out, raising a brow. "It is that, or I kill him now. Which would you prefer?"

I swallow hard, unable to break the stone of fear in my throat.

"Go," Ashe rasps, wet and weak. "I'll—" He coughs and I whimper. "I'll be fine. Go."

I can't leave him. How can he ask this of me? I can't let him sacrifice himself for me.

He holds my gaze, pleading filling them. Love and desperation ripple down the bond between us. Then, horrifyingly, I understand. I understand the pain that I caused him when I saved his life at the price of my own.

Tears run down my cheeks.

"I love you," I get out, sobbing the final word.

Ashe closes his eyes, his head lolling forward.

I run. I run from the room, unseeing from my tears. I don't know if anyone tries to stop me. I hear nothing as I burst from the estate. As my feet fly across the grounds and through the trees.

There's nothing but pain and terror shredding my very soul as I collapse on an asphalt road. Nothing but rage at Ashe and myself as someone lifts me into their arms. Even the pain becomes a dull sense of gray as the reality of losing my mate overwhelms everything else.

Then from the gray of desperation, I become nothing. A hollowed-out, soulless person without her mate.

Chapter Twelve

ASHE

A sharp stabbing pain lances through my right side as one of Aeternaphiel's lackeys yanks my arm up. I have at least one broken rib, likely more. I grit my teeth, breathing through the pain. Staying conscious is more important than fighting against the metal cuffs being slapped around my wrists. It's all I've been able to do since they dragged me here and threw me to my knees.

My thoughts are muddied by pain; my entire body is one large pulsating ache. My other hand is secured above my head, the fucker using the same amount of tender care as the first time. Even half out of it, the scent of his human blood is strong. He must be one of the guards I injured. Explains the hospitality, or lack thereof. If he gets close enough, I could sink my fangs into him. Drink him down and speed up my body's healing.

The dick of an archangel lurking by the steel door in front of me wouldn't let that happen. Best I could hope for is ripping the man's throat out with my fangs and getting a swallow or two. I'd end up in worse condition than I already am.

No. I clench my jaw as the lackey presses a button on the control hanging down from the ceiling. A moto engages and I'm lifted into the air until my toes barely brush against the floor. Aeternaphiel stands there, hands in his front pockets and watching me like I'm a fucking new zoo exhibit.

Rather than stare at the archangel, I do my best to take in the room they've brought me to. It seems like a pretty cliche barn turned interrogation setup. I'd snort if it wouldn't hurt.

"Welcome to your new home, vampire," Aeternaphiel grins.

It's a wolf's smile, all teeth and sharp angles. Makes me think of Ezra and how the demon vampire used to smile. Used to, because the version of him I fought was nothing like the male I considered a friend. I'm not even sure if Ezra's in there anymore. And I'm certain this male is directly responsible for it.

My fingers curl, the metal biting into my wrists and reminding me of the position I'm in.

"Don't worry," Aeternaphiel continues when I ignore him. "Your witch of a mate made it off the grounds safe and sound. Though she wasn't looking too good by then. I'm honestly impressed, and a bit disappointed, that she left you. I could have had so much more fun with the pair of you." He lets out a dramatic sigh. "Alas, I am a merciful angel. It's why they call me the Benevolent after all."

I jerk against the chains, snarling at his words before I can wrestle my control back.

"Now, now," Aeternaphiel taunts. "None of that."

His words are lazy, his posture relaxed, but his ice-blue eyes are sharp and assessing. I bare my fangs at him, a sneer curling my lip.

"That's better," Aeternaphiel hums. He begins walking, a slow, casual stroll towards me. "You see, vampire, I'm your master now. The sooner you accept that, the easier your new life will be. My last guard—" he sneers — "the one who that fool of a vampire stole during his escape, resisted me for a long time. True, it is more entertaining for me. But it can be so dull."

Aeternaphiel waves a hand towards me and the same lackey steps forward and delivers a sharp punch to my diaphragm. I wheeze, the air being knocked from me; my entire core seizes, pain lighting up my nerves like a switchboard. I turn a glare to the man, vowing to myself that I'll kill him before I'm done with this place.

The threat must be obvious, since a flash of fear crosses his face, the sour scent reaching me even over the metallic tang of blood.

A wicked satisfaction curls in my stomach despite the situation. I don't have a reputation for violence and brutality as my fellow Nightshades do, but it doesn't mean I'm tame.

"Leave us."

At Aeternaphiel's crisp order, the guard turns on his heel and leaves through the metal door. I don't hear a lock, which means either the room is warded magically or his pride is that damn big. If I focus, I can sense guards beyond the room but my head spins when I try to count the heartbeats. Fuck, I must have a concussion. A bit pathetic for a vampire as old as I am, though not insurmountable. If I'd made it out with Cassandra, I could have fed from her. With my mate's blood, my body would be healed within a day or two.

I don't regret telling her to leave, though. Even if this bastard kills me. Even if the Nightshades never come for me.

A thought drips through the bruising haze of pain, bright and clear as crystalline waters.

This must be what Cassandra felt when she made the bargain with Eris to save me.

Just like I couldn't let Cassandra stay and be

subjected to Aeternaphiel, she couldn't have let me burn with the rest of my clan that night.

That understanding, more than anything, hurts the most.

The next time I see her, because I *will* see her again, I'll tell her I finally understand. I understand why, even as she begged forgiveness for the pain I endured, she'd make the same choice over and over again.

I fight the need to reach out through our mate bond, to seek comfort and to comfort her. I know all too well the darkness she must be experiencing. I'd been lost in it for months; it would have been years if it weren't for Malachi, Kasar, and the rest of the Nightshades. Even Landon, in his own way, drew me from that void. When Eris returned unsuccessful, declaring her intentions of keeping possession of Cassandra until the bargain is fulfilled, it would have been so easy to give up. I would have without my family.

Pain explodes across my face, and my head is snapped to the side.

"Pay attention when your master is speaking, beast."

I roll my head back to face him, spitting a mouthful of blood and spit between us. I don't deign to give any other response. I've met people like Aeternaphiel before. It doesn't matter if someone is human or supernatural, there are always those who believe in their superiority. Even as you crush their face into the mud, they die screaming degradations to the very end.

No fucking dignity.

Satisfied enough, Aeternaphiel repeats whatever I'd missed.

"Your mate said Eris is gone. Is that true?"

A stare is all he gets from me.

Irritation burns in his eyes but he doesn't rise to the bait. I'm sure anyone who is an old ancient archangel can handle some silent treatment. This room, with its stained concrete floors, hanging hooks, and single leather club chair set next to the side table, makes it clear I'm not the first guest to spend time here.

I'll be the gods-damned last one though, I promise him silently.

Cassandra may be hurting right now, but I know my mate and I know my vampire brothers. I can survive whatever this archangel tries.

The male sighs, as if disappointed in my refusal to cooperate. He moves towards the club chair, sinking into it and crossing an ankle over his knee. Looking at him, he could be back in the main house, enjoying the day with his guests.

"It doesn't have to go this way, you know." He gestures between us. "My last guard dog resisted for so long he'd almost been completely useless by the time he relented."

Guilt turns my blood to bile, poisoning and scalding me. Ambrose had exiled Ezra during a time in the Barrows where war between us and a demonic faction was a very real threat. Ezra had taken a human soul, something Ambrose and the rest of us vampires fought against. Ezra had never done such a thing before and we could never figure out -why- he had and then immediately came to confess to Ambrose.

Eris had been furious, nearly attacking Ambrose when the male had announced what'd happened. We had all wanted answers, Rhys especially. But Ambrose hadn't had any, or if he did, he kept them to himself.

I could have looked for Ezra. My duties would have allowed me to inquire discreetly. Ezra had been one of Cassandra's best friends. Knowing what became of him, I wonder if I'll ever conquer the shame of never looking. Of blindly accepting my king's orders.

"Working for me can be enjoyable, you know." Aeternaphiel's voice pulls me back to the moment. "Not immediately, of course. You still need to be housebroken after-all." His voice turns steely. "Make no doubt, for I will break you."

Breathing through my nose, blood still sluggishly dripping from my wounds, I know the male is right. Everyone breaks eventually. There's no avoiding it. There comes a point where someone will say whatever it is the person wants, just to stop the pain. The goal is to give them half-truths in the beginning. That way, when the pain gets too much, they never know what is true and what isn't.

I spit another glob of blood to the side before giving him a considering look. He knows he has my attention now. I ignore every ache, every slow healing wound, every cracked bone.

"Whatever you did to Eris before I stabbed you took her out of Cassandra," I offer. "After spending the last century and a half with the demon possessing my wife, I didn't give a fuck how it happened. I got my wife back."

He hums in consideration. "And why did you and your wife seek me out today?"

I give as much of a half-assed shrug as I can, hanging like this. "She has some misguided guilt and connection to the demon. I wanted my mate safe. Nothing personal. I'm sure you understand."

Aeternaphiel studies me. I don't look away, refusing to back down. I might be the one tied up here, but he wants something from me other than my subservience. I think back on what Cassandra and Eris have mentioned over the years, scouring history for any clue. I've never let myself think too long on that night when Cassandra summoned Eris. Now I strain to recall every word Eris and my mate exchanged. Finally, I had it.

"You were lovers," I say. He clearly wasn't expecting me to speak again but recovers quickly, raising a brow in expectation. "She said you mentored her, helped her rise through the ranks of the army or whatever. She believed in you. Sounded almost like she thought you were mates. Or she hoped you were. Then you betrayed her."

Aeternaphiel doesn't scoff as I expect. Instead, he freezes so completely I wonder if he's breathing.

Wait.

"Are you mates?" I ask, incredulous; shock has my pain completely disappearing from my mind.

"Enough of this," Aeternaphiel tries to deflect, and I let out a dry laugh, one completely inappropriate for the moment.

I give him a sardonic look. "If you two are mates, you'd know if she's alive or not. Even when my mate was possessed, our bond was there." I shake my head again. "If you and Eris are mates, how could you betray her? How could you try to fucking kill her?"

"She betrayed me!" Aeternaphiel roars, throwing himself up out of the chair, and charges towards me. Bright power slams into me, radiating out in waves from the archangel. Light bursts from his shoulders and it's gone in the same instant. All that's left is the floating after-image of wings.

He slices his hand through the air and begins to pace. I'm still reeling from this information.

"All she'd had to do was stay quiet. We both knew that our world was rotting from within, that something needed to change. But the Resplendents did not care that the princes of the underworld moved against us. She didn't agree with my plan, but had she kept her damn mouth shut, we could have ruled the celestial realm together."

Aeternaphiel is practically frothing at the mouth. The hatred coming from him is more than just...anger or hurt. It's deeper, bigger, more a part of him than the power he has control over.

He stops and rubs his face with both palms, gathering himself before facing me again.

"I had to tell them it was her. If they believed her to be the traitor, my plans could still work. I could have let the Resplendents execute her. Instead, I argued for her to be sent to the underworld. At least there, she had a chance to live."

"Bullshit."

I don't realize I've said it until the word is ringing between us. I barrel on. "If she was really your mate, you would have done whatever it took to protect her.

You'd have offered yourself up before ever casting the blame on her."

I see the moment stony shields come down in Aeternaphiel's mind. He's wrapped himself back up with the cold control of power he's so familiar with. There will be no more pushing him to the edge. I breathe deeply and let my eyes close. I find the bond between Cassandra and me, the one that has only been reopened for a few days after so long apart.

I focus everything I have on rebuilding that wall between us, using every year of experience I kept that wall up to build it even stronger. I hope I build it strong enough that when I break, it won't. It'll keep Cassandra safe from my agony. Even when all I will want is her.

"Now, vampire," Aeternaphiel's voice is lofty once more. I hear him open something to the left of me but I don't allow myself to look. "It's time to begin your training."

1866

Ashe

Agitation fuels my pacing. Only Ambrose's stern order is keeping me from rushing from the house to my mate's side. Malachi had escorted Cassandra to town, since he'd had business there as well and I was needed in the stables. Lily Dancer had thrown a shoe and the hoof had contracted a strange infection within a day. I'm the only one the mare will let near so I spent the afternoon with her, applying poultices, heat wraps, and anything else I'd learned over the centuries of my life.

I trust Malachi with my life, and with Cassandra's, I remind myself as I make my way to the window overlooking the drive. It was nearing dusk, and while the two weren't late, the unease I feel through the mate bond has my fangs elongating.

Something is wrong. Not enough for Ambrose to allow me to rush off and risk causing a scene.

Not with the increased focus on us.

Resisting the urge to gnash my teeth, I think of the bastards who spit vile declarations at my wife after she'd saved a woman and her new babe. I'd wanted to tear out their throats in that moment, but Josephine had helped me hold back.

Maybe if her son, Lan, had been with me, the men wouldn't be an issue.

A blur appears, shooting down the lane, before slowing to reveal Cassandra in Malachi's arms. The sight of my mate in another male's arms—regardless of who it is—is too much. Ignoring Ambrose, I'm out of the room and then the house a heartbeat later. Malachi is in the process of setting Cassandra on her feet, when I take her from his arms, only partly successful in tempering my possessive snarl.

He holds his hands up in surrender, his face more serious than his typical easy grin.

I look down at Cassandra, her heartbeat soothing my anxiety better than any draught or tonic. Her unease has lessened, but enough remains that I know it's not due to Malachi carrying her.

My eyes snap to Malachi, our gold gazes meeting. "What happened?"

My tone is harder than intended, but the male doesn't take it personally.

"Just a little scuffle," Cassandra says as she tries to wiggle free of my arms. She huffs and gives up when I grip her tighter with a rumble.

Malachi isn't as glib.

"Those so-called devil hunters have started riling up the townspeople." Malachi nods towards the house and, to Cassandra's tangible relief, I set her down and we walk beside him. I keep my arm wrapped around her, tucking her into my side. The primal urge to protect my mate demands no less. Next to me is where she is safest. I can kill anything before it touches her. It's worrying when she doesn't try to step away, her own arm coming around my lower back.

"Did something happen?" I asked as we re-enter the house. Malachi closes the door behind us and Cassandra steps away from me. Not far enough to be out of reach; alarm shoots my brows upwards as she breathes out a warding spell and places her palm against the door. The air ripples as her ward settles into place.

She looks up at me, her expression grim. "Just a precaution." Her smile falls flat.

"We need to speak with Ambrose," Malachi says in lieu of explaining further. Cassandra looks resigned but doesn't disagree. I catch her hand, threading her fingers with mine and she gives me a grateful squeeze.

Ambrose is standing at his desk, arms folded, when we walk in.

"Explain."

His order is succinct and firm. He'd have heard everything and felt the wards rise. I won't be surprised if the others join us soon, curious to know why Cassandra had cast protective magic.

Malachi nods once, the move sharp. His normal arrogant demeanor has disappeared. In its place is the soldier and general I first met years ago. As he reports, I grind my molars. Ambrose's expression never changes but his anger is clear in the stiffening of his shoulders, the tight squeeze of his fists where his arms are crossed. I don't realize how tense I've grown until Cassandra presses a hand against my bicep.

As predicted, others join us during Malachi's accounting of their experience in town. Kasar slips in, with Josephine on his heels—the woman as silent as the Lion. Her son, Lan, follows moments later with less subtlety but doesn't interrupt. Rhys and Ezra are the last to enter the study, both of them wearing concerning expressions.

When Malachi finishes, a poignant silence packs the room.

"We should strike first," Lan says in a bored drawl.

"I don't see why we don't take care of these men before they turn the town into a mob."

Kasar huffs through his nose, sending a scalding look to the blond vampire leaning against the wall across from him. "If we kill these men, it will only prove what they are saying. We will be the monsters they claim."

Lan cocks a brow at Kasar. "We are monsters, or have you forgotten?"

"Landon!" Josephine chides her son and Lan purses his lips but stays quiet. Josephine looks at my wife. "What of Charity and her babe? Of Johnathan?"

A wave of unease reaches me through the bond and I look down at her, worry weighing down my chest. Cassandra rolls her lips, torn, before speaking.

"Johnathan wouldn't let me see them," she admits at last. "He said they were sleeping and didn't want to disturb them. But he was different. I got the impression he was lying, but I didn't want to push too hard." Cassandra looks between me and Ambrose. She's practically shaking in my embrace. "I'm worried about them, if I'm honest. I remember, in too vivid of detail, what witch hunters have done to my people and those they consider witch lovers."

I'm speaking before realizing it. "It won't come to that. I'll kill every single one of them before letting them touch you."

Rhys and Ezra give a quiet hear-hear in agreement, but Cassandra shakes her head. "You don't understand, my love. These people... they can't be stopped, not if they're true devotees."

Ambrose interjects then. "What do you mean?"

Cassandra meets his hard stare head-on. "I'm shocked you aren't familiar with them, given your age. Though I guess witch hunters must all be the same to you." She holds up a hand, her eyes crinkling in apology. "I don't mean to cause offense. It's just... these are the people I was raised being warned about. They're a witch's boogeyman so to speak. You know of demons and those who make deals with them? There are these hunters who do the same, except instead of demons, they seek out those people called angels. During the witch trials years ago, we believed that there was a large conflict in the celestial realms. It overflowed to our realm, and both sides used humanity."

"As above, so below," Ezra mutters quietly, shaking his head.

Cassandra gives him a solemn look. "Just so."

"It sounds familiar," Kasar says, looking at Ambrose. "We've had a few run-ins with groups with supposed holy patrons. These are whom you're talking about?"

"Most likely," Cassandra answers after a moment of consideration. "I can't exactly say. They're dangerous, though. More dangerous than any group of humans with pitchforks and torches."

Ambrose looks out of the window, his eyes going distant as he ponders the situation.

"We should leave," I say, pulling everyone's attention to me. I don't cower under my sire's hard stare. Not when it comes to protecting my mate. "We don't need to stay here. Why risk a bigger confrontation?" Someone snorts, probably Lan, but I don't stop. "We've already accomplished what we came here for. If the town is already turning against us, we aren't as well liked as we thought."

"And run like rats, scurrying to safety in the dark?" Malachi says with disgust. He cuts his hand sharply through the air. "That has never been our way and you know it."

"When you have a mate to protect, you stop giving a shit what you did in the past," I snap back. Irritation and the primal need to protect Cassandra skitters under my skin.

Malachi rolls his eyes and I take a step forward, lip curling up in a snarl.

"Stand down." Ambrose's command is quiet, no more than a breeze through the trees, but filled with enough power to freeze Malachi and me in place. The smallest tug has me stepping back beside an irritated Cassandra.

"I don't want to be run from my home, Ashe." Her words are more confident than the emotions I sense through our bond. "Besides, there are things I can do to stop them."

Ambrose straightens off the desk, his entire focus on my wife. "How so?"

Cassandra spares a short look up at me, and I immediately know I'll hate anything she says. She doesn't look away from Ambrose while she answers.

"If they are, in fact, working with a patron, as they call it, then it depends on the power of the patron. If they've only been given minor blessings, then I don't think we need to worry about a direct confrontation with them."

Kasar is the one who speaks next. "And if they've more than minor blessings?"

I can hear my wife's hard swallow. "Then there is very little even the most powerful being in our realm can do."

"In this realm," Ambrose repeats, but his question is clear.

Cassandra nods. "The best way to fight a being from a different realm is to seek the help of one from the same realm."

"You're talking about deals with a demon?" Josephine's voice is quiet with fear. "No, darling. That is too dangerous."

Nausea sours my stomach as Cassandra's fear threatens to overwhelm me through our mating bond. I've seen humans who've made bargains with demons, even ones who believed they'd figured out a way to outsmart a demon's abilities to twist words. Every time, the demon wins. The mortal gets what they wished for, but every single one I've witnessed has regretted the deal in the end.

I cannot let my wife make the same mistake.

A deep beating rhythm is faint at first but grows steadily louder. Drums. Only Cassandra doesn't hear them approaching. She can't send out her senses to count the shocking number of heartbeats marching towards the house.

She does notice, however, the way each of us straighten and bristle.

We're too used to what the sound means. It means we won't be able to avoid a battle, not with a mob already coming for us.

"Arm yourselves, gentlemen," Ambrose orders, swiftly turning and going to the polished wooden case and opening it. He retrieves two bone-hilted daggers, relics of his human days. When he turns back to us, fitting the sheaths to his belt, he's adopted the hard expression of the man who turned me on a bloody battlefield. "Cassandra, set what wards you can. Then, you and Josephine must prepare the livestock's blood in the event we need it. The rest of you, meet me in the foyer to prepare ourselves."

Everyone files out as the uncertain threat becomes reality. I take Cassandra by the hand, leading her quickly to our room. When I've closed the door behind her, I wheel and grip her by the shoulders, bringing my face close to hers.

"Whatever you do," I grit out, "whatever happens, do not summon a demon."

She trembles, grasping my wrists like a lifeline. Her fear sours the air around me, drowning out the sweet scent of her.

"Ashe," she begins and I shake her, rattling her into silence.

"No," I snarl. "Swear it. I would rather die by your side if that is our fate. I will not lose you to a demon's schemes."

Her eyes are wide and water-lined. I sigh and close my eyes as I press my forehead against hers. I slide my hands from her shoulders to cup her neck and jaw. "I love you, my mate. I cannot lose you."

"And I cannot lose you," she replies, her words wobbling. Her fear hurts more than any wound.

"Swear it," I plead, ghosting a kiss over her lips. "Swear you won't do it, no matter what."

Her heart stutters at my words and I brace myself, readying myself to tie her up and put her in the wardrobe if I must. The only reason why I haven't sent her away is I know she's too stubborn to listen, and if she's tied up in a wardrobe... if the worst happens, I want her to be able to fight until the end.

She presses her petal-sweet lips to mine. "I swear," Cassandra breathes out. "I won't summon a demon."

Her words are rushed, but the drums and heartbeats are close enough that she must hear the mob herself. She guides my mouth to her neck, tilting her head away to submit to me.

"Feed. You need it for the fight ahead."

I should say no, knowing if I feed from her too much, she'll be weakened. If she's right, though, that these men have abilities granted to them by a higher power, we need every edge we can get. I breathe in the scent of her, imprinting it on my senses, vowing this will not be the last time I have her. Then I sink my fangs into her flesh and drink down her intoxicating, empowering blood.

Chapter Thirteen

CASSANDRA

Something pats at my cheek, almost hard enough to be considered a slap. I wince, trying to turn away from the abuse but something else catches my chin. My face is rattled until I groan, feebly pushing at whatever it is to get it to stop.

"Uh-uh, witch," a smoky voice says, almost as if they're annoyed with me. "I need you to wake the hell up. I might be able to kick their asses, but I don't want to waste my time. So, you need to wake up and be on your own two feet so Ambrose doesn't try anything stupid. They're all already buzzing around like a pissed-on hornets' nest."

Blearily, I crack my eyes open. There's a ceiling light bright enough that I raise my hand to try to block it out. Someone is silhouetted above me and I don't recognize the voice. I peer around, trying to get a sense of location when the smell of ground coffee hits me. Combined with the exposed bricks and eclectic furniture, I realize I'm at Black Death Beanery—but how?

"Are you always this slow on the uptake? I swear you never were when I was in you," the same voice grates out and then strong hands grip my shoulders and forcibly pull me up into a sitting position. My head spins; I throw out a hand to keep my balance but it's not necessary for more than a moment. I blink, clearing the spots from my vision and it's not Darcelle in front of me.

"Wha—who?" I rasp out, my mouth filled with sand.

The woman with warm brown skin and pitch-black hair rolls her eyes. Eyes that are a wine red, with a cat-like pupil, framed with thick black lashes and perfectly arched brows.

She raises a hand between our faces and snaps a couple times. I go nearly cross-eyed as I stare stupidly at the two-inch talons painted a matte chartreuse. My eyes running from her hand to her arm, up to her shoulders and across her tight, black leather-clad torso, I finally look at her face again. A face I haven't seen for over a hundred and fifty years.

"Eris?" I blurt out, no doubt sounding like an idiot. "But how? You were gone. We were dying? I failed to kill the soul and—"

She presses her hand to my mouth, shushing me. "Were you always this dimwitted? I swear you were intelligent when we first made the bargain."

I jerk my head back, frowning. "You don't have to be so rude, you know."

Eris rolls her eyes. "Yes, yes, manners and all that. I've always found manners get in the way when time is of the essence, and if you want to save your mate and finally finish this bargain of ours, I need you to pull your shit together fast."

A door opens and in walks Darcelle with a tray filled with a couple bowls and a stoneware mug that steam rises from with an enticing smell.

"Ah, so she's awake, good," Darcelle says as they cross what I realize is a small living room. It must be above the coffee shop, since I have vague memories of it from when Eris possessed me. They set the tray on the small art deco table beside the couch I'm on and press the mug into my shaking hands. "I really wanted to avoid having to use the bitters. Always makes my nose itch for days after and I'm useless when it comes to any mixings or roasting the beans. Go on, drink up."

Confused and discombobulated, I do as the witch tells me. To my relief, it's nothing more than herbal spiced tea. It wipes the last of the fog from my brain and my last recollections slam into me.

"Ashe!" I stare at Eris, wild-eyed.

She nods, eyes half-lidded with satisfaction. "There she is," she says, standing from where she was crouched in front of me and snagging her own cup from the tray. "So, shall I catch you up from the point you passed out from shock after exiting the wards? You can say thank you any time for waiting for you, by the way."

I set the cup down with a tight smile directed at Darcelle, before I rub my temples. An ache is forming behind my left eye and it's directly related to the demon in front of me.

"I think—" I cut myself off and move my fingers to pinch the bridge of my nose. Finally I let out a breath, shaking my head in hopes to jostle more understanding out of the dark crevices of my mind. Failing that, I shoot a narrowed look at the demon sitting there, blithely drinking some sugary concoction. "I need you to explain what the hell is going on." I gesture to her. "How are you like this? I felt you die!"

Eris smacks her lips and cradles the drink between her hands while giving me a look better suited to a misbehaving child. "You didn't feel me die; stop being so dramatic."

I scoff and Darcelle settles on the other end of the couch, taking up an embroidery hoop and threaded needle. They give Eris a pointed look before turning their focus to their project.

Eris rolls her eyes, sighing loudly as if she hadn't just accused me of being dramatic. "Yes, I was dying because of Aeternaphiel's siphoning blade. When you found his soul—cunning bastard—you also found where I was being siphoned to. I was able to guide you to use a blade that's called—" whatever she said twisted in my ears, sending chills along my spine, and a coil of despair to tighten around my organs. She must have noticed because she frowned in annoyance. "Forgot how sensitive you mortals are."

Even Darcelle tutted at her this time. Eris holds up a hand as if in apology, but everyone in this small room knows better.

"Essentially, the blade is a bond breaker," Eris comes up with. "That's an understatement of an explanation, though. It's from another realm, not even my own. Aeternaphiel should not have it. It doesn't so much as break bonds as devours them. Undoes them so completely as to erase them from existence. It could never have killed his soul. By the time you and your mate got there on your, frankly, idiotic scheme, I'd been in the room long enough to know nothing in there could kill him. But I did know that blade would sever me from him and free me. So I had you do that."

"So glad I lost my mate while freeing you, idiots we are." My retort is dry as sand.

"Dramatic."

"Eris, we talked about this," Darcelle says, not bothering to look up from where they threaded the needle into the white cloth. A gentle caress of magic, like the touch of a falling leaf, matches the rhythm of their stitches. "The vampires will be here soon."

That has me sitting up straighter. "The Nightshades?"

Eris sneers. "No, some other clan of vampires have taken over in the couple of hours you've been drooling on Darce's couch."

I close my eyes, gripping the edge of the couch, and focus on taking deep, hard breaths. When I'm certain I won't explode at the demon, I open my eyes and give her a hard look.

"I would greatly appreciate it, Eris, if you could hurry the fuck up and get to your point."

Eris blinks for a long moment, her eyelids closing horizontally rather than vertically. Then she grins. "I knew I had a good influence on you."

"Eris," I growl her name.

"Yeah, yeah," she huffs and takes another long drink. "The long story short? The blade severed me from Aeternaphiel, along with some other bonds. What it also did was sever the spells protecting his soul. As far as he knows, nothing is different. Only way he could tell is if he inspected the spells himself, but he doesn't have that type of power. I doubt he has a pocket warlock hidden away. He's never liked being around others with any sort of power. Can't lose a pissing contest if you're the only one who can piss."

A hollow twang, almost tangible but not quite, has both of us looking at Darcelle. They set their embroidery to the side and stand, smoothing down their billowy pants as if wearing a formal gown. "That would be the vampires. I'll see them up."

I don't see the look they give Eris, but given the demon sticks out her tongue at the witch before nodding, I can imagine it.

I slump against the couch, blindly grabbing my tea, the mug's warmth seeping into my palms. I'm grateful to not have the heightened senses of a vampire. It means I have a few more moments to erect walls around the ache in my soul. Goddess, leaving Ashe behind the way I did.

I press the heel of a palm into my eye, gripping my tea tightly with the other hand. If I drop the mug now, it might be the final thing to break my sanity. Now is not the time to be clumsy.

The moment Ambrose enters the room, even without looking, I can tell. The vampire king has this energy, the same energy of a beast of the night lurking in the shadows. But when I look up, it's Eloise hurrying over, concern and sympathy in her eyes. Ambrose's mate sinks next to me on the couch, immediately taking me into her arms.

Goddess, I don't realize how much I need a hug until the shorter woman has me squished against her. A sob hiccups free and Eloise hums with understanding. She runs her hand through my hair, gently avoiding any tangles.

"We're getting him back, Cassandra," she murmurs, fierce yet tender. "We don't abandon family."

"Unless they refuse to grovel at Ambrose's feet," Eris snarls. The air turns frosty. Heart caught in my throat, I look up to see the vampire king and demon in a glaring match. At some point, Eris had gotten up and now she stands with her arms folded, looking at Ambrose in condemnation.

Ambrose is a mountain, impervious to the storm of Eris's anger. "You speak of Ezra. It is ... unfortunate what happened to him after he left—"

"After you exiled him, you mean," Eris interrupts.

"However, he made his choice while knowing the consequences," Ambrose continues as if she never spoke. "That being said, we will not abandon him in his current condition."

Eris rolls her eyes. "Oh, yes, wouldn't want a feral half-vampire, half-demon running around. It wouldn't be good for your reputation." Her sarcastic tone makes her thoughts of Ambrose clear.

"Eris," I chide her gently, easing Eloise's arms from me and rising.

Malachi, Lan, and Kasar flank Ambrose, their expressions hard. Each of the vampires are tense, ready to leap if necessary. How often have these males wanted to go to blows with the demon, but held back because she possessed my body? It's the shock I need to focus on defusing the situation.

Boldly, I take Eris's hand, ignoring Ambrose for the moment. Her red eyes meet mine, accusatorially. I speak before she can, knowing that once Eris gets on a roll, it's nearly impossible to stop her.

"Ezra is my friend. Ambrose is not without honor, entirely," I amend and ignore his huff. "When this is finished, I will help him. Not for Ambrose or the Nightshades, or even the city. I'll help him because I consider him my brother, even if we do not share blood. I love Ezra and I will not leave him to suffer."

Eris watches me for a long moment, before blinking in that reptilian way she always has. She grunts and yanks away her hand, muttering something I choose to ignore. Satisfied there isn't about to be a catfight between the two, I turn and fist my hands on my hips.

"We need to get Ashe back. Now."

Ambrose raises an elegantly arched black brow at the command. My cheeks suffuse with heat but I refuse to back down.

"Of course we will," he says after a moment.

I let out a long breath, unexpected relief almost making me dizzy. I rub my chest, just above my heart where Ashe marked me as his mate. "Good, good."

When he realizes I'm not going to say anything else, he directs a look to Lan and steps aside.

After mating Wren, the sadistic glint in Lan's eyes had tempered. Now it is back in full force as he steps forward, a hand resting casually on the butt of a handgun. It's that precise moment I realize the vampires haven't arrived in their usual expensive custom suits. All of them, even Ambrose, are wearing black tactical pants and jackets over vests. They're armed with modern weapons and look ready to make war.

It's sickeningly familiar to the night the witch hunters pinned us in the mansion before setting it on ablaze.

"Before we can make any plan, there's something you need to explain," Lan says, his voice smooth as whiskey and melted chocolate. I think he's talking to me at first, but he's staring at a broody Eris. She flicks her eyes to him after a moment. When he has her attention, he tilts his head. "When were you going to tell us this archangel of yours, the one you made a bargain with Cassandra to kill, is your mate?"

The rush is like the floor disappearing under me, as I snap wide eyes to Eris. She's bristling and snarling, like a pissed-off cat tossed in a bath.

"How do you know that?" She shakes her head. "It doesn't matter. We are not mates. We were once, but he chose himself over the bond. When he cast me to the underworld, our bond rotted. It's gone. It doesn't matter."

"Eris?" My voice is gentle and she turns her glare on me.

"Oh, don't look at me like that," she spits. "Not everyone with a mate gets a happily ever after. Aeternaphiel has always loved himself and power more than me. Even as his mate, he only ever saw me as a tool. Our bargain still stands, witch."

"Eris—"

She cuts me off with a growl. When I pinch my lips together, she turns her attention back to Lan, then Ambrose. "If we're going to take him down, we need to act now. He's probably already called in reinforcements. You cannot underestimate him."

"We won't," Kasar rumbles as he folds his arms across his broad chest. "Malachi's called in the foot soldiers. Lan's surveillance hasn't been detected yet, and you're right. He's called in at least fifty more guards. At least half of them are shifters of some sort. None affiliated with packs in the city."

"They know better," Malachi states. "We have more than enough with the clan, but I can call in a favor with the Knights of Hades if you want. Chainz is still here. By himself, he's as good as ten of the street crew."

Ambrose seems to weigh the decision before shaking his head once. "No. Better not involve them in our business. I don't want to owe Reaper anything." Ambrose looks back at me, studying me. I stand straighter under the close inspection.

"If you're coming with us—"

"I am!"

"—then you need to be outfitted properly. Kasar, get the witch set up with something more appropriate. And for god's sake, make sure you find a Kevlar vest for her." He looks each vampire in the eye before gesturing to me. "Our primary goal is to rescue Ashe. Malachi, you keep Cassandra at your side every moment. If she gets hurt, you'll be the one explaining it to Ashe."

"And what about me, oh, mighty vampire king?" Eris asks, inspecting her talon-sharp manicure.

"You can take care of yourself," Ambrose responds dryly. Then Kasar kicks a metal case I hadn't noticed at his feet, sending it sliding across the floor. "Darcelle made us aware of your situation. I figured you'd want some blades."

Eris crouches down, flicking the case locks open and revealing at least half a dozen different knives and daggers. She gives him a sadistic grin. "You do care."

He grunts. Eloise moves beside me, giving me a side hug. "You'll get him back."

I nod once, cold determination replacing the blood in my veins. A darkness creeps from behind my heart, one I always associated with Eris. It's me, though. Even if I'd never wanted to claim it. Even if I recognized it long ago as something inherited from my family.

If I must embrace the savage side of my wild magic to save Ashe, I will.

Aeternaphiel will rue the day he took my mate from me.

1866

Ashe

Drumbeats fill the spaces between pounding heartbeats. Smoke, blood, and the rotten stench of fear and death have replaced the comforting smells of horse, hay, and clean leather.

Malachi snarls a curse, slamming his shoulder against the door keeping us locked in stables. It splinters under his assault but does not fall.

"Leave it," intones our king, our sire. The male who turned me centuries ago as I lay dying on a battlefield. He stands tall, as resolute as a cliff against the waves, in the central aisle I'd swept earlier that morning.

Like the rest of us, he's covered in blood—some of it his own. These humans, these self-proclaimed deliverers of Heaven's justice, have weapons we've never encountered before. Blades that make the wounds inflicted burn as if coated in acid. The hunters from out-of-town wear a talisman that shields them from our attacks and have donned white tabards emblazoned with an iron cross in the center of a collar with spikes pointed inwards.

Rhys had snarled at the image, flying into a frenzy as he tried to attack one of the hunters. His family had died wearing those collars, used for torture. When his vicious attacks did nothing, each swipe repulsed by an unseen barrier, the townspeople who'd joined in the mob attacked.

I sink down the paddock door, scrubbing my face in anger and shame.

Men, and some women, who we considered friends once, had swarmed us. They had armed themselves with kitchen knives, hunting daggers, and family heirloom swords. Even fucking pitchforks and torches, as gods-damned cliche as it was.

Vampires may be faster and stronger than humans, but we were outnumbered four to one. It's like every damn person had joined the mob.

And we'd killed them, defending ourselves.

I killed them.

Benedict, the grizzled old man who I'd swapped stories with of horse escapades. Danny, the baker, who always had a soft spot for Josephine. Thomas, practically still a boy at seventeen who pestered Rhys with questions about the world.

Johnathan. Tears of anger and hurt roll silently down my cheeks as I look up at the top of the barn. Jonathan, the man who'd begged Cassandra to save his wife and babe. Who had allowed himself to be convinced that Charity had given birth to a devil and given her soul away. Who'd allowed her and their child to be killed for the sake of purifying the world.

Kasar had called in a retreat and we'd been harried towards the stable. Whatever magic these humans were using created a ward stronger than any I've experienced. We were trapped in here, all us males. I can only be glad Cassandra and Josephine had remained in the main house.

Cassandra's fear has remained near choking levels and even now, I dredge up the energy to send my love towards her, promises that it will all be okay.

Josephine will get her out and keep her safe. The mob has no idea that the two females aren't in here with us.

"It looks as if we're to be roasted alive," Lan says blandly, as if discussing the next week's weather or the upcoming harvest.

Rhys and Ezra lean together against a support post and look up at the hayloft. Kasar leaps from his position next to Ambrose to join the blond vampire at the hay door, Ambrose following his second's every move. Malachi comes and stands over me, his fists clenched, knuckles bloody and bruised. He looks around the stables and holds his hand out to help me up.

"We should let the horses have a chance," he says quietly. "The far door might open since there's an overhang. Maybe they'll be able to pass through the ward even if we can't."

I grab his hand and let him haul me up, ignoring the dull ache deep in my side. Someone had gotten a lucky blow, penetrating deep in my side. The bleeding is sluggish now, my tattered shirt and pants growing stiff with dried blood. I don't say anything and Malachi doesn't seem to expect me to. He lets me go the moment I'm on my feet and turns to the nervous horses across from me.

I turn to face the stall I'd sought refuge in. A sob chokes me as I realize I'd sought Lily Dancer out, the spirited mare I'd been riding the day I met Cassandra. Unlike the other horses, she was calm watching me with trusting eyes. I slide open the bolt, pulling the door open and stepping in with her. She butts her head against my chest, seeming to not care about the blood covering me.

"Hey, beautiful," I murmur, unable to speak any louder. I pray to anyone who might be listening that she not be condemned to burn alongside me. I steal a moment to scratch under her chin, swallowing back the grief wrapping around me. "I'm going to need you to do a favor for me. I know you love to run, and that's what I need you to do. I need you to run, and take the rest of them with you. Don't stop until you find someone who will treat you the way you deserve. Can you do that for me, girl?"

Lily Dancer's warm brown eyes are bright, as if she understands everything I'm saying. She tosses her head and stamps a hoof before pushing me hard enough with her nose that I'm forced to take a step back. I shake my head, doing my damnedest to not let any of my heartbreak travel to Cassandra. I don't want her to feel my pain at this loss or my fear for her own safety.

I shake my head. "I'm not joining you this time."

"The horses can make it!" Malachi shouts from the other end of the barn. Whatever ward they have surrounding the stables must not be pressed directly against the back door.

"Hear that?" My voice is more jovial than I feel and Lily Dancer stamps her foot again. I bolt behind her, slapping her rump hard enough to startle her. She rears, only a handful of inches off the ground before jolting out of the stall.

I follow her out, arms out wide and herd her in the direction of the open door. Rhys and Ezra have joined us in opening the stall doors and chasing the horses out.

Lily Dancer prances in place, tossing her head and huffing with irritation while she glares at me. I can't help going to her one last time, wrapping my arm around her strong neck, breathing in the comforting scent of her hair. I step back and meet her brown eyes one last time.

Then she turns towards Malachi and the open barn door, picking up speed as she leaves. By the time she's passing through the massive doors, her mane and tail are flying behind her. Even in the dark, I can see her charge through the paddock filled with milling horses. At her passing, the rest follow, ready to be led as they charge through or over the simple fence.

Peace settles over me, blunting the edges of the agonizing pain.

It's easy to ignore the growing shouts of the mob, their beating drums so similar to those I've heard on battlefields. They're surrounding the stables now; they had to have spotted the fleeing horses.

I turn my back on the dark doorway, not wanting to look at the faces of people who once treated us with kindness.

Instead, I reach for Cassandra through our bond. I wish we would have had more time together. Forever wouldn't have been enough, though. I sink into my love for her, thinking only on my favorite moments with my witch.

The smell of burning wood grows stronger; the crackle of fire racing across the front of the barn is as loud as gunfire.

"Burning is a hell of a way to go."

I open my eyes at Malachi's defeated words. I hadn't realized I'd closed them.

"Not the way I'd choose to go, that's for sure," Ezra adds. He and Rhys join us in the center of the stable. It'll take some time for the fire to reach us, which is almost worse. A realization freezes me and I must stiffen since my three vampire brothers all look to me.

"I need one of you to kill me, quickly." The words rush from me. I keep going, ignoring the mixed looks of shock and horror. "For Cassandra," I explain, desperation claiming me. I grab Malachi's bicep, pleading, "I can't let her feel me burn. I won't be able to keep the wall up between us. I— I can't do that to her."

"Ashe—" Malachi starts but is cut off by Ambrose shouting my name.

"Get up here," Ambrose orders and I find the energy to sink into a crouch before leaping to the loft. I stride over to him, a question on my lips. Ambrose, Kasar, and Lan are all looking in the direction of the main house. I follow their gazes.

Through the rising smoke, over the milling crowd bellowing and cheering a shouting man standing in his stirrups, in the pale light of the moon, is Cassandra.

She's on the roof, Josephine standing back, shouting at her.

I claw down our bond, reaching out for her, only to be met with an adamantine wall. Horror turns my stomach to stone, sinking me to my knees. I shake my head. She can't. She swore she wouldn't.

"What's she doing?" The other males have joined us at the hay door, but I don't know who asked the question.

"Summoning a demon, it appears." I recognize the solemn, authority-filled voice as Ambrose.

"No," I croak out, unable to take my eyes off of my wife. Someone grips my shoulders, and I realize they're holding me back from the ledge of the door. I struggle and more hands grip me, keeping me from attempting to rip through the ward imprisoning us. "Cassandra!" Her name rips from my chest.

She stands tall, her sleeves ripped from her blouse; the moon's light turns the trails of blood along her arms to silver. Josephine still shouts, pushing against an invisible barrier.

One of the men below us turns to see where we looked, then begins pointing and shouting. Half of them separate from the crowd and surge towards the house.

Cassandra's commanding shout is as clear as if she'd spoken in my ear. Air rushes outward from her, blasting the mob and us. I throw a hand up to shield my eyes, struggling through the dust and smoke to see. There's a new presence standing in front of her, a malevolent darkness that seems to swallow any light.

"Don't," I plead with my wife. "Gods, anything but this, Cassandra."

Josephine is gone now, likely dealing with the assailants.

"You promised," I shout at my wife, not caring that she can't hear me. She's blocked me completely through the bond. Did she plan this? Did she swear to me she wouldn't summon a demon, knowing it was a lie? Or have I failed her so spectacularly that she felt pushed to this? I'd sworn these men would never touch her and now we were separated, the stables going up in flames around me.

"Not like this," I plead, voice growing hoarse. "Anything but this."

As if she can hear me, she looks in my direction. Her eyes find mine across the distance. My soul is buffeted by a tidal wave of love and sorrow. Then it cuts off as she looks back to the void, so fast and completely I question if I'd imagined it.

The void crashes over her body, enveloping, devouring. Screams rise around me, only for me to realize I'm the one who is making the sound. The sound of a dying beast, full of pain and suffering.

I think it's Ambrose himself that wraps his arms around me, holding me tight against him as my world is ripped away before me.

Cassandra—or whatever she summoned—leaps from the roof and into the crowd. Whatever they see when they look at her sends them into a panic, even the demon hunters as their magic fails them.

The ward around the barn falls, and the rest of my vampire brothers rush outside. Malachi and Kasar are shouting about putting the fire out.

My mind is filled with... nothing. It's impossible to think, to be horrified as the slaughter below us grows. As the scent of terror is quickly overwhelmed by the scent of blood and death.

I don't resist as Ambrose moves me, sweeping me into his arms like I've fallen in battle. My king, never one to be tender, leaps from the loft to the ground filled with puddles of crimson red. He's careful to angle me so I can't see Cassandra and I'm not sure if I'm thankful for that kindness or furious.

He carries me from the scene, too tired to use the speed I know he's capable of. Josephine meets us in the doorway, her gray dress speckled with blood and half of her silver hair falling around her shoulders in disarray.

I look away when her eyes meet mine. I can't handle pity.

Ambrose sets me on a chaise lounge in the sitting room, while Josephine rights a table near me. He says something to his daughter and goes to leave. He hesitates and turns back to me.

I meet his eyes, my own senses dulling.

"She saved you," Ambrose speaks, keeping his voice low. "She saved all of us with her sacrifice."

I turn away from him, squeezing my eyes shut. He leaves me, Josephine following a moment later. I'm grateful. She doesn't deserve my anger, even as I want to rage that she should have stopped her. I know she tried.

I'm left alone in the deafening silence, a part of my soul missing, cut off from me.

I weep until the black claims me.

Chapter Fourteen

CASSANDRA

The first time I rode along with Ashe to the Haven, intent on destroying Aeternaphiel's soul, I was nervous. That was hours ago, but it felt like a lifetime.

Now, sitting in the back seat of a large SUV beside Eris with Ambrose sitting up front, I'm strangely serene as Kasar turns us towards the gated entrance to the Haven's estate. Night has fallen and we're the first of four vehicles. Lan and Josephine drive the two SUVs behind us and Malachi brings up the rear in the last. Each one is full of the street soldiers of the Night-shade vampires, vampires young and old who've found a place to belong in the Barrows under Ambrose's rule.

I turn and look over my shoulder to the cramped third row. These are vampires who may not survive the upcoming fight to save my mate. It feels disingenuous to not even know their names, so I ask.

The one in the middle, a brunette woman who looks severe enough to be a governess, raises her brows but answers, "I'm Caroline. This one," she inclines her head towards the male on the left, "is Jack and he—" inclining her head towards the other male— "Is Grant."

I smile at each of them in turn. "Thank you for coming with us. It means a lot."

Eris scoffs and looks back at them. I don't miss Grant's flinch, as much as he tries to hide it. He's got such a boyish face, he couldn't have been older than twenty when he was turned. Eris smirks, her face twisting in sheer arrogance, and I shove her shoulder in rebuke. I swear one of the vampires behind me gasps, but I'm too busy meeting Eris's incredulous eyes with a glare.

"Stop it," I say. "We need their help and there's nothing wrong with thanking them, especially when this isn't their usual duty."

"We really don't mind, ma'am—miss—uh," Jack stumbles over a reply. He looks older than Grant, but not by much. "Any time we get to fight is a good night. This'll be more fun than dealing with idiots high on Rapture or drunk and belligerent."

Unlike Ambrose and the males he considers his inner circle, these vampires are wearing more casual clothing. They aren't even wearing the suits I'm more familiar with, and they aren't dressed in the same tactical gear as the inner circle. I was given more appropriate clothing, borrowing the gear from Kasar's mate, Deidre. The woman is more slender than me, so the pants are a bit tight, which was awkward at first. I knew I couldn't go in wearing my dress, and my preferred skirts would only get in my way.

Even Josephine has traded in her dress and arrived in steel gray wide-legged pants and a black long-sleeved shirt. I worry for the female, even knowing she will only fight if she must. Her primary role is to help those injured, if possible. I helped load the back of her SUV with insulated crates of blood and rudimentary medical supplies.

The bullet-proof vest Malachi had fitted me with gives me a sense of safety, but I know bullets may be the least of my worries. Fortunately, Darcelle was able to equip us with cantrips and a few other items from their magical armory. I'd had no time to prepare anything, so whatever magic I perform today will be as wild and uncontrolled as nature itself.

The SUV comes to a stop, all of us looking out the front window. Four men, each of them resting their hands on rifles slung across their chests, stand in front of the closed gate, illuminated by our headlights. I glance over my shoulder, trying to see where the other drivers are. I see one stop behind us and assume it's Malachi. Josephine and Lan should have pulled off the road by now.

"Wards are up." I keep my voice quiet, in case the guards at the gate are more than human. Aeternaphiel had warded the property against vampires when we'd breached the wards around his treasury.

Eris leans forward, peering at the wrought iron gate with disdain. "Hundreds of years on earth and he still has no goddamn taste. The wards are weaker than they should be."

"Trap?" Ambrose asks as one of the guards steps forward, walking to Kasar's side.

"Maybe," Eris answers, her brow bent in thought. "I should be able to take them down, but then he'll know we're here."

"If he doesn't already," Kasar says before rolling down his window.

"Mr. Egress isn't home tonight, sir." The guard tilts his head back towards the road. The partial view I have of him makes me suspect he's human. "I suggest y'all turn around and don't cause any trouble."

Before Kasar can respond, Eris is getting out. Ambrose lets out a long-suffering sigh but says nothing. The guards' attention snap to her, the tension making my mouth go dry.

The demon saunters around the front of the SUV,

wiggling her fingers to the three guards still maintaining the line before the gates. She comes to a halt in front of the guard, her back to the rest in a pointed message about her opinion of their danger. She meets the guard's eyes and blinks. A strangled noise slips from him as he takes a step back.

Eris grins, and a smile with fangs would have been less terrifying than hers. She cocks her hip, her dark hair fluttering around her shoulders, and props herself against the hood with a hand. She drums her fingers on the side, her nails clicking with a sound that makes unease grow inside me. Kasar stays silent, letting this play out.

"Here's the thing—" she peers closer at the man's chest, as if the dark impacts her vision. "Murphy, Mr. Egress probably hasn't told you the truth about himself. Why would he? Have you ever fought a demon or vampires before? I'm going to guess not, considering you reek of fear."

Faster than he can process, she moves. She grabs him by the throat with one hand, lifting him up high enough he must be off the ground. The guards in front of us shout and scramble for their guns. Ambrose and Kasar are out of the SUV in the next blink, bodily blocking the demon.

Eris lowers the man to her face, his own going pale enough even I can tell he's afraid. "I'm not typically merciful. In fact, I'd enjoy killing you humans just because. Except you're not who I want. You're just a delay. So I'm gonna give you boys a choice. You can let us through, easy-peasy, or you can irritate the fuck out of me and we'll kill you. Either way, we're getting in."

When the man grunts, holding his hands up as if in submission, I roll down the window and stick my head out.

"He can't answer if you don't let him breathe," I remind her, giving a pointed look to where her talons dig into his flesh enough that trickles of blood have appeared.

As if she'd forgotten how fragile humans are, she huffs in exasperation and lets the man go.

"We'll go," he gasps out, forcing himself to speak before gulping in deep breaths. "We don't get paid enough for this shit."

He waves the three guards to move aside, and one lingers. It's clear from his expression he's debating putting up a fight, but then one of the others grabs him by the shoulder and yanks him along. He follows, all the fight leaving him, and I breathe out in relief.

"Smart choice." Eris slaps the hood, looking ahead at the two vampires. "What are you two waiting for? Let's get this show on the road."

Mutters from the vampires behind me have me curling my lips fighting a smile. They're clearly not used to anyone ordering around Ambrose or Kasar. Ambrose, too used to Eris's ways, ignores her and comes to the back door the demon had left open. He folds down the seat and jerks his head.

"Time to get in position," he says, and the vampires are moving before he's even finished. The SUV rocks as they climb onto the roof. I'm sure the others behind us are doing something similar.

"Eris?" Ambrose calls a question in his voice.

The demon hadn't let the Nightshades involve her in their tactics, saying she's got her own agenda and telling Ambrose to keep his little soldiers out of her way.

"I'll take down the wards," she says, turning to the iron gate. The human guards have disappeared into the night and she grumbles. "Would have been nice of them to open the gate. No manners these days, I swear."

I roll my eyes. She's the last one to talk about manners. Rolling the window back up, I watch her stride to the gate as Ambrose and Kasar return to the SUV. Pressure builds in my head as the demon stands still. Eris punches the gate with both fists. My ears pop as the pressure vanishes. The gate explodes inward, tumbling across the drive and into the grass, carving deep grooves into the dirt. One part of the gate is stopped by a tree, the momentum warping the metal around the thick trunk and sending the oak swaying.

Eris doesn't say anything as she bolts forward, disappearing down the long drive.

I scoot to the middle of the bench seat and meet Kasar's golden gaze in the rear-view mirror. I nod once, confirming that the ward is now down.

Ambrose presses a finger to the earpiece he wears. "Move in. Remember, our goal is to secure Ashe. Our secondary objective is to find the soul or the archangel. Stay clear of Eris. Malachi, you're in command."

I hear double. This time I've insisted on having an earpiece, even as uncomfortable as it feels.

I know Malachi wanted to be with us as we search for Ashe, but his position as the general for their forces is too important. He's set his feelings aside and will lead the vampires in securing the estate.

Rhys isn't with us since someone needed to keep Ezra contained at a secure location. I don't even know where they went. Ambrose knows, but refused to tell me.

Kasar puts the SUV into gear and we start towards the house, much faster than the sedate speed Ashe drove at earlier.

Then we come under attack.

Chapter Fifteen

CASSANDRA

Lycans, a type of werewolf, drop down from the skeletal trees and charge us. They're too fast for me to count and Kasar never slows. Gunfire comes from above, but only one falls to bullets. The trio of vampires we'd ridden with are dark blurs as they leap towards the rushing creatures and slam into their targets midair.

Malachi's SUV rushes in beside us, Kasar moving over enough to let him in. The ride turns bumpy, two tires off the smooth asphalt. Ambrose lowers his window, a large handgun in hand. I slap my hands over my ears as the loud cracks reverberate through the SUV.

Gods above and below, modern battles are horrible. Tremors rattle me more than the rough ride and I grit my teeth. I remind myself that I've been through plenty of fights, even if it was Eris who was in control of my body at the time. I refuse to give into the fear urging me to hide on the floor between the seats.

"We've got Lycans in the front," Malachi's voice is unruffled in my ear. "Lan?"

"The same," the other vampire responds after a moment. "They weren't expecting us to move in on foot or approach on multiple fronts—" his voice cuts off with a grunt, then snide insults. "I hate fucking Lycans."

"We're approaching the front," Kasar says, still not slowing. I hadn't noticed Malachi moving in front of us. "Coming in hot."

"If you've got something to shield yourself with, witch, I suggest you do so quickly," Ambrose says, holstering his handgun at his side. He draws the two bone-hilted blades that have been with him since he was human. "Stay close, but out of our way. Understood?"

I don't have time to respond as the tires squeal as Kasar cranks the wheel to the right, sending us sliding across the pavement of the drive. I throw my hands out, grasping the back of both seats to keep myself from tumbling over. I should have buckled myself in again once I scooted over, a disconnected part of me thinks.

Kasar turns the SUV off and then he's out, opening my door while keeping his eyes trained on the front double doors. Ambrose is out too, going around the front, matching a jackal shifter's growl with one of his own.

Kasar fires towards the now open doorway, where more jackals bolt out. They're shifters, so their canine forms are massive, and there seems to be an entire pack.

"Cassandra." Kasar's sharp tone snaps me out from the freeze. I grip the pendant at my neck, a simple stone carved with runes but humming with Darcelle's power. A mental twist and I crack open the magical shell. The magic wraps around me, a protective coating that tingles against my skin. Darcelle said it wouldn't stop bullets or a shifter's physical attacks completely, but it'll protect me from all but the most powerful of magical assaults.

I hurry out of the car, keeping behind the opened door until Kasar pulls me forward. I stay behind him, like I'd been told, crouching down to make myself as small of a target as possible. Ambrose is in front of us, along with Malachi and the vampire, Grant. They're flanking their sire, clearing a path in the jackals for Kasar and me to advance through.

"Can you get a sense on his location?" Kasar asks,

cool and unbothered by the savage shifters doing their best to get to us.

I don't close my eyes, but I focus hard on Ashe's and my mating bond. It's still closed off, limiting my ability to accurately find him. Unless he opens the bond, all I have is a general sense that he's within proximity of me. No direction, no glimpse of his location, nothing but the knowledge that my mate still lives.

"Not yet." I stick close to Kasar as we finally make it through the double doors. The entry foyer is markedly different than it was hours ago. The once pristine marble floors are now splattered with blood, the red bright against the white stone in the light. Some of the credenzas are pushed out of place, while another has crumbled under a blow. One of the oil paintings hangs askew on the wall but is otherwise untouched. The one beside it hasn't fared as well, with the canvas curling apart where claws have gouged through it.

Behind us, the sounds of snarls and gunfire echo into the spacious hall. I move to the wall, backing myself against it and hunching down as fear lacerates me. Goddess, I hate violence. Even when Eris was using my body, I hated the muted experience of her in fights and taking lives.

Eris appears at the top of the velveteen-covered grand staircase, not a speck of blood on her. Ambrose and Kasar force the front doors closed, leaving Malachi and the other vampires to finish the remaining shifters. The stench of blood and death clogs my nose and I press the back of my hand to my mouth. I refuse to be sick.

"They're not in here," Eris says and begins to stride down the stairs towards us. Rather than looking annoyed, she looks like the cat who got the canary. Or, considering the familiar box tucked against her side, the demon who got the angel. "He's close, though. He wouldn't run without trying to get this."

The heels of her black boots clacking against the floor somehow cut through the sounds of struggle we'd barricaded out. She walks towards Ambrose adjusting until she has the miniature ark in both hands. Kasar keeps a shoulder against one of the doors, pistol in hand. His body is loose but in the same way a predator is, prepared to strike without hesitation at the slightest provocation.

I push away from the wall, stepping over the limp leg of a dead jackal. I wince when I step in a puddle of blood and it squelches as I almost slip. Now is not the time to be clumsy. I reach the two of them as Eris flips the lid open.

"Are we certain this is the right soul?" Ambrose asks, the skepticism dripping from his words. "It seems rather. . . ill-advised to have left such a vital part of him unguarded."

Eris laughs; it's almost a cackle and the sound sends gooseflesh over my arms.

"It is the right soul," Eris assures us. She trails one chartreuse green nail along the heart. It doesn't give the same way a real heart would. It's almost uncomfortable to look at it, so wrong it is. "Our mating bond may have withered, but only death will truly sever it."

"Then is it trapped?" I ask, prodding it with my magic. "It doesn't seem to be."

"I told you," Eris says as she scoops the heart-shaped soul from the box and tosses the gilded container to the side without care. "Aeternaphiel is beyond arrogant, while also being completely unwilling to allow others with a semblance of power around him. The wards you tore through were haphazardly repaired with a patchwork spell. Even when I worked at his side, Aeternaphiel believed in his intellectual superiority to the degree of fallacy. If he left this here, it's because he truly did not believe you would make it to the room."

Ambrose and I share a look, questioning what could have made the archangel so certain. Then we both scan the room, searching for anything out of place.

"There's nothing magically. Just the wards I felt earlier." I focus and push further across the house. I send my magic in a flurry of tendrils, searching for any trap or danger we may have missed.

Ambrose's eyes are focused, no doubt searching his own senses. His nostrils flare and my gaze snaps to him.

"Do you smell that?" he asks Kasar. His top enforcer takes a deep breath, furrowing his brows as he concentrates.

"It's slight, but there," Kasar agrees and gestures for me to go to him.

"What is it?" I ask, hurrying over, my heart starting to race again.

Ambrose is the one who answers, "An accelerant. Magical in nature. We need to get the fuck out of here."

Kasar wrenches the door open and we're greeted with a gruesome sight. Dead Lycans and jackals litter the ground, with a dozen bloodied vampires standing over them. It's a scene straight from modern horror movies, with some of the vampires casually finishing off the dying guards. Malachi appears before us, a cut from his left eyebrow crosses the bridge of his nose and continues to his right jaw.

"What is it?" he asks, ignoring the wound. "Where's Ashe?"

"Not here," Ambrose answers and starts to cross the viscera-covered drive. "And the place is set to go up in flames. We haven't determined the trigger, so we need to fall back."

Malachi relays the message, the gathered vampires falling back into the dark meadow between the trees. Kasar and Malachi each get into an SUV, driving them off the pavement and into the manicured grass, following the others.

Ambrose takes me by the arm, gently but forcibly pulling me with him until we're on the soft grass ourselves. We turn, looking back, as Eris saunters through the battered doorway, the heart containing Aeternaphiel's soul still in hand.

"I imagine it's in case this happens." She takes a large step over the threshold, and the air seems to vacate the space around us. The next moment, the air returns as an electric rush. Blue-green fire ignites at the foundation of the house, speeding along the outside. From the flickering lights in the windows, the fire's been unleashed along every wall.

Worse, a line of flames spread out from the double doors, containing Eris in a semi-circle. It's not a protective circle, but I don't recognize the magic. From Eris's bark of laughter, I imagine Aeternaphiel once again made a stupid choice.

Rather than stepping across the flames, she raises the heart as if in toast. Then she brings it to her mouth, her jaw distending, opening wide. I watch with wide eyes as she swallows it whole.

Her head remains tilted back, eyes closed as if savoring the taste. Then she opens her eyes, gaze landing on me, and strides towards me. The flames part for her, never growing close.

Her eyes are bright with determination. "I know where they are."

Chapter Sixteen

ERIS

The mate bond had withered away nearly to the point of no existence. I could have let it, over the centuries I spent fighting for my life as an angel cast out of the heavens and into the dark depths of the celestial realm. I refused, though. I would not let Aeternaphiel take my best chance to deliver him to justice, so I held tight to it. I held onto the mate bond even as my celestial soul, once full of righteous fury, turned dark and tattered from the corruption of darkness.

All that effort of keeping that bond there, maintaining the last delicate strings tying me to the angel who was supposed to love me, is worth it now. That spiderweb-thin connection pulsates with the powers of fate. Gods, divinities, nature—whatever it is that creates the bonds of mates. Consuming Aeternaphiel's soul revitalizes the bond between our bodies. Because my mate's soul is within me, I can track him in a way I couldn't since he threw me into the pits of the underworld and slammed the grate shut.

I'd sworn to have my justice that day, as he didn't even bother looking at me while closing the grates and leaving me to the denizens of our enemies. I had been a high-ranking general in the celestial army, fighting and killing demons and the rest of the creatures of rot and ruin. Life had not been easy in those first few months, but I survived. I became a demon after once being renowned for killing them.

Fuck justice. Now I only want revenge.

"Where?" Cassandra asks, the poor witch. Even though I'm no longer possessing her body, I can feel her concern for her mate. One of the worst parts of possessing her for so long was enduring the love of her mate as it spread through our connection. I would never allow myself to feel such love for another. It's impossible, anyways.

I incline my head towards the east. "That way," I say, turning and striding along the drive. The home Aeternaphiel had settled in as William Egress burns behind me. The only sadness I feel about that is that he isn't hog-tied in the middle of it.

Cassandra races to catch up to me, her heart erratic as she strains to keep up with my stride. I could be there within the next heartbeat, so she should be grateful I'm leading her there.

Ambrose follows, along with his pet Kasar. So long as they don't interfere, I don't give a fuck what the vampires do.

"Leave Aeternaphiel to me," I growl. "Don't be stupid and try to go right to Ashe. He'll use him for leverage and if you want your precious mate alive or mostly intact, I suggest you hold back that temper I know you have."

I grin at her sputters but don't bother looking at her. She doesn't deny it. She can't. I know her better than even her mate at this point.

A single-story, long barn with shiplap siding comes into view as we cross the manicured lawns and weave between leafless trees. Cicadas buzz in the night and the heat of the day lingers even as the moon moves higher into the sky. It's fitting that I confront Aeternaphiel in the dark of night, since he's the reason I've become a creature of chaos and darkness. The only lights are the two barn lights illuminating the area in front of the door, insects swarming the yellow light.

"He has basic wards up," Cassandra says. The brush of her magic is familiar as it ripples out from her and seeks out weaknesses in Aeternaphiel's protection. "Want me to take them down?"

"Not yet. Not until we're about to go in. I want to take him by surprise."

"No doubt he's aware of the house going up in flames," Ambrose observes as he and Kasar arrive on either side of us.

I incline my head. "Nice of you to join us," I say first. The vampire king walks easily beside me, hands in his pockets as if he's on a midnight stroll with his own queen. "Aeternaphiel will know his fire trap was triggered, but he is likely to assume whomever triggered it has perished in the flames. That fire was spelled to consume anyone that was not him."

Kasar snorts. "Clever."

Cassandra nods in understanding. "You ate his soul, so the fire let you pass."

I click my lips, pointing at her. "Exactly."

When we approach the area illuminated by the barn lights, I incline my head to the witch. She steps forward, raising both of her palms. The air swirls around us, the sound of nonexistent leaves rustling in the wind drowning out the real world. With a hard tearing motion, Cassandra's magic rips down the bright magic coating the building. Brutal but effective.

"Remember, he's mine," I say once more for the vampires.

"Our brother is our priority," Ambrose states, readying himself, daggers in hand.

I don't wait another moment. I raise my knee and slam my foot in the center of the barn door, sending it splintering inwards. Ambrose and Kasar are on my heels as I sprint inside. Cassandra follows behind us, her magic writhing around her and eager to be released. I find my target immediately, baring my teeth and hissing.

"Eris. How unexpected."

Aeternaphiel, the male who'd once meant everything to me, greets me as if he hadn't destroyed my life for his personal gain.

I breathe deep, settling myself. Aeternaphiel wants me to lose control. It was the only way he could ever best me in training. I cock my head, ignoring Ashe's bloody body hanging limply by his wrists behind him. "Why? Because you cast me to the depths of Hell for your crimes? Or because you thought that siphoning blade of yours would have drained me of my life force on your behalf?"

Cassandra is tense beside me but I can't look away from the archangel for a moment. Not when he's so unpredictable. Any suggestion of distraction and he could strike out. He was the master of patience when it came to combat.

Aeternaphiel purses his lips in disappointment, but then raises a brow as he sees the witch. "Perhaps I was too hasty when I judged you innocent of this demon's aberrations."

I'll give Cassandra credit. She doesn't cower.

"Release my mate. You've no right to keep him."

The male watches her, then looks at Ambrose and Kasar. He shrugs, indifferent. He takes three steps to the side where a long industrial cable hangs with a button box at the end and presses it. "He's more trouble than it's worth, it seems. Pity. We were having fun."

Ashe, his bindings suddenly released from where they were attached to the chains, crumples to the floor. His body hits the cement with a loud thud, drawing a gasp from Cassandra and twin snarls from the vampires. When she steps forward, I catch her arm, keeping her back.

"Step away from him," I order Aeternaphiel.

He backs away, hands raised, with an expression of innocent cooperation. I keep ahold of Cassandra while Kasar and Ambrose approach the injured male. Kasar keeps his gaze on the archangel the entire time, while Ambrose rouses Ashe enough to get the male to loop his arm over his shoulder. Ambrose hauls him upright; Kasar steps into Ashe's other side under his arm. Ashe is weak but conscious enough to attempt walking. Broken, haggard stumbling is more accurate in my opinion.

When they finally turn their backs on the

archangel, Aeternaphiel slowly resumes his place at the center of the room, hands in his pockets. He's wearing expensive tailored pants and a shirt, the shirt sleeves rolled neatly up. No doubt to try to spare his clothing the stains of Ashe's blood.

I let go of Cassandra when the vampires are in front of us. She goes to Ashe, cupping his bloodied face with her hands. She murmurs something I make a point not to hear and meet Ambrose's eyes. He nods once in silent understanding. With a nudge, he moves them forward. Cassandra sends me a concerned look, an offer in her eyes to stay. I decline in a quick, sharp shake. This isn't her fight. It never was.

In the end, it was always going to be just me and Aeternaphiel.

I return my attention to the male I'd loved as the four make their way out of the barn. The sounds of engines and then doors opening and closing let me know that they weren't alone out there.

"I never intended for you to suffer," Aeternaphiel states when it's only us.

I cut him off with a snort. "Save me the bullshit. I know you as you really are. You were willing to sacrifice your mate to gain control over the celestial realm." I tilt my head with a sickly-sweet smile. "Doesn't look like it worked out too well for you."

Aeternaphiel's once beautiful face twists in rage.

"You could have been my queen!" he spits out. "You were the one who betrayed me. Going behind my back to whisper in the council's ears. Poisoning them against me. I *saved* you. They wanted your head on a pike."

I scoff. "Only because you'd convinced them I was the one planning a coup. Better my head than yours?"

He raises his chin in arrogance, the righteous anger I used to admire burning in his eyes. "I was meant for more. I could still help our people, even if it cost me you."

I raise my hand to idly inspect my sharp talons, then turn the hand palm out and study my nails. "All for nothing, as it seems. Else you wouldn't be here on Earth, turning to dark magic to prevent your death at another celestial's hand." I drop my hand, looking at him with wide eyes. "Oh, right. That hasn't worked out for you either."

He furrows his brows, eyes flicking in the direction of the house. His nostrils flare with agitation and he takes several steps closer, only stopping out of reach. "What did you do this time?"

I drop the act and meet his glare with one of my own. I'm done playing this game. "Cassandra severed the protective spells on your soul. Interesting thing about demons, Ae. We eat them. Yours was surprisingly better than I expected. Not much taint of rot."

"You lie."

I cock my head. "Do I?" I let out a humorless laugh. "Why don't you let me slit your throat and you can find out."

Either my taunt pushes him too far or he's determined to truly kill me, but Aeternaphiel snaps his hand to the side and summons his celestial blade.

I don't have mine, thanks to him melting it away when I was still in Cassandra's body. I do have the bone-hilted obsidian blade Ambrose passed me when he clasped my hand.

I roll my neck with a pleased sigh, before raising the dagger and meeting Aeternaphiel's stony face. "I'm going to enjoy this."

Chapter Seventeen

CASSANDRA

Y ou're going to be okay," I promise Ashe, wringing my hands as I wait for Kasar and Ambrose to help settle him on the back of one of the SUVs after Malachi opens the hatch. He looks awful. He was only in the archangel's clutches for half a day, but the damage is extensive. I'm terrified that I may lose him yet.

I step up to him the moment the other vampires move away, looking him over and trying to triage his wounds. My mouth is dry and I'm cursing my lack of preparation. I knew he'd be hurt, but I never expected it to be this bad.

Ashe tugs me between his legs, suppressing a wince. Before I can protest, he runs a shaky hand down my hair and cups the back of my neck.

"I'm okay, mate," he murmurs. His golden eyes are clear and bright. "He didn't want me dead."

I swallow, the lump in my throat painful. "Still. You're badly hurt."

Ashe smiles and rests his forehead to mine. "Nothing time and a good feeding won't cure," he promises. "Now, how the hell is Eris here? That is her, right?"

I hesitate, wanting him healed and rested before telling him anything, but the other vampires are returning and Ambrose is watching us. Another black SUV pulls up, the headlights turning off along with the engine. Josephine steps out, a large duffle slung over her shoulder.

"Yes. It's her," I answer, and gesture for Josephine to bring the supplies over. "I'll tell you more if you let us look over you."

Ashe sighs, dropping his head to my shoulder before limply waving a hand. "Go ahead and fuss, then."

"Foolish boys, the lot of them," Josephine says and we share an affectionate and aggravated look. "None of them like to think they're hurt and could do with some help."

The ground rumbles and Ashe slides from his position, standing and trying to put himself between me and the barn. He's shaking, his arm already lowering towards his body as what little strength he has slips from him.

"Sit," I tell him, trying to coax him to do my bidding. I cast an uncertain look at the barn, where Ambrose stands in front of the door. Malachi, Kasar, Lan, and the other vampires have joined him, forming a line between us and the two battling it out.

With a grunt, Ashe slumps back into sitting. When I raise a brow pointedly, he offers a sheepish grin.

"All right," Ashe concedes, "some fussing may be necessary."

Josephine sets the duffle next to him in the back of the SUV and opens it, the picture of serenity. As if the sounds coming from the barn are not growing more thunderous, the ground shaking as if giants are river dancing fifty feet from us.

"So, Eris?" Ashe asks, weakly grasping my fingers. I tangle our fingers together, desperate for the grounding he provides.

"Right." I swallow and shoot another look at the barn. "According to her, the blade I'd used to try to kill the soul is meant to sever bonds and magical ties. It released her from the soul, and me, if I understand correctly. It also severed her possession of me, allowing her to materialize in a body of her own. She's the one who found me after I fled—" my sob takes me by surprise. I fling my arms around his shoulders, squeezing him tight. He grunts but doesn't protest. Instead, he wraps his arms around me, holding me as tightly as he can.

A metallic, coppery scent hits me and I freeze. "I'm hurting you," I protest as I try to pull away.

"Cassandra," Ashe growls my name, squeezing me tighter. "If you try to move, I will turn you over my knee and spank your ass."

Blood rushes to my cheeks even as heat builds in my core. Embarrassment wins when Josephine's snort preludes her speaking.

"You won't be spanking her anytime soon unless you let us stop some of this bleeding. What in the blazes did the male think you were? A colander?"

Ashe reluctantly lets me go, giving me a crooked smile before turning the look onto Josephine. Despite his face being mottled with bruises, blood trickling from a split lip, his nose, and a gash above his left eyebrow, he's still the most handsome male I've ever seen. His sandy-brown hair is unruly and has lumps of dried blood in it. His chest is bare, revealing more dark purple bruises across his muscular chest and abdomen. My own heart aches for my husband as unnatural protrusions suggest multiple broken bones. I also see what Josephine means.

He's covered with multiple puncture wounds, some of them larger than others. Some of them have already stopped bleeding, but others still have blood sluggishly running down them.

"Oh, my love," I breathe out, horrified all over again that I left him with Aeternaphiel.

Josephine motions me aside and begins wiping the worst of the blood away from him, muttering underneath her breath.

"I should never have left you," I say, bringing his hand to my lips and pressing a kiss against his swollen fingers.

He growls, and I meet his fierce golden eyes. "I didn't want you to stay. I could endure it, knowing you were safe." Then those eyes soften, love and understanding replaces the determination. "I get it now, Cassandra. I know why you made the bargain."

I bite back the tears, giving him a wobbly smile that is more painful than humorous. "And I understand just how badly I hurt you. Goddess, what you had to go through for a hundred and fifty years. I only had to endure the pain for hours. I don't understand how you don't hate me."

Ashe chuckles before cutting off with a grunt as Josephine presses a sterile pad over a slice on his bicep. He shrugs her off, to her exasperation, but she primly sets the bandages down and leaves us to join the rest of the Nightshades.

"I could never hate you, not truly," he assures me, gathering me close. "I hated the choice you made. Because I was selfish. I only thought about my pain. Not what you'd have to endure watching me suffer before dying."

He brings my arm up to his lips, running them over my inner wrist and kissing my racing pulse. I press my wrist closer. "Feed, my love," I urge. "You need it."

It's a testament to his injuries that Ashe doesn't hesitate. He pulls his lips back, sinking his elongated fangs into my flesh with a tear-inducing tenderness. As he takes my blood, I reach for him through our bond. No longer am I met with a solid wall, but with his own soul reaching for mine. I take him into me even as he takes my blood into himself.

It's bliss, a kind of love that is impossible to understand, only experience.

He pulls away after only a few swallows, licking once against the puncture wounds. The sight of his tongue traveling along my skin sets me on fire. He meets my eyes, his own pupils blown wide with matching desire.

"Later," he promises me, beating my insistence that he drink more. We both know he needs more to heal.

He eases me back, standing on his feet more easily than he had minutes before. His vitality is already returning. "We need to help Eris, if we can."

I slide my hand around his back, satisfying my own need to support and embrace him. He drapes his arm over my shoulders, holding me tight. He's steady as we walk to the line of vampires.

Malachi twists towards us; he'd found the time to clean his face of blood, the facial wound already healed.

A crash of unnatural thunder implodes the barn in front of us. I turn, hiding my face in Ashe's chest as he bends over me, arm up to block potential debris from slamming into his face. Many of the other vampires have jolted backwards, crouching from the unexpected blast. The air is full of dust when we straighten.

Ambrose and Kasar had not flinched away, though they lower their arms to see better. I can't see through the thick haze, the only light now coming from the partial moon above us and one SUV's headlights.

I want to ask Ashe what he sees, but a moment later I don't need to.

"Holy shit," Ashe breathes, and I follow his gaze upwards, staring in awe at the figures rising above the destruction. "When did Eris get wings?"

To my shock, she does have wings. Blacker than the

night sky beyond her, black whip-like tendrils have spawned from her back and undulate in the air. She's larger than before, a deep red aura surrounding her. My hindbrain, the part of every living soul, recognizes the absolute danger she is, urging me to flee, hide, and hope she never sets sight on me.

Aeternaphiel is her opposite, wings of prismatic white feathers beat behind him. The golden sword he wields is almost too blinding to look at.

He bears down on Eris, aiming for her neck, but she parries his strike with her arm, the tip slicing deeply.

I can't tear my eyes away. Fear builds in my chest. Not of the two celestial beings, but *for* her.

"Eris was holding back on us," Malachi mutters, almost in awe.

A shudder goes through me as I picture Eris using this power while possessing my body.

"If she's devoured his soul," Lan begins, drawing my attention. He's still watching the two fighting, a puzzled expression on his face. "How does she expect to kill him? Wouldn't she need to return the soul to his body first?"

I blink, confused, and turn my attention back to them. My mind races, working through everything I knew about demons before I was possessed and what I learned from Eris.

"A demon in possession of a mortal's soul binds them together," I say in a measured tone, trying to work out what will happen. "If the demon dies, so do any mortals bound to them. If the mortal dies, they're sent to the underworld."

"So, another angel in hell?" Kasar asks, looking at me. I shrug.

"He wasn't mortal, originally," I remind him. "I have no idea what will happen if Eris kills him."

The figures clash against one another, the crack of lightning rending the sky. Each blow sends a gust of wind towards us, buffeting us with dust.

"She's losing," Ashe states, voice urgent. "Look at her."

I do, and I realize he's right. Eris is slower, her strikes weaker. She's taken multiple blows from Aeternaphiel's celestial weapon, slices and cuts marring her arms and torso.

"Is she, though?" Lan's voice is cool. "Or is she playing him?"

We're a captive audience to the fight above us. All we can do is watch and speculate.

"She's baiting him," Malachi agrees. "She's stronger than she's letting him believe."

"But not strong enough," Ashe growls, the arm around my shoulders tightening. "She's getting weaker."

My gut churns, conflicted. Aeternaphiel swings his sword, the movement too fast to see. Eris blocks it, but only barely. Aeternaphiel's sneer is visible as he leans in and shouts words I can't hear. Eris shouts something back, using a language I can't understand or recognize.

Whatever she's said to him sends him reeling back, retreating out of arm's reach. He looks horrified for a moment, stunned at whatever she told him. She laughs, the cackling sound belonging in the worst of night-mares. It snaps him from his daze, but Aeternaphiel is too late.

Eris launches herself forward. I slap my hands over my mouth, a scream trapped in the back of my throat as she arrows herself directly at the archangel. He manages to raise his blade in time. She doesn't slow, even as the blade pierces her body and bursts from her back. She grasps him in her talons, the black tendrils wrapping themselves around Aeternaphiel, binding him to her.

He struggles against her hold, his wings hampered and unable to move. They begin to plummet from the sky.

"She never planned to survive," I whisper, my hands sinking from my face as understanding dawns.

As if the wind carries my words to her, Eris turns her head towards me. Aeternaphiel still struggles against her hold. I swear our eyes meet across the distance. That second of time stretches into eternity.

Then, before they slam into the devastation of the barn, a burgundy light explodes from them. It barrels towards us, the wind so intense it pushes us backwards. I'd have fallen had Ashe not braced me against him. Even Kasar is forced to a knee to stay upright. Scorching heat and sulfur envelops us when the light reaches us. Echoes of hellhounds and tortured screams blend with the rush of the wind.

As quickly as it appeared, the light is gone. The sounds have disappeared, the silence left being ear-piercing. Multicolored spots float across my vision and a primal, animalistic part of me sighs in relief. Whatever that was, that part of me is grateful to have avoided that fate. Even the once noisy insects have quieted, unwilling to emerge from hiding for now.

"They're gone."

Ambrose's voice is quiet, more unsteady than I've ever heard from the vampire king. I blink rapidly, trying to peer through my spotty vision to where I'd seen Eris and Aeternaphiel last.

All of us stare at the ruined barn, the world finally settling around us. Slowly, one cricket begins their performance, others quickly following. Collectively, we seem to take a breath and collect ourselves.

Distant sirens wail, growing closer. We turn back

towards the front of the estate, the house now swallowed up by violent flames. Any trace of magical fire is gone, leaving the house and all of its treasures to be devoured by the blaze.

Ashe leans heavier against me, and I catch him around the waist. "Ashe?" Concern replaces everything else.

He gives me a pained smile. "Nothing a bit of rest won't take care of."

Ambrose waves Kasar and Josephine towards us. "Get back to the house," he orders us, the strong, stoic vampire king of the Barrows once more. "Malachi and I will handle the authorities. Have Deidre ready to manage the newspapers. Lan, monitor the police lines and chatter. We need to know who, if anyone, knew that William Egress was an archangel. We need to be ready for any fallout with those justicars."

"Oh, what fun," Lan drawls but Ambrose ignores him. He shifts his attention to me.

"Heal your mate. Then I want you to record everything you know about demons and what may have occurred tonight. I need to know if there will be potential consequences of Eris's and Aeternaphiel's disappearances and presumed deaths."

I manage to jerk my head in an approximation of a nod, my mind already oscillating between caring for Ashe and deliberating over what Eris's fate is. My mate distracts me when his breath tickles the shell of my ear just before he speaks.

"You can solve that mystery tomorrow. I know exactly what I need from you to heal." His words are warm and smooth, promising pleasure.

I turn my head towards him, our faces inches apart. "Behave," I chide him before prompting him to walk towards the SUV Kasar has started. Josephine sits in the front passenger seat, watching us with amusement.

"Why?" Ashe's question is thick with humor. "It's so much more fun to tease you."

Something about his words breaks something tense inside of me. Relief and understanding that it's finally over, that I'm finally free and we're both alive, has me tossing my head back and laughing bright. I feel so light, so much happiness, I swear Ashe is the only thing keeping my feet on the ground.

I reach to open the backdoor for us and peck a kiss against his smiling lips. "If you be good for me, I promise you'll like the reward."

"Well then," Ashe says, suddenly completely serious. He releases me and gets into the back seat on his own. He reaches forward between the seats, slapping Kasar on the shoulder. "Let's get going, brother. I've got to prove that I can be the perfect patient to my mate."

Rolling my eyes, I get in the other side. Kasar meets

my gaze in the rearview mirror as he pulls out. Amusement and camaraderie fill them, and I grin before buckling in and looking at my mate.

Goddess, I'm so glad to have tripped over my own feet in front of this male so many years ago.

Chapter Eighteen

ASHE

Cassandra stands in front of the window, back to me. The early morning sunlight silhouettes and surrounds her in a warm light that belies the winter weather that's settled in around the Barrows. I drink in the vision of her from where I lay in our bed, in our room at the clan house.

It's been two weeks since that day at Aeternaphiel's home. Two weeks since I risked losing her forever.

She's wrapped herself in a thin robe, the sunlight revealing her figure through the material. My cock thickens at the innocent temptation she is. I've spent every moment since our return once more memorizing the curves of her waist, the slope of her neck, her pert ass, and the swell of her breasts.

Sometimes I still find myself gripped by the fear

that she'll be taken from me without warning. That I will go to take Cassandra in my arms and find Eris instead.

Each time that happens, Cassandra is there, banishing it with her sweet words and sweeter kisses.

I slip out of bed, not bothering to dress. She jumps when I slide my hands around her soft waist, pressing against her and dropping a kiss on her shoulder. "Where were you, mate?"

She laughs, a sound as beautiful as a creek babbling over rocks in the sunlight. Damn, having her back has turned me into as much of a romantic as Rhys typically is. She leans against me, her ass trapping my growing erection between us. The sigh that comes from her isn't one of pleasure, though. I rest my head against hers, waiting for when she's ready to speak.

"Is it strange that I worry about her?"

I don't have to ask who she means. A part of me wants to respond immediately, to tell her that there's no reason for her to concern herself about Eris anymore. But I give the question true consideration.

"No," I say after a long moment, and squeeze her tighter to me. "Eris was a part of you for the majority of the time you've been alive. You've never fully explained the bargain, and she didn't either, but I know she had to preserve your mind and soul. Which meant you were aware a lot of the times, right?"

She nods, the movement barely jostling me. "I knew the risks with summoning a demon. I wanted to make sure I survived, which meant getting her to swear to protect my health." Cassandra pauses, her thoughts practically chugging aloud, so I wait her out. I can be patient. I've waited over a century and a half for a morning like this, so I cherish this moment.

"I wouldn't say I was awake, most of the time," she starts, her words not quite absolute. "When I try to recall memories of certain times, they're hazy. I have a vague sense of them, but like I'm trying to recall a story someone told me. When she'd let me have control, either to preserve my mind or help the Nightshades, I remember those clearly."

I press another kiss against her head. "See? It makes sense that you're concerned about her. It's as if a friend—well, maybe not a friend, of yours is gone now. You remember their stories and now they aren't around, so you worry about them."

Cassandra laughs, a little watery sound, before sniffing. "I think she was my friend, in the end," she admits. She holds herself stiffly, as if waiting for my judgment. How can I judge her for something I have to admit I also felt?

"I think we were friends, too," I reply quietly. Then louder, "Definitely a strange friendship, and not a healthy one at all. But, yeah, definitely friends. I started carrying around hair ties, because she'd always break hers by yanking too hard and she'd threaten to cut your hair off. Or if she was in a foul mood, I'd get Darcelle to make me a ridiculous coffee drink to shove into her hands."

Warmth builds in my chest and I let out a soft laugh. "I'm convinced I saved a poor shifter's life once by asking Eris if she wanted to go get her nails done. She'd been questioning the shifter for Ambrose, but over something petty. Eris decided her nails were more interesting than the terrified shifter."

Cassandra laughs with me and the tension in her dissipates. "She was ridiculous, wasn't she?" She shakes her head, still looking out the window across the Barrows with me. "I just wish I knew if she's dead or not."

I nod; there's no other way to answer, not without sounding trite or apathetic. Instead, I change the topic.

"Get dressed," I tell her and head towards the walk-in closet. "I have a surprise for you."

"Oh?" she looks over her shoulder, her warm brown eyes meeting mine without a drop of sadness in them. Her inquiring touch trickles between our bond and I bare my teeth at her in admonishment, growling with empty threats.

"No trying to figure it out." I skip over my tailored suits and pull on a pair of black boxer briefs then dark denim over them. I pull a burgundy tee off a hanger, the material luxurious despite being a casual piece of clothing. "Or I won't show you for another month!"

"Beast!" Cassandra calls to me.

The shower turns on, so I finish dressing and shrug on a heavy gray jacket with a hood and head out into the main house.

As I descend the stairs, I can hear Ambrose and Eloise speaking in his office and Deidre trading barbs with Lan on the opposite side of the house than the kitchens. I head towards the kitchen; Josephine's singing a calm litany only interrupted by firm directions to the two staff assisting her.

I push open one of the doors to enter Josephine's domain and see I'm not the first one to seek her out this morning. Malachi leans up against one of the counters, a powdered beignet in one hand and a porcelain mug of coffee in the other. He raises the mug in question and when I nod, he sets his food down and pours me a fresh coffee.

I take it with thanks and settle in beside him. Josephine wastes no time in coming over, plate in hand, with freshly powdered chocolate beignets.

"I had a craving this morning," Josephine says in lieu of a greeting as she offers me some.

I happily snake a few, shooting her a smile. "When

you have cravings, we feast like kings. So please, never resist!"

She sets the plate between us males and pats my shoulder before returning to the center island where she and one of the vampires who work under her are marinating and seasoning venison.

"Heard from Rhys yet?" I ask Malachi and take a bite of the beignet. I groan in pleasure, earning an indulgent smile from Josephine.

Rhys had taken Ezra and gone dark. I suspect Ambrose and Kasar are aware of where they are, but they haven't deemed it necessary for anyone else to know. If I had to guess, Ambrose is funding anything Ezra may need in Rhys's attempts to bring him back to himself. Rhys struggled to forgive Ambrose for exiling Ezra, which is why he left so soon after Ezra disappeared.

I think all of us are feeling guilt over Ezra's fate and the individual parts we played in it. I want to think Ambrose wouldn't have sent Ezra away if he'd known the demon vampire would have landed in Aeterna-phiel's clutches. Except I know Ambrose too well, and I don't envy his position as the king of vampires. He has the steel heart to make horrible choices for the betterment of the clan and the territory we control.

"Nope," Malachi answers, staring down into his coffee mug for a long minute. "But that's just like Rhys.

Show up out of nowhere, cause a little chaos, then leave town before the dust has even settled."

There's an edge to his words, but one that's been dulled with time and experience. It's always been Rhys's way, ever since the Nightshades took him and Ezra in. It's why Ambrose lets him roam the country with a rock star persona, so long as he occasionally checks in and completes any assignments Ambrose may need.

"How are the guys recovering?" I ask, knowing the Rhys and Ezra topic will lead to nothing but frustration. "You said we didn't lose any in the fight, but a few took some nasty bites?"

Malachi barks out a laugh, full of real humor. "Tommy-boy and Silas are absolute degenerates who are milking their supposed near-death experiences for all they're worth. You'd think the two of them had lost both legs and an eye for how I've heard them going on, just to get the sympathy of a pretty woman at the bar."

I snort, thinking about the two street soldiers. "But otherwise, everyone is whole?"

He nods, gesturing to his face. "I don't even get a scar from the paw I took to the face. The rest of them are fine. I figure I'll give them another week of commiserating before kicking their asses into gear. I've got too much shit going on with this restaurant to deal with bitching and moaning."

Familiar footsteps tease my ears and I eat the last beignet in my hand. I wipe my hands on one of the kitchen towels, before sliding around the cooks and grabbing a glass container and lid. As I slide about a dozen of the chocolatey treats into it, I ask more about Malachi's project. He'd never been interested in his own venture before, satisfied to let the Nightshades handle his money and grow his fortunes through investments.

He waves a hand, dismissing the question. "It's fine, just a pain in the ass as every business is. There was a hiccup with the small batch brew from Tartarus Taps, but Cinder's pulled through and it'll get here before doors are ready to open." Then he grins, one better suited to Casanova. "Though I am interviewing the burlesque dancers next week. And a dance producer to handle all of that."

I huff a silent laugh through my nose, securing the lid on the container. Cassandra walks in, stealing my breath as our eyes meet. God, I'm so damn lucky this woman is my mate. Beautiful inside and out, I know I don't deserve her, no matter what she says.

She's slowly adjusting her wardrobe to modern fashions and I can't help enjoying her. She's opted for a brown, scoop-neck, long-sleeve sweater paired with wide-legged pants in a deep green, and her new favorite brown heeled boots. She's only pulled back the front of her hair in a clip, leaving the rest of her hair to drape down over her shoulders.

I move to her, drawn in like a moth willing to burn in her flame. I capture her waist in my hands, tugging her close before dropping a kiss onto her smiling lips.

"Have I told you how beautiful you are today?" I ask and she gives me a stern look.

"Not yet, I'm afraid," Cassandra teases and Malachi laughs at our antics. She sends him a glare without heat. "One day, you'll have a mate and you'll be the sappiest of them all. You're the one who watches all of those romance reality TV shows."

"Nah." Malachi pushes off the counter and swipes up another beignet from the plate. "I watch those shows specifically as a reminder of how awful relationships are. Any woman I'm with is after the same thing I am and there are never any hard feelings the next day as we go our separate ways. Speaking of separate ways, I'm off. I've got profiles—I mean resumes to go through for potential dancers."

I roll my eyes but give him a tilt of the head as he leaves. I turn back to Cassandra, pressing the container of beignets into her hands. "Ready for your surprise?"

Chapter Nineteen

ASHE

W hat are you doing?" Cassandra asks as I pull off onto the gravel side of the highway. We're in the country, with fields on either side of the highway and nothing else in view. Cars rock ours as they fly by, and she looks warily towards the road.

I reach across and pop the glove box open. I retrieve the black silk sleep mask I'd hidden there and hand it to her.

She raises a brow. "You're serious?"

"Completely," I tell her, urging her to put it on. "I'm not driving another foot until you can't see anything."

We've been in the car for hours and it's been a true effort to keep her from sensing the maelstrom of emotions warring inside of me. Excitement, trepidation, doubt, jubilation. My emotions are a damn roller coaster that has derailed and refuses to stop. I've kept the surprise to myself for so long. Not even one of my nightshade brothers has seen it in decades.

With a good-natured huff, Cassandra tugs on the mask and sticks her tongue out at me when I double-check that she can't see anything. I kiss her, pulling back before I'm tempted to deepen it and delay our arrival. I want to make sure we have plenty of daylight when we get there, and it's already mid-afternoon.

Pretty soon I turn us off the highway and onto a two-lane road where farmland gives way to an older town. Homes built earlier that century are set back a dozen feet from the road and then the houses give way to the center of the town itself.

My nerves wind tighter each stop sign or blinking red light. The main street is lined with brick buildings that are stores that haven't changed much since they were first built. Old iron lamp-posts have been updated to use electric lights rather than gas. Then the street curves around the manicured park in the center of town.

"Are we almost there?" Cassandra asks impatiently.

"Almost," I tell her, pulling my eyes away from the restored fountain and turning off the main street. "Just another minute or two."

The narrow street takes us away from the main town, the meadows rising along either side of it. Bare trees tower over the road; when their branches are full with leaves, it feels almost tunnel-like.

I reach up to the visor, pressing the right button on the gate remote I'd clipped there before we headed out. Just ahead, where a chain-link fence loses the constant battle against vines of ivy and honeysuckles, a gate rolls open. I turn the car onto the gravel driveway, my heart in my throat as I use the remote again to close the gate behind us.

Fuck, I'm struggling to breathe. What if Cassandra doesn't want this? What if, rather than bringing her happiness, it tears open old wounds and traumas? I put the car into park, leaving the engine running while I try not to panic.

"We're stopped," Cassandra says after a long moment, breaking the silence and startling me. Her brow furrows behind the blindfold. "Is something wrong?" She reaches blindly for me, and I capture her hand, lacing our fingers together and pressing a kiss to the back of hers.

"I'm just nervous is all," I confess and am rewarded with a smile.

"I'm sure I'll love it."

I take a deep breath, steadying myself. "Right. One moment, then."

Releasing her, I turn off the car and get out before hurrying over and opening her door. When I take her hand and help her out, she's got an enormous grin on her face. It's infectious enough that maybe, just maybe, she'll like this as much as I've hoped.

"Can I look now?" Cassandra pleads, sounding more like an anxious child than a grown witch.

"Almost," I answer, voice just as light. Eagerness overtakes my nerves and I take her by both hands, walking backwards while I guide her into the perfect position. I move until I'm behind her, the air between us practically vibrating from our combined excitement.

I hook my fingers under the elastic of the mask and begin to count, "One. Two. Three." I slide the sleep mask up and off of her, hold my breath and wait.

Cassandra's quiet for half a heartbeat then gasps as she realizes what's in front of us. She doesn't turn from the sight as she breathes out a single word, "How?"

I rub the back of my head, anxiety battling against my dwindling excitement. I have to see her face, her expression. I move around to face her; her wide eyes brim with tears but her face is so shell-shocked I can't tell if they're good tears or if I made a horrible mistake.

I look over my shoulder at the stone cottage I've maintained for the last century and a half. I shove my hands in my front pockets and clear my throat.

"After you saved us with the bargain, most of

Willow Creek didn't want anything to do with us," I explain. "I think they were afraid of us, not that I can blame them. A couple of them, though, had never bought into what those witch hunters were preaching. Before we left, I met up with Charity's brother, Ezekiel. He hated what Jonathan had done and wanted us to know he was grateful for what you did for his sister. I paid him a lot of money to keep the property safe and keep up with the grounds."

When I pause, she steps forward as if in a daze, and I follow behind her as she approaches the white-washed walls and now shingled roof. The wooden fence we'd had then had been replaced with white pickets. The gardens are bare for the winter, but in spring and summer, flowers line the gravel pathway. The same herbs and vegetables we'd planted still fill the garden rows in the front yard.

"Ambrose helped with the legal paperwork. He created a trust and put the house into it. Then when Charity's brother was too old, he passed the care to his son, and so on. I'm pretty sure Kaitlyn, the current caretaker, is his great-great granddaughter."

I stop speaking as Cassandra pushes through the white gate and into the gardens we'd spent so much time in together. My own throat constricts as I follow her, realizing now how I'd never truly expected to stand here again with my wife.

She slowly turns, taking in everything and finally meets my eyes. Her smile almost makes me collapse with relief.

"You're happy then?" I ask, needing to be sure.

"This—this is incredible, Ashe!" Cassandra says and then throws herself against me, wrapping her arms around my neck and kissing me soundly. "I can't believe how well you've taken care of our cottage!"

I hold her close, needing to feel her soft body against my hard one. "How could I leave it? It was our home after our wedding. I'd lost you already. I wasn't going to lose this."

Cassandra kisses me, and her gratitude and love rushes over me through our bond. Her lips are soft and sweet, tasting faintly of the beignets we'd shared on the road. I deepen our kiss, holding her tighter against me as I drown myself in her taste.

She whimpers, her mouth yielding to mine, and my cock thickens as the sound. Her scent turns into something more warm and spicy, like cinnamon and allspice, as her desire grows. By the time we pull apart, I'm as hard as steel against her stomach and we're both struggling to breathe.

"Are you going to show me the inside, husband?" Cassandra's voice is husky and my hips thrusts against her in response. "Perhaps the bedroom?"

My lips curve upwards with wickedness and in the next breath, I've swept Cassandra up into my arms.

"I think you'll like the new bed I chose," I answer as I carry her to the front door. It's only a moment of careful movement before I've got the key in the new lock of a modern door. Then I'm carrying Cassandra across the threshold of our home.

I don't bother showing her the rest of the house right now as I make for the loft. Now that she's here in my arms, it really hits me.

We have all the time in the world together now. And I plan to enjoy every moment of it.

EPILOGUE

Malachi

I need a damn drink. A proper one. And yet, I'm here at Noir because I promised Ambrose I would keep an eye on the place while he and Eloise are off on some romantic vacation.

Hell, now that Cassandra is back, I'm the last single male of the inner circle. Shame twists my guts. The last one if I don't take Rhys and Ezra into account. Which seeing as Rhys fucked off with a wild Ezra without so much of a heads-up, I don't.

The fast music, heavy with base, from the dance floor spills into the quieter front bar of the place. Even as I walk through the bar, packed with a surprisingly large crowd on a weekday evening, it's like everywhere I look are couples. Everyone seems to have someone else to be with and it just pisses me off even more after the day I had.

This restaurant has become such a headache, I'm beginning to wonder if it was a bad idea. I've grown bored, though. With the modern world, Ambrose doesn't need me and my skills as his general as much. Helping Cassandra and Ashe take on Aeternaphiel was the closest thing to a real battle we've had in decades. Ever since Ambrose brokered a peace deal with the demons, the Barrows have been settled. Sure, there've been some scuffles between various packs or a few upstarts need to be reminded of the proper hierarchy.

After years of strife, of leading men and women into battles, countless injuries and losing friends, I'd never expect to feel this way. I remember longing for a peace like this, longing to just be able to rest and not think about when the next attack might be.

I'm such a fucking asshole for being bored when everyone around me is settling down and getting to enjoy some peace.

Two males yank me out of my brooding as they face off at the bar, squaring up on one another. Finally. Something to actually do, other than walk around and look intimidating. One of the males, a tall, lanky pretty boy facing off with one just as pretty, goes to throw a punch. Except then one of the vampire security guards I've assigned to Noir is already there, getting between them.

The fight stops before it even begins. I'm left with an all too familiar restlessness. I won't do anyone any favors sticking around. The guard who's broken up the fight starts herding them to the entrance, his golden eyes meeting mine. I nod in approval, and the man returns it. It's not fair for me to be pissed at a man doing the job I gave him.

My men have Noir well in hand. There's really no reason for me to be here.

I head towards the door that leads up to Ambrose's office, ignoring the interested smiles women throw my way. It used to be I'd happily take a woman up on the silent offer and spend a night of mutually beneficial debauchery. Except along with peace, sex isn't... it just isn't doing it for me. Not that I'd dare let any of my brothers know. If they knew I haven't actually fucked a woman in the last three months, they'd make Cassandra search me for curses.

I push open the heavy door, slipping into the stairwell and leaving the club behind. I bypass Ambrose's empty office and the hall that'll take me out of the building. Instead, I head up the rarely used roof access.

As I walk onto the roof, the cool air is heavy with the promise of rain. The sun set hours ago and clouds have blocked out the moon. Tension slips from my shoulders and spine as I tilt my head back, letting the city around me wrap me in its embrace. Discordant sounds blend together in a nightmare symphony. Cars driving and honking at one another. People hurrying along Blood Street, humans and paranormal alike. Street vendors and performers are slowly returning to the sidewalks as winter turns to summer in the city. It'll only be a matter of weeks until the sounds are twice as overwhelming, twice as demanding.

It doesn't matter that the sky is dark, the Barrows glows with its own lights. An aurora of reds, greens, yellows, all shifting and waving as the city thrums with the life that only comes out at night.

In the distance, across the river, is Topside—Newgate. Top of the river. The city where humans tried to establish their own settlement without us lesser beings. A city where they can ignore our existence, until they can't fight the temptations of the pleasure we offer. We make sure they pay handsomely for the experience.

Topside. Where I'm opening my restaurant and burlesque theater at the top of one of the tallest buildings. We've always had our people Topside, sending their secrets and plans to Ambrose through the shadows. With this restaurant though, the Nightshades will have an official foothold in the city that once refused to grant us access.

I argued for this opportunity. I did my research,

found potential locations, vendors, and anything else I could imagine might sway Ambrose to my side. When he agreed, he only had one condition. To not fuck this up and tarnish the Nightshades' reputation.

And here I am, seeking refuge on the roof of Noir, because it's only been one problem after another, with no fighting or fucking to take the edge off.

I haven't even come up with a goddamn name for the place yet, and we're supposed to have the soft opening in three months.

"For fuck's sake," I mutter to myself. Then I shake the wallowing thoughts from my head. I've been alive for five hundred years. I'm too damn old to be pulling this bullshit.

I stride to the side of the building, stepping up onto the ledge. The wind is stronger here, catching my unbuttoned suit jacket and making it whip and jerk out behind me. It's the warning of a worse storm, one promising to deluge the city within the hour. Below me, people walk closer together but don't yet seek out shelter.

One figure, a woman, walks alone though. I watch her, like one would watch an insect as it makes its way along a tree branch. She's not dressed for the weather, in a dress meant more for sunny days with its fluttering skirt and cheerful yellow flowers.

Intrigued, and with frankly nothing better to do, I walk parallel to her, easily leaping across the narrow allies. She's holding her purse tight to her stomach, staring at something on her phone, occasionally looking up as if searching for someone.

It seems I'm not the only one who's found interest in the human woman, as I realize the three males twenty feet or so behind her are following her. Stalking her, more like, considering I can scent their wolf forms from her. Looking ahead of the woman, the busy part of Blood Street ends at a crossroad, the rest of the street growing dark with closed businesses.

She pauses at the end of the sidewalk, not venturing across the crosswalk just yet. The road is clear, so maybe she does have some sense of self-preservation.

I move to the corner edge of the building's roof I'm on, propping one foot up on the ledge. I consider inter-vening as the wolf trio finally catches up to her. I tilt my head and listen. My enhanced hearing makes it easy to follow their exchange despite the growing storm.

"Are you lost, pup?" the tallest one asks, a smile on his face. He must be the leader. The other two males smirk and rib each other, maneuvering around to her other side without her noticing at first. It's clear the moment she does, as her shoulders tighten.

"No," she answers, glaring at the leader. "I'm waiting for someone, actually. They should be here soon."

"Oh, yeah?" One of the others asks and makes a show of looking around. This close to the end of Blood Street doesn't get much foot traffic; most clients of the surrounding establishments don't want to be caught lingering in front of them. "Pretty shitty to leave a pretty girl like you alone."

She hesitates, her body shifting. She wants to move, but she's boxed in. Any way she turns, she'll give her back to one of them.

The leader tells the other one to back off, giving her an easy smile. I huff out a silent snort. He's playing the chivalric hero to their villains. "Really, though," he says, stepping closer. She can't back up unless she wants to get closer to the others. She holds her ground and, strangely, I feel a bit of pride in my chest. "It can be dangerous for a human out here alone. Why don't you let us take you somewhere safer and you can meet your friend there."

She gives him a hard smile. "No, thanks." She waves her phone a bit. "My boyfriend will be here any minute to pick me up."

I sigh, disappointment making me shake my head. I can hear the lie from here, hear her quickening heartbeat. As close as they are, the wolf shifters won't miss any scent of fear.

"What if we weren't asking?" one of the villain-playing wolves says, adding a growl under his words.

The tension I'd lost earlier returns, and my fangs itch to elongate, priming to fight. I should pull my phone out and send a couple of the foot soldiers walking the street to deal with this. One text, and they'd be here in a minute, two at the most.

"Then I'd say you're pretty rude," she answers with a sniff before tucking her phone into her small purse. "I'd also have to let you know I took martial arts for years, if you're expecting an easy mark."

The wolves are quiet for a long moment. It's as if the world is holding its breath as I wait for their reaction. I still don't reach into my pocket for my phone.

The leader laughs, breaking the silence, and the other two join in. He cocks his head at her, raising a hand as if to touch her face. "We like a bitch with fight in her, don't we, boys?"

Her eyes widen enough for it to be clear even all the way up here. Then her brows furrow and before the wolf shifter's hand can touch her, she knocks it out of her way with one arm and then lands a solid punch to the male's nose. His head snaps back and he staggers a step, before turning hate-filled eyes onto her.

Her heartbeat stutters, pure fear claiming her.

Thunder breaks across the sky, or maybe it's just the blood rushing in my ears. My feet are slamming into the pavement before I'd even decided to intervene. In another instant, I crossed the distance between us, slamming my shoulder into one of the lackeys. He goes flying with a yelp, slamming onto his back and skidding further up the road. I sweep out my leg, catching the other at the knees and sending him flailing. I help him to the ground by gripping his face and shoving downwards, satisfied from the crunch of bones fracturing.

Turning from him, I grab the woman by the arm and move her behind me as I step up into the glaring shifter's face, baring my fangs with a snarl. He tries to take a step back, confusion dampening the rage. I snap my hand out, gripping him by the throat, squeezing in threat.

"Give me one good reason, mutt, why I shouldn't rip out your throat for touching my girlfriend." My blood is racing, every instinct screaming for me to do it, to sink my fangs into his throat and destroy the male. To do what I do best, kill and feed.

The male on his back staggers upwards, hurrying behind his leader with his nonexistent tail between his legs.

"We didn't do nothing," the male gasps out, ignoring the blood running from his nose. "We were just trying to get her somewhere safer, honest. Didn't know she was a Nightshade's girl."

I snarl again, dragging him closer, ready to end the wolf right then.

A gentle hand against my back stops me.

Grunting in disgust, I release the male with a shove backwards, sending him into his friend. "Get the fuck out of my sight."

The males retreat, giving us a wide berth as they head towards the last male still struggling to get to his feet.

I close my eyes, breathing deep and forcing the disappointed blood rage down.

"Thank you," comes from behind me, the two words shaky. I turn and take her in, but she's shaking out her fist. Without thinking I catch it, making her gasp. I bring it up, angling it so it's in the soft yellow light coming from the corner lamp post. The skin is torn on her first and second knuckle, the metallic copper of her blood sweet to my nose. I run my fingers over her hand, before meeting her eyes.

"Nothing seems to be broken," I say, keeping my voice calm and low. "But you'll want to get ice on that tonight and it'll probably hurt like a bitch tomorrow. It was a good punch, though. Solid."

She tugs her hand away and I release it, startled at how soft her skin is as it brushes mine. She gives me a strained smile. "I know. It's not the first time I've punched someone."

We look at each other for a long moment, then I clear my throat. "So, not to sound like those jackasses, this end of Blood Street really isn't the best place for a human woman on her own."

She lets out an annoyed sigh and retrieves her phone, grimacing at the screen. She unlocks it and pulls up her messages. I look away, shoving my hands in my front pockets. But my gaze is drawn back to her like a compass pointing north.

In the waning lights of the street lamps and red glows of neon signs hung in the windows above us, I take the moment to study her. I should walk away, her being safe now, but my feet refuse to move. She's got pink hair, the color deepened by the neon signage, but if I were to guess, her hair is rose pink in the daylight. It's cut in a sharp bob just below her jawline, and when it falls into her face as she glares at her phone screen, her small hand tucks it behind a delicate ear that has three earrings in her lobe.

She's goddamn adorable, I realize.

When she swears and looks up, she startles as if she'd completely forgotten my presence.

"Oh. You're still here."

I arch a brow, then incline my head towards her

dark phone screen. "I take it you haven't gotten the response you're waiting for?"

She blows out between her lips and then nods. "My baby brother is proving again just how unreliable he is." She looks up and down the street, searching for something. Whatever it is, she doesn't see it if the scrunch of her lips is anything. She looks back up at me. "Could you point me to the closest bus stop? I'd rather not walk home if I can avoid it."

"Bus doesn't run this late, especially if you're headed across the bridge to Topside." I hate the way her shoulders slump. After seeing her stand up to those shifters, it makes a weird feeling scratch my gut.

"I don't live in Topside." Another sigh before she visibly rallies and gives me a firm smile. "Well, then. I should be off. I've got a couple miles to walk. Thanks for the help."

She grips the strap of her purse and steps around me, heading back towards the busier part of Blood Street. I watch her go, telling myself she'll clearly be fine.

I hold back a groan and let my head fall back. Then a fat raindrop smacks me in the middle of the forehead. With resignation, I jog to catch up with her, a bit impressed at how far she's already made it.

"Look, it's about to be pissing buckets," I tell her as I reach her side.

She doesn't slow down, glancing quickly up at the sky before staring resolutely ahead. "I can handle a bit of rain."

I don't miss the goosebumps that cover her arms as a gust of wind winds between us. I pull my wallet out from the inside pocket of my jacket, pulling out both my ID and an official Nightshade business card. With my other hand, I catch her arm making sure to be gentle but insistent. She looks down at the cards when I hold them out to her.

"My name is Malachi," I tell her. "My car is one block over. You've had a shitty night, no need to suffer more. Let me drive you home. Take a picture of my ID and card, and send it to a friend or someone, so you know I'm not going to try anything."

She studies me, her sharp eyes a bright blue even in the dim lighting. It strikes me again at how damn cute this woman is, with her button nose and round cheeks. She looks way too innocent to be hanging out on Blood Street. I've half a mind to ask her what she's doing here, but I've already involved myself in her business too much. I'm not trying to be her friend, I remind myself. Just trying to keep the Barrows safe for visitors like the Nightshades are supposed to.

In the end, I think I'm pretty sure it's the sudden rain that gets her to agree. She whips out her phone with impressive speed and takes a picture of each card with the flash on. Then, to my surprise, she grabs the cards from my hand and shoves them in her bra.

"There, I sent it to three different people and my boss. And I'll hold onto these until I'm at my place, safe."

I can't help but grin at her cleverness. I pull off my jacket and wrap it around her. "Here, use this so you aren't soaked," I say before gesturing to her to cross the street with me. She hurries along but grabs my hand when we reach the opposite side, making me stop.

She holds up my suit jacket above her head like an umbrella. "We can share it. No point in you getting wet either."

I find myself taking her up on the offer, hunching down until I'm crowding her. I didn't realize how short she was until now, with her barely coming up to my chest.

Once she's satisfied both of us are protected by a jacket that probably costs way more than she realizes, she raises her voice to be heard over the worsening storm. "Okay, let's go!"

Together, we hurry along the sidewalk along with everyone else trying to get inside somewhere and out of the storm. When we're close to Noir, I nudge her towards an alley, gesturing with my chin towards a floodlight that lights up the middle of the alley. "I'm parked in there."

She doesn't say anything because the wind whips at the jacket, the rain spraying us. She shrieks before laughing, grinning up at me. I find myself smiling back, feeling ridiculous and light. I tug her closer to my side, telling myself it's to keep her drier. We rush down the alley, trying to dodge the growing puddles and failing terribly. She's not complaining, though. If I weren't a vampire, I probably wouldn't hear her soft giggle over the rain.

I press my thumb to the biometric lock and yank open the metal door the moment the light turns green. We rush inside and I pull the jacket carefully away from her, shaking off the water. In the light of the parking garage, her cheeks are rosy, strands of hair (lilac, it turns out , a part of me notes) cling to her face, and her lips are parted as she breathes with exertion.

I wonder what else I could do to make her look like this. My cock twitches to life, interested in a woman for the first time in months. I swallow hard and make myself think about anything else. And definitely don't let myself notice how her dress is plastered to her, showing off her toned thighs and firm ass.

"Here, this is me," I make myself say and grab the keys from the box beside the door. I use the fob to remote start it, wondering if I had the heater on last. I cross the short distance to the first space, where my hunter green custom Range Rover has purred to life. I open the passenger door for her. "Hop in."

"Fancy," she says, her eyes no longer as bright as the moment before. She gets in though, easily scooting in while avoiding brushing against me.

I jog around the front and get in, pressing the ignition before hitting the button for her seat's warmer. "If it gets too hot, just press this."

She's stiff after she's buckled herself in, her hands on her knees. As I pull out of the space, the garage door sensor recognizes me and opens.

"So, where to?" I ask, hoping my light tone will help break down whatever wall she's suddenly shored up between us.

She hesitates, then gives me cross streets that are on the south side of the Barrows. There's a bear shifter pack in that area, but they typically keep to themselves. Still, it's far enough away I'm glad she's not walking, especially in this storm.

I try to think of something to talk about to break the silence, but everything sounds too stupid. At least she's seemed to relax into the warmth of the car, her fingers idly playing with the hem of her skirt. I swallow hard, reminding myself and my cock to look straight ahead. We're just giving her a ride. I don't even know her name.

So we pass the short drive in silence, only the

sounds of the windshield wipers and rain battering the roof of the car between us. It's harder to keep my thoughts clear the more her scent fills the space. I'm not sure what it is, but it's something sweet and flowery. Maybe honeysuckle? Gardenia?

After I turn onto one of the cross streets she gave, she points me towards an old boarder house that's seen better days. "That's me," she says, and I pull up to the curb, glad that at least there's a bright porch light and a cheery spring wreath hung on the front door.

She turns towards me as she unbuckles, giving me a grateful smile. "Thanks again for the ride. And earlier."

"No problem," I breathe out, unable to look away from her eyes. It's on the tip of my tongue to ask her what her name is when she surprises me yet again when she leans over the console and presses a kiss to my cheek.

Her lips are cool from the rain but soft as down. She pulls back, her cheeks flaming red, and looks away as if she can't believe she kissed me either. I'm struck stupid still when she looks at me again, our eyes catching.

I don't know if she moved or I did, but we're suddenly kissing. She's leaning towards me and I bury myself in her hair, tilting her head back as I deepen the kiss. Her lips part on a quiet moan as my tongue chases the sound. One of her hands comes up to my neck, the other on my shoulder as our kiss turns hungry. I shift towards her, needing more, craving more. I need to touch her.

I'm forced to a stop when my seatbelt locks me in place.

The moment is broken as she pulls back with another soft laugh.

"Bye," she says as she slips out, her voice husky. My cock screams at me to chase her but she's already shutting the car door and hurrying up the short steps to her door.

I've only got the presence of mind to roll down the window and shout, "What's your name?"

She's already unlocked the house door and it's halfway open when she looks back. Instead of answering, she gives me a cheeky smile and waves, disappearing into her house. The porch light turns off, leaving me to slump back in my seat with a laugh.

It's only when I make it back to the clan house and pull my wallet out of the jacket that's almost certainly ruined do I realize she still has my ID and business card. With a smirk, I toss my clothes into a pile and climb into bed naked and alone. But the mystery woman's smile is all I can think about as I fall asleep.

Grab Malachi and his mysterious yet adorable woman's
story here:
Vampire Soldier

Or turn the page to read the bonus Epilogue for
Cassandra and Ashe!

EPILOGUE

Cassandra

Many Years Later

"Anthony!"

Even inside the cottage, I can hear Josephine's exasperation. I can't help grinning as I work the basil in the mortar and pestle at the kitchen counter. A moment later, my rambunctious seven year old squeals and giggles just outside the kitchen window. Glancing up, my heart radiates with a joy I never considered possible at the sight of Ashe holding our son up high and spinning her around.

He must sense me, looking up as he twirls one last time in our gardens and meets my gaze with a smile of his own. He hitches Anthony on his hip and boops him on the nose as Josephine walks up to the pair with affectionate irritation on her face. Anthony is the

335

perfect blend of us, with Ashe's sandy brown hair and my eyes. To our surprise, he wasn't born a vampire, seeming to take after my side of the family. His magic has already caused the entire Nightshade clan much mischief.

With Emily, Lan and Wren's daughter, as his best friend, it's become a full time effort for the clan to keep the children in line. Emily had inherited both of her parent's keen intelligence and Anthony has shown he's following in his father's footsteps seeking out adventure.

I look down at my round stomach, patting the bump affectionately. "You'll be the sensible one, I can tell," I murmur before scraping out the basil into the glass bowl. "Now, so long as Eloise's child is also sensible, we'll only have to worry about those two."

Ambrose had turned his mate, Eloise, over two years ago now, truly making her the vampire queen. Now, she is due any day with their first child. I'd never seen the king so tense. His hovering has annoyed Eloise so much lately, that she's threatened to go on a vacation from him.

It's adorable, honestly, to see the normally so stoic and unflappable Ambrose brought to the state of a shaking kitten from his wife's pregnancy.

Cold shock and surprise shoots down the bond from Ashe and I nearly drop the dish with the beginnings of pesto as I hurry to the front door. Pushing through, I see Josephine taking Anthony from Ashe and rushing towards me. Following Ashe's gaze, my breath sticks in my chest.

"Is that..." I trail off and Josephine looks over her shoulder again.

"He certainly thinks so," she answers. "I'm taking Anthony inside. Be careful, you two."

I nod absently, walking towards my mate. She closes the door behind her, and when I reach Ashe's side I can do nothing but reach for his hand. He laces his fingers with mine and squeezes.

We watch the woman strolling casually up towards our cottage on the gravel drive, her hands shoved in her front pockets.

She looks as if she hasn't changed since the last day we saw her.

She stops just outside my wards, unable to cross them without my permission. She makes a point to look at the stone fence and raises a dark, elegant brow.

"What's wrong with you two?" Eris asks, her voice dripping with disdain. "I thought you had better manners than warding against old friends."

I'm moving without thought, pushing through the gate. Then I'm throwing my arms around Eris as I hug her tight, the demon grunting from the impact.

"Fuck. When did you become so sentimental?" Eris

grouches but her arms come around me, giving me an awkward pat. "And you let the male knock you up, eh?"

A sound that's half laugh, half sob comes out of me and I let her go, shaking my head. "Twice, if you can believe it," I answer, then shove her shoulder. "And I've always been sentimental."

Ashe comes up beside me, wrapping an arm around my shoulders and tugging me into his side. "So, not dead then?"

"Not dead," Eris confirms. "I'm surprised too. But, ehh, Hell wasn't done with me yet."

"Aeternaphiel?" Ashe asks.

She shrugs. "In Hell stripped of all his archangel powers and currently serving as the lapdog to one of the dark princes. The Resplendents up in the heavens have abandoned him, as he deserves."

I sniffle, cursing the pregnancy hormones for making me so weepy. With a twist of my fingers, my wards part to allow her through. I point with my thumb over my shoulder. "I was just about to make an early dinner. Would you like to join us?"

Eris looks like she's about to decline but then shrugs. "Why not. I did come all this way after all."

"Why did you come?" Ashe asks, gesturing for Eris and I to go first back through the gate. He's wary, as he should be considering Eris is a demon.

She looks over her shoulder at him and winks. "Oh, have I got a story for you."

Eris hooks her arm through mine and I shake my head at her teasing my mate. It doesn't matter why Eris is back, even if I suspect she's made up some excuse just to visit. She knows me and the possession went both ways. I know her better than anyone else in the realms.

"Whatever the reason," I say as I push open the door. "We're glad to have you. I missed you, if you can believe it."

The demon scoffs. "Of course, I can believe it. I'm fucking wonderful."

Even Ashe laughs at that. I shake my head again and push her towards the hearth, where Josephine sits with Anthony. I head back to the kitchen to finish preparing dinner, smiling broadly as my son starts peppering Eris with questions. To my surprise, she answers patiently... for now.

My world settles, as if a long missing piece has finally returned. The babe in my stomach kicks, as if in agreement. I pat my bump and reach for the olive oil, listening to the sounds of my family, and get on with making dinner.

Thank you for reading Vampire Runner! If you enjoyed this book, please leave a review on Amazon. Then, don't forgot to grab Malachi's story! This reality show loving vampire is about to go on the ride of his life.

Get it now: Vampire Soldier

ALSO BY ROWAN HART

Nightshade Vampires

Vampire King

Vampire Enforcer

Vampire Savage

Vampire Runner

Vampire Solider

———

Knights of Hades MC Security

BLAZE

BONES

ABOUT THE AUTHOR

 Rowan Hart is a potty-mouthed romantic who is obsessed with all paranormal monsters. It all started with Goliath and Demona.

Since then, Rowan has fallen in love with all different vampires, werewolves, gargoyles, demons, and well... you get the picture.

She's written over twenty books featuring romances between a woman and multiple heroes, or anti-heroes in some cases.

Now she's dedicating Rowan Hart to her love of gritty romance with dark heroic monsters who have to deal with feisty women who refuse to run from the big bad wolf.

Made in United States
Troutdale, OR
11/08/2024

24564965R10212